"Dylan, do this for us."

If Dylan was even going to consider hosting the Behrs' Christmas party, he had plenty of ground rules to lay down first. "If we're throwing the gala here—"

Caroline bounced a half step off her feet, a squeal escaping her throat. "I knew you'd see it my way! We will throw the most beautiful gala this town has ever seen!"

She shoved a file of paperwork into Dylan's hands and sprinted for the doors.

"Hey!" Dylan called after her. "I didn't agree to— Where are you going?"

"We'll hammer out details later!" she called on her way out. "You made the right decision, Dylan!"

Dylan blinked, mouth agape. She had come into the room like a lamb and blown out like a lion, and he felt woozy about what had transpired in between.

Dylan opened the file folder. An early twentieth-century drawing of Santa Claus stared up at him. "Big guy," Dylan breathed. "I don't know what just happened...but I think I'm in for a whirlwind of a ride."

Dear Reader,

Ah, Christmas. Oh, how I love the anticipation of this time of year. Whether baking cinnamon rolls, watching old movies or decorating the tree, I find the Christmas season is always a dance between nostalgia and anticipation.

Caroline and Dylan's story is much the same. The nostalgia of their childhood "friendship" (only Dylan's word, of course) grows into something more as they team up to make their own entrepreneurial dreams come true. But while I loved both Dylan's and Caroline's ambitions, what I most enjoyed writing was how carefully they enfold McKenna, Dylan's three-year-old daughter, into their plans. Over the years I've had the pleasure of watching parents go to great lengths to meet their children exactly where they are. To be loved and accepted just as we are? Now that's what I call a love story.

I hope some part of this story resonates with you. If it does, I'd love to hear from you. You can follow the Elizabeth Mowers, Author page on Facebook or visit my website, elizabethmowers.com.

Wishing love to you and yours,

Elizabeth

HEARTWARMING

His Daughter's Mistletoe Mom

—

Elizabeth Mowers

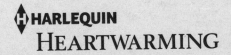

HARLEQUIN
HEARTWARMING

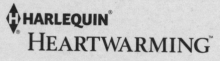

HARLEQUIN®
HEARTWARMING™

ISBN-13: 978-1-335-58469-4

Recycling programs
for this product may
not exist in your area.

His Daughter's Mistletoe Mom

Harlequin Enterprises ULC
22 Adelaide St. West, 41st Floor
Toronto, Ontario M5H 4E3, Canada
www.Harlequin.com

Printed in U.S.A.

Elizabeth Mowers wrote her first romance novel on her cell phone when her first child wouldn't nap without being held. After three years, she had a happy preschooler and a hot mess of a book that will never be read by another person. The experience started her down the wonderful path of writing romances, and now that she can use her computer, she's having fun cooking up new stories. She's drawn to romances with strong family connections and plots where the hero and heroine help save each other. Elizabeth lives in the country with her husband and two children.

Books by Elizabeth Mowers

Harlequin Heartwarming

A Promise Remembered

Little Lake Roseley

Where the Heart May Lead
Her Hometown Detective
Her Veterinarian Hero

Visit the Author Profile page
at Harlequin.com for more titles.

To Grandma Mary with love

CHAPTER ONE

CAROLINE WATERSON KNEW the phrase "blast from the past" was something a person could potentially feel when standing up as maid of honor in a friend's wedding. With a church full of three hundred people, many of them folks she had known her entire life, the nostalgia had come on quite suddenly, making her vision a bit blurry and unreliable. It was why she refrained from doing a double take when she thought she had seen the face of the one person who had frustrated her all throughout her childhood: Dylan Metzger. Blast from the past? More like blast to her senses. One glimpse of his face had sucked the oxygen from her body after slamming into her like a freight train.

As the ceremony continued, Caroline maintained the pleasant smile she had perfected over the years. As a wedding planner, or unfortunately as the assistant wedding planner who ended up doing the brunt of the work for a sliver of the commission, she always tried to disguise the disdain she felt for big weddings. The perfect disguise started with the right facial expression, and it was a lifesaver at a time like this.

Caroline mentally scrolled through the guest list Tyler and Olivia had given her. She had spent long evenings with her best friend, addressing envelopes and writing table place cards. Not once had she ever seen the name Dylan Metzger. *That* was a name she would have remembered.

Caroline squeezed her bouquet a little tighter and reassured herself that there was no way Dylan was in the church, staring at her. No way. The stress was causing an overactive imagination. Yes, she thought, drawing in a slow breath as Tyler and Olivia finished their vows. She was seeing things.

She stood silently, running through a list of things she needed to fix. She planned to kick out of her heels, at least for a few minutes, and scratch that place on her back that felt like it was abraded by poison ivy. She likened her visions of Dylan to her body being squeezed into a rhinestone dress half a size too small; he sure was pretty to look at, but heavens, if he wasn't a monster pain in her back.

Caroline watched Tyler and Olivia kiss, each smiling tenderly at one another. After Olivia lost her husband a few years earlier, it was good to see her find love again. As it turned out, the local veterinarian was a perfect match.

After the ceremony ended and the pictures were taken, Caroline waited outside the reception hall for the MC to announce the wedding party as her cousin Faith slid up behind her and smacked a loud kiss on her cheek. As Faith had moved away from Roseley as a teenager and Olivia had only spent summers visiting, to now have both women living in town again and becoming close friends felt like a wish fulfilled.

"I have to tell you," Faith said, "harvest orange is not one of my favorite colors, but you made this late-autumn wedding work. If John and I had waited to get hitched, I might have chosen a formal affair like this too."

"Yeah, right," Caroline said. "You wore blue jeans under your wedding dress, for heaven's sake."

Faith considered this for a moment before breaking into a laugh.

"That's true." Faith leaned close to now whisper in her ear. "Everyone knows *you're* the one who pulled this thing off, by the way. I think I spotted your boss throwing back a cocktail when we first arrived."

Caroline gave Faith a "you have got to be

kidding me" look. Sheila, her boss, sometimes acted less like an event planner with a small business at stake and more like the guest at the party who gets everyone dancing. She was the person you invited as a fun buffer, not the person you hired to coordinate one of the biggest days of your life.

"I'm desperate to get out of there," Caroline said. "If I could have total control of planning events—"

"None of them weddings."

Caroline gave her cousin a nod. Faith had for a long time listened to her both bemoan large weddings and daydream instead about planning swanky galas.

Faith continued. "I overheard Sheila talking to the Behrs about a Christmas party."

"Tex and Bianca Behr?" This was an interesting detail that Caroline appreciated hearing. With Bianca on the hospital board, she wondered if the Behrs wanted to throw a Christmas party for the hospital. "What did she say? Specifically."

"Bianca said something about it being too bad that Sheila already had a wedding scheduled for Christmas Eve. The big-city event planner she had lined up fell through and now she's scrambling to find help."

"A Christmas Eve party for the Behrs…"

Caroline said, pondering out loud. "If I could land a contract with them—"

"You mean two of the most prominent people in Roseley?"

"It could be a game changer for me, Faith. I should pitch her."

"Do it," Faith said. "Tonight. Here."

"Here?" Caroline whispered as fresh nerves of excitement rose in her gut like champagne bubbles escaping a fine-stemmed flute. She waited for Faith's final nod of encouragement even though she had already decided to do it.

Caroline glanced around the vestibule outside the entrance of the hall. At the MC's announcement the wedding party would be entering soon, everyone had slowly moved inside the hall to take their seats, but something about the entire situation didn't feel right.

After Faith squeezed her arm and darted inside to find her seat, Caroline found the vestibule too empty. The only "simple" thing about Tyler and Olivia's wedding was that they had chosen a small wedding party: Caroline and Olivia's fifteen-year-old son, Micah, who was nowhere to be seen.

Olivia gazed lovingly into her husband's eyes as Caroline hurried toward them. Both seemed unaware that the teen was missing in action right before they were to be announced.

"Tyler," Caroline said. "Where's your best man?"

Olivia blinked as if surfacing from a dream.

"Micah?" she said. "I thought he was here. He followed us from the limo into the hall and then…"

Tyler kissed Olivia's hand. "I'll find him. We can't go in without my best man."

"You'd better not," Caroline said. "Isn't it better for *me* to walk in without an escort than Olivia?"

"True," Tyler said, frowning. "I thought this would be easier with only two people in the wedding party, but now half of you is missing."

"Ideally, your wedding planner should go find him." Caroline sighed, scanning the hall for Sheila. "But it might take longer to find her than Micah."

For several years Caroline had kept Sheila's business afloat by taking care of the details and managing most events, sometimes single-handedly. She had told Sheila that she was planning to leave, planning to start her own event planning business, though she pointed out that she had no desire to poach any wedding clients. If she had her way, she'd never have to plan another wedding for the rest of her life. She had such high hopes for her friends' marriage, but in general, weddings felt like a big flashy show to celebrate a commitment that didn't last. At least, that's what personal experience had taught her.

"This was exactly what I didn't want to happen, Caroline," Olivia said. "You're supposed to be my maid of honor, not the wedding planner. I wanted you to enjoy the day too."

Tyler peeked into the reception hall.

"I think Sheila is talking to the disc jockey," he said. "She's laughing with them about something."

Caroline muttered to herself. "Of course she is."

Tyler continued. "Everyone in there has to be pretty hungry. Who knew a photo shoot would take so long? If it comes down to waiting for Micah or appeasing our guests…"

"Knowing my son, he probably sneaked into the kitchen to eat, unaware he's shirking his escort duties." Olivia winced at her friend. "Sorry, Aunt Caroline."

Caroline's face broke into a warm smile. As irritated as she was with Sheila, she loved how Micah now called her Aunt Caroline. Ever since Olivia and Micah had moved to Roseley, Caroline's friendship with Olivia had deepened from friendship to something of a sister. And when Micah had started calling her Aunt

Caroline, she'd felt solidified as a permanent fixture in the Elderman extended family.

"Don't worry," Caroline said. "I'll find him."

Caroline hustled around the perimeter of the reception hall, scanning the tables for any sign of a teenager in a tuxedo. She paused outside the men's bathroom and cracked the door a hair before calling inside. Aside from a few strange looks…

Nothing.

The kitchen was bustling as caterers prepared plates of chicken cordon bleu and pot roast. Just as she had scurried back into the hall, she ran smack-dab into Sheila.

"Caroline," Sheila said in a huff. "You're supposed to be with the wedding party. We're announcing you in *two minutes*."

"I'm looking for Micah."

"He should be there with you."

Caroline glared at her boss, wondering if Sheila didn't think she already knew that. Sometimes the woman lacked common sense. As best as she could understand it, Sheila was great at failing up.

"Hence," Caroline said, her tone tense, "my searching."

"I'll just make an announcement," Sheila said, wafting her hand in dismissal. "He's got to be around here somewhere. I'll tell him to come to the vestibule immediately."

"Don't you dare," Caroline said. "That'll look bad. Just give me a minute to find him."

"Are you sure?" Sheila called. In lieu of a response, Caroline spun on her three-inch heels and marched through a set of fire doors leading to an empty, adjacent reception hall.

The heavy metal doors clicked shut behind her, ceasing the chattering of the crowd, leaving nothing but the sound of her heels clicking across the tile floor, echoing through the empty hall.

Recently, she'd spent more time in giant halls like this than she'd ever thought she would. Her childhood had been filled with long days of digging for worms, catching fish, climbing trees and trying to snag some of her dad's attention, which had always been so focused on her brother, Trig. As much as her mother had wished she would "play nice" and "wear something suitable," it was her father whom she had most wanted to impress. That wasted time hadn't done her a lot of good. How ironic that she now spent her days "playing nice" with a boss she could not stand while trying to impress clients. Though, if she could impress the right people in Roseley, word of mouth, particularly from the Behrs, could help get an event planning business off the ground—eventually.

When she reached the back doors, she pushed out into the parking lot and strained her eyes looking for Micah hiding among the rows of cars, covered with a dusting of snow. The beautiful autumn leaves had all fallen from the trees ages ago. It felt more winter than fall, occasionally snowing during the day and most nights. Caroline thought it a less-than-ideal season to tie the knot, but once Tyler and Olivia had gotten engaged, they were anxious to get married. They had booked the first date available at a reception hall big enough to accommodate their guests, and they still had to wait six months to wed.

Off in the distance Caroline could hear a basketball bouncing off the asphalt. She believed she'd found the best man. As Caroline was the only female attendant in the wedding, Olivia had let her choose her own bridesmaid dress. The strapless number had looked beautiful during the fittings in a warm bridal shop but as the brisk wind whipped off Little Lake Roseley, she now regretted how revealing it was. The November chill was not forgiving on her bare shoulders. Then again, she hadn't expected to run around the parking lot without her wrap or a coat.

Wrapping her arms around herself, she hurried outside and fought against the unrelenting cold. Following the sound of hoots and hollers, she darted around the side of the building to discover Micah and another man playing basketball. Her teeth chattered from the cold. Goose pimples prickled every inch of her arms. As she approached the court, Micah spotted her.

"Hey, Aunt Caroline!" he called before turning and tossing a fade-away shot into the net. Under different circumstances she might have warmed at his greeting, but Aunt Caroline was flirting with pneumonia.

"Micah," she said, wanting to keep her words few and direct. "Come on. Everyone is waiting."

"Aren't you cold?" he said, cocking his head to the side as if it just occurred to him that her dress was strapless.

"Freezing. Let's go."

Through her chattering teeth, she heard the voice of Micah's companion.

"You need a coat, Red," he said.

Caroline did a double take at the man offering her advice. She had been so concerned with getting Micah back to the reception she had not looked past her nephew to identify his friend.

Tucked into a black wool peacoat with the collar flipped up, the man before her snatched her breath away a second time that day. It was now clear that he hadn't been a figment of her imagination. He was the real thing. Dylan Metzger.

A playful smirk curved Dylan's mouth as he continued.

"As history has taught us," he said, "I doubt you'll accept mine."

She couldn't see his eyes at her distance, but Caroline instantly recalled how blue they were. They were the color of the sky after a storm had cleared to brighter horizons. She had not seen them, nor that devilish grin, in nearly twenty years, but with one glance she now had something other than the cold wind to rap tingles up and down her skin.

"Dylan," she said, her brow pinched so tightly it might have frozen in place. "What are *you* doing here?"

Her obvious disdain made Dylan laugh so heartily even Micah chimed in.

"Now *that's* the Caroline Waterson I remember," he said. "Still living up to your redheaded temperament, I see."

"I'm not living up to anything," she said, finding the feeling in her lips had all but disappeared. If she had a stick, she might have swung it if only to wipe his smug face clear. "I—I...it's *cold*."

"That's Michigan, honey."

She blinked hard. Dylan appeared like an apparition after all these years yet could instantly slip back into his old routine of irritating her.

"I *know* it's Michigan." She shook her head. "I've lived here my entire life."

His build had changed—taller, broader. He had facial hair; that was new. It looked good, though he had always excelled in anything he had attempted back when she'd known him. God could certainly be unjust sometimes.

"But still no coat, huh?"

Though deeper, richer, his voice had the same familiarity as when she had been thirteen. It had always caught her in a constant emotional tug-of-war where he was concerned. And that darn smirk of his...

She pursed her lips in defensiveness.

"Micah, we have to go. *Now*."

"Wait, one more shot," Dylan said, jagging and dribbling around her. "Three-pointer!"

He released the ball and sent it soaring through the air, only to ricochet off the rim straight to Micah.

Micah rebounded and dribbled a few times

before taking his own shot and cheering as it sank through the net.

"Nice shot!" Dylan called, beckoning Micah with a high five. After their hands collided in a loud smack, Micah darted to retrieve the ball.

"Now," Caroline said, hating her brash tone but also knowing nothing in the world had prepared her for seeing Dylan Metzger again. Though, she thought as she studied his profile and the faint dimple in his chin, she could no sooner have prepared for winning the lottery.

Caroline shook her head as if to shake away the analogy. Winning the lottery would be an amazing thing, a dream come true. Dylan Metzger had teased her all throughout grade school and middle school and deserved no better comparison than…than…a tsunami leveling cities. Or at least, she thought as she squeezed her arms tighter around herself, he was somewhere between those two options.

"You look like you're ready to shatter," Dylan said, striding toward her.

"Still as observant as ever, Dylan," she said. She tipped her chin up a notch. "I can make do."

"Nonsense," he said, peeling off his coat. With a masculine grace she had only ever seen in the movies, he had it wrapped over her bare shoulders quicker than a heartbeat. His body heat still clung to the wool and warmed her skin. She wanted to strip off his coat out of sheer pride, but she couldn't. On cold nights when she stole out of bed for a moment, she couldn't wait to dive back under the warm, inviting covers. His coat felt that way now, too cozy and comfortable to refuse. And his scent lingering on the wool…

"Am I supposed to thank you now?"

"Maybe when your lips are no longer blue."

Caroline pressed her pink-stained lips together as Dylan tipped his head and studied her.

"I take it you didn't know I was coming to the wedding." It was true, though she refused to admit it. How she had missed his place card was baffling. "I was a last-minute addition," he said as if reading her mind. "My, uh, date couldn't make it, but I wanted to see the old man get hitched."

"I didn't think you and Tyler were close."

"Close enough to get invited. We reconnected when I moved back to Roseley earlier this year."

Caroline was baffled. Dylan Metzger was back and here to stay?

"Keeping it under the radar?"

"From you? Never." He grinned, making her tug the coat tighter to keep from tingling.

"The way I heard it," Caroline countered,

"you were climbing the ranks at that big law firm… What's it called again?"

"Zaggart, Pointe and Hildegarden."

"Couldn't cut it?"

Dylan's eyes twinkled as if he got energy from a little row with her.

"Not quite. I made partner last year."

"Your dad would have been proud."

He shrugged and glanced back at Micah. "Maybe."

Caroline noted the line that had formed between his brows before he turned his attention back to her.

"Are you really home for good?" she asked.

"I'm back indefinitely."

Caroline pulled the coat tighter around herself. Dylan Metzger had returned to Roseley to stay? Why, oh, why was she just learning about this now? Tyler had most definitely kept this important bit of information from her, just like he must have hidden Dylan's place card too, though she couldn't imagine why. He didn't even know about her history with Dylan. In fact, since Olivia hadn't grown up in Roseley, neither did she. "New York City wasn't all it was cracked up to be, huh?" There was a bit of a jeer in her tone. From their history, she knew he expected nothing less. The corners of his mouth lifted.

"Something like that. Disappointed to see me again?"

"Something like that."

This made him chuckle, which only made heat rise in her cheeks. He was always laughing at her, jesting for sport.

He turned as he led her to a side entrance of the hall. "Let's get inside, Micah," he called. "I think you're holding up the buffet line."

"Actually," Caroline said, "it's a sit-down."

"Then we'd better hustle." He grinned from over the top of the messy, hand-knit scarf wrapped around his throat. It did not scream "yuppie from the city." He was the same old Dylan and yet the scarf signaled that something about him had changed, not that she was going to spend her valuable time trying to figure out what. "You look good, Red."

"Caroline."

"Mmm-hmm."

"No one calls me Red anymore."

"I'll see what I can do about that. I've always been something of a trendsetter."

She huffed out more annoyance than she knew what to do with. She knew he would settle back into calling her Red again, just as she would fight to keep him from doing it. She would refuse to answer to the name, refuse to acknowledge it, refuse to acknowledge him and the dreamboat jawline he had cut since they had last bickered.

Caroline squeezed her eyes shut and popped them open, determined not to fall back into the gawky girl who had tried to tag along after her big brother and his annoying best friend. Back then she had consistently tried and failed to assert herself as their equal. She had done her best to keep Dylan Metzger from getting under her skin and would have rather died by a thousand snakebites than let him know his teasing directed nearly every decision she had made back then.

Before they reached the door, Dylan sprinted a few steps ahead and pulled it open. Caroline, flooded with a heavy cocktail of adrenaline, annoyance and pride, shot past him and into a hallway that led back to the vestibule. She could see Olivia, Tyler and Sheila waiting for her. The sight of them reminded her of who she was now: a successful, confident woman who refused to let Dylan Metzger get the best of her.

"Save me a dance, Red," he called before darting into the hall. She wanted to call after him and say something to put him in his place, but he had already disappeared into the crowd. She turned her attention back to Sheila, who motioned for her to take off the wool coat.

"Give it to me," Sheila said, yanking it off her shoulders before shoving the bouquet into her hands and signaling the disc jockey to begin. Caroline's shoulders chilled at its absence and reminded her that there were more pressing things to focus on.

"I'm ready," Caroline said, readjusting her bouquet and slipping a hand through Micah's offered arm. She was ready for her bridesmaid duties, but Micah was all curiosity.

"Dylan said you two used to be friends."

Caroline's stomach flurried. During the wedding ceremony Dylan would have had a great view of her, but the fact he'd managed to bring up her name with Micah while playing basketball and then gone to the lengths to say they had been friends before she had even been certain he was back in town made her huff—loudly.

"Uh, no," she corrected. "He was friends with my brother, Trig."

"Why would he say that, then?"

"I'm sure he has a rosier view of the past than I do."

Micah soured a face. "Why?"

She didn't want to relive the teasing, nor dampen the admirable esteem Micah had for her. "People remember things differently, I guess."

"He's cool."

"Ha!" Caroline scoffed. *"Cool."*

Micah leaned closer, a taunt in his voice. "Should I call you Aunt Red now?"

Caroline's eyes set. She flicked a brow in challenge. "Not unless you want me to dip you in front of everyone during our dance."

"You wouldn't."

"Try me."

The disc jockey announced their names as the band struck up the music. Micah laughed as they entered the reception hall. "Aunt Caroline it is!"

CHAPTER TWO

CAROLINE PICKED AT her meal, too preoccupied with watching the Behrs to eat. When she noticed Olivia staring at her, she stiffened her spine.

"Are you enjoying the dinner?" Olivia said.

"Of course. I'm mostly enjoying how cute you and Tyler look together."

Olivia squeezed Tyler's arm, prompting him to wink at her.

"He's a keeper," Olivia said. "But I'm having the hardest time remembering why we decided on a big wedding. I'm secretly counting the hours until we hop the plane for the beach."

"When do you move into Tyler's house?"

"When we get home. I had to talk to Tyler and Micah about not turning the place into a bachelor pad before I moved in." Micah had already been living there for the last month, and Olivia had mentioned she wasn't sure who'd been happier about it—her future husband or her son.

"Well, you don't have anything to worry

about while you're away. Gary will keep a good eye on Micah."

Gary was Tyler's uncle and helped him run the Roseley Veterinary Clinic.

"Ha," Olivia said. "Gary's just as bad. Those two will probably spend every waking minute that Micah isn't at school working at the clinic."

"You married into the right family. That kid is a natural with animals." Caroline caught Micah's attention and motioned for him to stand and follow her to the disc jockey table. "Speaking of my escort, Micah and I have some fun dinner entertainment planned for everybody. It looks like the timing is now."

"Oh, no," Olivia said. "We've been over the itinerary for this reception a dozen times so there wouldn't be any surprises. I said I didn't want to do the garter belt thing—"

"And we won't." Caroline squeezed Olivia's shoulder reassuringly. "This will be cute. Promise. Right, Micah?"

Micah nodded. "Don't worry, Mom. You'll like this."

"Okay…" Olivia said. "As long as it doesn't embarrass me."

Tyler wrapped an arm around Olivia's shoulders. "They would never," he said.

"Listen to your husband," Caroline said.

"Husband," Olivia said, pecking a kiss to Tyler's cheek. "I love the sound of that."

Micah made a pretend gagging face before erupting into laughter as Caroline led him to the disc jockey table. It was such a joy to see her best friend and her son so happy, but as much as she wished for the same kind of happily-ever-after, she couldn't imagine a reality where it would happen for her. She knew every man in town and none of them interested her enough to distract from her goals.

For the last year, she'd been putting together a business plan and collateral and preparing herself, and Sheila, for the day when she finally broke off on her own. She had thought that she would make a move after the new year, but the thought of landing the Behrs' Christmas party as her first contract was enticing enough to jump the gun. She couldn't wait to take the plunge...in business. Love was much scarier.

Caroline grabbed a microphone and signaled the disc jockey, before getting everyone's attention by clinking a nearby water goblet into the microphone.

"Ladies and gentlemen," Caroline said brightly. "We have something fun cooked up for you while you finish your dinner. Please put your hands together for Dr. and Mrs. Elderman!"

The guests clapped as Olivia shot Caroline a warning look, but Caroline just winked to signal that everything would be okay. She would never embarrass her friends on their big day, and she had a feeling that Olivia would like this surprise.

Micah handed Tyler and Olivia each two paddles. One had Olivia's name on it and the other Tyler's name. Caroline explained that she would ask questions and both Tyler and Olivia had to answer blindly with their paddles.

"Let's kick it off with a question going back to the beginning of your relationship," Caroline said. "Which one of you made the first move?"

When Tyler held up a sign that read Olivia and Olivia held up a sign that read Tyler, the crowd erupted into laughter. It was a great first question to break the ice and Caroline could tell the laughter immediately put Olivia at ease.

"So, it's debatable." Caroline grinned. "Good to know."

As she scanned the crowd, pleased to find so many interested expressions on guests' faces, she caught herself when her eyes collided with Dylan's. There was an intensity in his gaze she'd never seen, and it made the heat in her cheeks rise several notches. Caroline cleared her throat and shuffled her game cards.

"Question number two," she said. "Who has the bigger sense of adventure?"

This time, they both held up both paddles, and then celebrated with a kiss.

As the game continued, Caroline scanned the crowd, carefully avoiding the direction of Dylan's table. She spotted Tex and Bianca Behr nodding to each other as they watched her. Apparently, they approved. She needed to strike while the iron was hot and talk to them about their party before the night was over.

After the couple had answered a dozen light-hearted questions, Caroline finished with the one she knew would get some hollers.

"And finally, the question that's on everyone's mind... Micah, we need a drumroll." Micah slapped his hands on the tops of his thighs as Caroline continued. "Who does Ranger prefer?" Ranger was Tyler's loyal German shepherd.

Tyler shot the paddle with Olivia's name high into the air and waved it madly before Olivia could even answer, making the guests cheer.

Once Caroline cued the disc jockey to play the next song and invited everyone to the dance floor, she locked her sights on the Behrs. The bride and groom had enjoyed their first dance before dinner so Caroline felt confident she could steal away for a minute to chat them up without neglecting her maid of honor duties.

As she moved her way through the crowd, she spotted Sheila hurrying to cut her off.

"Caroline, where are you going? We have to get the cake ready for the cutting."

"*You* have to get the cake ready," Caroline said. "I'm a guest, Sheila. The maid of honor, to be exact."

Sheila fluttered a wave to people a few tables away, either distracted or pretending to be distracted. After years of working for Sheila and learning her tricks, Caroline guessed it was the latter.

"If you're fine with that," Sheila said, "I'll just have them wheel the cake out at the end of this song."

"Not *this* song," Caroline said, her brows pinched in disgust. "It's too early."

"Fine. We'll wait a few songs. Thanks, hon."

"But, Sheila—"

Sheila darted to mingle before Caroline could stop her. With a sigh, she caught sight of the Behrs, making their way to the dance floor. Though she knew she could set up a meeting with them later in the week, she couldn't shake the feeling she should at least introduce herself before the reception ended.

"Why so glum, Red?"

Caroline refused to turn around and acknowledge the owner of that voice. After Dylan's stare had made her falter during the game, she wasn't anxious to see him again.

"I'm not glum," she answered, staring straight ahead. Not one to be ignored, Dylan slid around her and leaned back against one of the empty dinner tables. He had loosened his necktie and rolled his shirtsleeves to the elbows. It was a traffic hazard to let a man as good-looking as him go walking around on the street looking the way he did, not that she'd ever tell him, or anyone, she thought so.

"Did no one ask you to dance?" he said, tipping his head closer.

"What?" Caroline scoffed. "Is that what you think?"

When his face broke into an amused grin, she knew she had taken the bait.

"Dylan, why are you still trying to get a rise out of me after all these years?"

"I'm just making conversation."

"Like you were with Micah earlier? You and I were not friends back in the day."

"We weren't enemies."

Caroline glared. He still had no idea what

kind of love-hate battle she had had back then. Whenever she saw or thought of him, all she really wanted was for him to give her some attention, other than teasing her.

"I have to get back to the kitchen to get the cake cutting started."

"One dance. For old time's sake. Come on, Red."

"Forget it," Caroline said, avoiding his offered hand. "Why don't you dance with your date. Oh, that's right. You're flying solo tonight. What's the deal?"

Dylan leaned in as if sharing a secret. "I'm a wedding crasher."

"Ha, ha," Caroline said, sarcastically. "Though I wouldn't be surprised if you were."

"I came stag."

"Now I know you're lying. I would have remembered seeing your name."

"Looking for me, were you?"

"Until an hour ago I didn't know you had moved back to Roseley so…no. But I did help Olivia make all the table seating cards and your name wasn't on any of them."

"I was my mom's date, but she couldn't make it."

That explanation made sense. Caroline recalled seeing the name Delia, though with a different last name. Perhaps she had returned to her maiden name after her divorce.

"Does your mom know Tyler too?"

"She knew his dad. Everyone in this town did. I'm surprised the reception wasn't bigger. Big weddings are fun."

Caroline rolled her eyes. "If you say so."

"That's a funny response coming from a woman eager to run wedding interference all evening. You barely sat down long enough to shovel three bites of dinner into your mouth."

Caroline's breath hitched. Had he been spying on her all evening? Every time she managed a look in his direction, she had thought he was watching her, but she thought it'd been wishful thinking.

"It's my job, Dylan, but back to your mom. Why didn't Delia come?"

"Some things came up with my baby sister, so Mom offered to stay home and…" He stared out toward the dance floor. "Isabel was feeling under the weather. That's what moms are for, right?"

"Right…" Though Caroline agreed, she caught an edge of sadness in Dylan's voice. "How old is Isabel?"

"Twenty."

"Gosh, where does the time go? Is she in college?"

"She was attending school in Ann Arbor but transferred back here at the start of the semester."

"Both of you are home again? Delia must be ecstatic."

"I hope so."

Dylan contorted his mouth as if unsure. When his stare set on her again, he crossed his arms and brushed a finger over his lips as if sizing her up.

"What?" Caroline said, presenting herself as more self-assured than she felt.

"You were staring at someone when I walked over. I'm sure of it."

"No, I wasn't—"

"If you don't want to dance with me, perhaps I can be your wingman, for old time's sake."

"That's not what I was doing and even if I was, I don't need your help, Dylan."

"Do you have a boyfriend?"

"That's absolutely none of your business."

"That's a *no*." Dylan tipped his head back as if rethinking. Caroline pursed her lips. What was it about this man that made her blood boil?

"If you must know," she said flatly, "I wanted to talk to the Behrs before they started dancing."

"Ugh," Dylan said with a grimace. "What on earth for?"

Caroline blinked. "You don't like the Behrs? Everyone likes the Behrs."

"Not everyone. Have you met them?"

"Not officially."

"Then why do you want to talk to them?"

"That's also none of your business."

Caroline looked past Dylan and almost thought Bianca Behr was looking straight at her. Perhaps someone had already mentioned that she was an event planner and could organize their Christmas party for them.

Dylan held up his hands defensively.

"I was just curious, that's all. Why don't you and I take a spin around the dance floor, and you can pretend like you don't want to tell me about it."

"I can't," Caroline said, her eyes set solely on Tex and Bianca. "Cake cutting is next and I'm—what did you call it?—running interference."

Dylan sauntered to stand next to Caroline, both of them facing toward the dance floor. Her breath hitched as Bianca waved to her.

"Yes, I can see I lost that argument," Dylan said. "And by the looks of it, you're about to get what your heart desires. Grizzly Behr is heading toward us, eleven o'clock."

Bianca had slipped away from Tex and was beelining through the crowd toward them.

"She's not a…" Caroline said, frowning. "I'm sure she's a lovely person."

"If you say so."

Dylan strode off, making a quick exit out the back doors of the reception hall as Bianca closed in. It was just as well because she wanted a moment of privacy to speak with Mrs. Behr. Besides, the less time she spent talking with Dylan the better. She didn't need to stumble into any old irritations with him, no matter how charming he could now be.

CHAPTER THREE

DYLAN SLIPPED OUT of the wedding reception and into the quiet of the vestibule to call his mother's cell phone. He expected Delia's honey-warm voice to come over the line, so he was surprised when his sister answered.

His sister coughed a few times and cleared her throat. "Dylan?" she croaked. "Hi."

"Isabel? Is everything okay?"

"Yup. Still sick as a dog."

He could hear Delia calling to her in the background.

"Isabel, is that D-Y-L-A-N?" she called. "Ask him about the wedding."

"Mom wants to know how it's going."

Dylan grasped the back of his neck. It had been a long time since he'd gone out to do anything solo and, to be quite honest, he was still getting used to it.

"Fine," he said, dryly.

"Having fun?"

"Time of my life."

Isabel giggled. "Meet anyone new?"

"Is this you asking or Mom?"

Isabel lowered her voice. "What do you think?"

Dylan knew his mother had his best interest at heart, but the last thing he needed right now was to meet anyone new, at least in the way Delia wanted. The second-to-last thing he needed was his mother's interference.

"I *think* someone is having a meltdown because I'm out for the night, but you're trying to distract me with talk of the wedding."

"No," Isabel said quickly. "No meltdown. We're fine. Really."

Dylan strained to listen for noises in the background, but all he could hear was Isabel's gravelly breathing.

"Sis, do you need anything while I'm out? Soup? Medicine?"

Isabel hummed a happy note. "Mom made me a pot of chicken broth, but I'd love dessert."

"I'm sure I can wrangle up something. I'll head home now."

"No, no, no. Mom is handling everything. Stay."

"It was nice to get out for a couple hours, but I don't have to close the place down."

Dylan peered through the door window to the hall and spotted Caroline front and center as Tyler and Olivia cut their wedding cake.

It had been a long time since he'd seen his friend's little sister, and she certainly wasn't the freckle-faced kid tagging along after them anymore. He could barely tear his eyes away from her.

"Dylan?"

"Hmm?" Dylan was distracted by the captivating way Caroline's dress swayed as she sashayed around the cake table.

"We're heading off to bed shortly so there won't be anything for you to do when you get home. You might as well stay. Just don't forget my dessert."

After they had said goodbye, Dylan pocketed his phone. He was torn between a desire to return to the reception and a sense of duty to go home and check things out for himself. He decided on the latter, but would snag Isabel some cake before leaving. Plus, if he went home too early, he'd probably never hear the end of it from his mother and sister, not that either of them was the person he was most concerned about.

Hanging back until the crowd around the cake table began to dissipate, he moseyed closer and accepted a plate of cake and a fork from Caroline.

"You missed the cake cutting," she said, grabbing a plate for herself.

"By the looks of it, I'm right on time." He took a bite. "I'm glad to see Tyler and Olivia didn't smash cake into each other's faces."

"I don't like that," Caroline said. "Who wants to start off marriage with frosting up their nose?"

"I'm with you. Especially because it would be a waste. Buttercream is my favorite."

"Mine too." She beamed up at him, her cheeks rounding in a way he hadn't seen yet that evening.

"You're in better spirits," he said. She was glowing and had a bounce to her step he hadn't seen before.

Caroline shimmied her shoulders. "Maybe I am."

"Did you meet Mr. Right?"

Caroline motioned for him to step away from the group. Once they were out of earshot, she explained.

"Way better. I officially met Mr. and Mrs. Right. I set up a meeting with the Behrs to discuss their upcoming Christmas gala."

"*You're* throwing the Behrs' gala this year?"

Caroline scraped the frosting off her cake and took a bite, closing her eyes to savor either the sweet taste or her new business venture.

"Not yet, but I plan on it. If I can impress them at our meeting, they might hire me and if that happens, well…" Caroline sighed. "The sky's the limit."

Dylan enjoyed the satisfied smile on Caroline's face. She certainly had more self-confidence than the last time he'd seen her, though the last time he'd seen her he had literally been yanking her strawberry locks just to see her screw up her face and shriek at him.

Still, he hated to see her get involved with the Behrs. They had a way of bulldozing people to follow their agenda and he didn't want to see Caroline get hurt.

"How can you handle an event as big as their gala if it's just you?"

"That's the best part. The hospital has a crew of people to do the heavy lifting and decorating. Bianca just needs a point person, like me, to come up with the vision and manage everybody."

Dylan could see the allure of that. Even though the gala would be huge, Caroline would have the help she needed, at least until she could get on her feet and start to hire employees.

"Look," he said. "I can see you're excited. But if you sign a contract with them, make sure you have someone read over it first."

Caroline cocked her head. "What's that supposed to mean?"

"It means you need to treat your relationship with them as a business, no friendly verbal agreements. Get everything in writing. Don't assume they'll do the right thing when the time comes. And make sure—"

"Ah," Caroline said. "I forgot. This is the big shot, New York City lawyer talking. Thanks, Dylan, but I can take care of myself."

"I didn't say you couldn't," Dylan said. From what he remembered about Caroline, she had been resilient as a kid, and he could already see she'd gotten even better with age. "I just know the Behrs and they're…"

"What?"

Dylan didn't want to dredge up ugly history, but he also knew enough about the Behrs to know what he was talking about.

"Meddlers."

Caroline arched her brow. "Am I supposed to know what that means?"

She wasn't. Nobody in town would. As far as the people of Roseley were concerned, the Behrs were generous with their wealth and very well liked because of it. If he was going to carve out a life in Roseley, it was probably a good idea not to speak poorly of them, especially at a giant wedding where they were invited guests. Discretion was better than a cautionary tale.

"Look, if you need someone to read over your contract, I'd be happy to do it."

"Really?" Caroline said.

"Absolutely."

"Hmm," she said. "What's the catch?"

"No catch."

"Yeah, right. The last time you offered to 'help me' you stole all my good Halloween candy and replaced it with the gross candy no kid ever wants to eat."

"That does sound like something I would do…" Dylan chuckled at the memory. "Didn't I ever apologize for that?"

Caroline glared at him. "Your mouth was too stuffed with king-size chocolate bars to lob much of an apology."

"They were delicious, and I am sorry. Truly."

"Whatever. Anyway, I don't think I could afford your services. Don't lawyers charge for every minute they're even *thinking* about a client?"

Dylan avoided eye contact with Bianca, who was obviously studying the two of them from several tables away. The way her eyes followed every move he made, he wanted to tell her she'd make a lousy spy. Instead, he turned to Caroline, who was oblivious to the fact they were being watched.

"There's never a charge for old friends." He grinned. "Didn't you already know that?"

"We're *not* old friends, Dylan. You were friends with Trig, not me."

"You were always hanging around back then, so how do you think of us? Mates? Pals? Bosom buddies?"

"Bosom buddies?" Caroline cringed. "Ick. Heavens, no."

"Comrades? Chums?"

"Now you're just being ridiculous."

"Aha!" Dylan said, snapping his fingers. "I've got it. You were the kid sister sidekick."

"I was *not* a sidekick."

It wasn't exactly true. She'd always been tagging along when he and Trig had run off to find something to do. Sometimes she'd made her presence known and other times they would catch a glimpse of her, trailing behind as they rode bikes to The Lollipop or fished off the dock.

As he watched her cheeks redden now, he couldn't for the life of him remember why they hadn't let her catch up with them. He didn't mind having her around now and by her sudden reaction, a blaze in her eyes that burned brighter by the second, he realized, perhaps because of his new perspective as an adult, that he was poking at some sort of old wound. It wasn't just his maturity that made him notice how angry his words had made her. Life had changed him in many ways, especially in the last three years. But for now, he didn't want to think about those reasons. Instead, he wanted to cool the heat on her expression.

"I'm joking," he said, genuinely sincere. "I never thought of you as a sidekick."

"Yeah, right."

"Nope. It's true. You are not anyone's sidekick, Red. Not then, and certainly not now. If you're in a position to throw the Behrs' Christmas gala on your own, you should go for it full throttle."

Caroline visibly relaxed.

"Well…thanks."

"You're welcome."

"And it's *Caroline*."

He was about to make a joke about still pushing her buttons when Micah approached.

"Come on," he said. "Are you guys going to dance, or what? Everyone's out there."

It was true. The disc jockey had started playing some fast-tempo songs that had lured most of the guests to the dance floor. Olivia and Tyler were in the center of the group, and by the sweat on Micah's face, it was clear that he'd been enjoying every minute of dancing and was eager to return to the fun.

Dylan shook his head. "I'd like to, but I need to get home." He snatched another plate of cake from the table.

"Well, *Caroline*," he said. "I'm sure we'll think of the right description soon enough. But until then, I'm sticking with 'old friend.' Call me when you get the contract."

He scooted past her and made for the door as Caroline called after him. "Dylan, I still don't agree to the old friend label. And you already had a piece of cake!"

He smiled to himself, pleased. He didn't need to tug on her beautiful hair to get under her skin anymore, but something about talking to Caroline made him wonder if she wasn't the one who would get under his skin if he wasn't careful.

DYLAN RETURNED HOME to discover Isabel on the couch watching an old movie.

"What'd you bring me?" she whispered hopefully.

Dylan handed her the plate of wedding cake before glancing up the stairs.

"What time did she go to bed?" he asked.

"After I talked to you."

"How did things go tonight?"

"Just fine."

"Honestly, Iz. If we're going to all live here

together for a while, we have to trust each other. I need to know."

Isabel set her plate on her lap and peered up at him. "It wasn't perfect, but we all did okay. This is manageable, Dylan. I know you have your doubts, but it really is."

He nodded, though more to end the conversation than to agree with his sister. He'd had his reservations about leaving his life in the city to move back to Roseley. Moving in with his mom and sister ten months ago was proving to be a bigger readjustment than he'd ever anticipated—for everyone.

He climbed the stairs quietly, like he had a million times as a kid. When he reached his old bedroom, he paused at the door before cracking it open.

The room was dark except for a rainbow butterfly night-light on the nightstand. The sound of soft rain emulated from a sound machine in the corner. Delia dozed in a rocking chair, her head resting against the back.

When Dylan touched her softly on the shoulder, she awakened and immediately pressed a finger to her lips. They had gotten pretty good at silently mouthing conversations, so even when they made it out to the hallway, they didn't let their voices rise above a whisper.

"Thanks for watching her," Dylan said. "I'm sorry you had to miss out on the party."

"I'm not. Isabel felt really bad about getting sick and shirking her babysitting duties, but I know she didn't feel well enough to handle things on her own."

"I appreciate you stepping in so I could get a night off."

"How did Olivia look?"

"Beautiful. And Tyler looked very happy."

Delia clasped her hands under her chin. "He was such a sweet child. I'm glad he found a good one in Olivia."

"Me too."

Dylan could almost feel the second part of Delia's thought, left unspoken out of kindness. He had managed to find a beautiful wife as well, though as it had turned out, she hadn't really been one of the good ones. At least, that's how it felt these days.

"She struggled at bedtime," Delia continued. "But we talked about what she wants for Christmas this year and that gave her something to focus on as she fell asleep."

"What did she say she wanted?"

Delia giggled. "Tic Tacs."

"I'd give her the world, if I could, and all she wants is Tic Tacs."

"Orange flavor, to be exact."

"I think I can handle that."

"And…"

Dylan's gut sank as he waited for his mother to finish her sentence. He already knew the second thing his baby girl would want to see on Christmas Day, and it wasn't something he could so easily deliver.

"Giana?" he finally said.

Delia winced. "Maybe they could FaceTime tomorrow, if McKenna brings her up again."

Dylan nodded in agreement. There was nothing he would like more.

"I'm going to turn in for the night, Mom. Thanks for watching her."

"It was my pleasure."

After Dylan got ready for bed, he returned to his bedroom. McKenna, his three-year-old daughter, was sleeping peacefully in the twin bed across from his. In the dim light, she looked like an angel, dark eyelashes resting on full round cheeks. Her chest rose and fell, the rhythm as predictable as the tide.

He leaned over and brushed a kiss to her forehead before slipping into his own bed.

He pulled out his cell phone and scrolled through his camera roll, admiring pictures of McKenna's last Christmas in New York City. At almost two years old, she'd still been very much a baby. She'd changed so much in just one year, though everything in both of their lives had changed dramatically since that Christmas.

When his phone chimed with a message from an unknown phone number, he perked when he read it.

Hope it's OK. I texted Trig for your number.

Who is this? he texted back, though he already knew it was Caroline. In lieu of a proper answer he received…

You're in trouble for taking two pieces of cake.

Dylan's face widened in a smile.

Gonna tattle?

Already did. Police on their way.

Old friends wouldn't do that.

The seconds ticked by as he waited for a response. He was just about to follow it up with another jest when Caroline finally responded.

Were you serious before?

About?

Contract.

Yes.

Dylan hoped Caroline would heed his advice enough to at least proceed cautiously with the Behrs. As he waited for her to text back, he glanced over at McKenna, sleeping beside him. His little girl was the most important thing in his life, and it was a life at a crossroads. He figured he should take his own advice and move a bit more cautiously where Caroline, or anyone else, was concerned. Even if he had noble intentions for wanting to see the strawberry blonde beauty again, that didn't mean he should. He had more than enough reasons not to entertain romantic feelings, especially for his friend's little sister.

Seeing Behrs Monday.

Good luck, he texted back.

The seconds ticked by, one after another. After a minute, he was about to put his phone away when it vibrated with a new text message.

Can I call you?

Dylan knew that Caroline was referring to a call after she met with the Behrs, but some part of him wished for her to call right then. He might have admitted earlier to himself that talking to her had been the highlight of the evening, but if he were honest, it had been the highlight of his week.

Yes.

Thanks.

You're welcome...buddy.

For a long time only three blinking dots, the indicator that Caroline was deciding how to respond, glared back at him from the phone screen. Finally, after what felt like an eternity, she replied.

That's not going to work either.

Dylan smirked to himself, considering what other word substitutions for *friend* he could text her. Finally, he settled on...

We'll think of something.

CHAPTER FOUR

CAROLINE QUICKLY SWUNG her car into her father's driveway with enough umph to bring his neighbor, Joan Baskins, out of her house. The widow had begun renting the house next door after she and her niece, Paige, had moved to Roseley to start a new life. Paige had gotten married and Joan had made fast friends with most of the town.

"Mornin', honey!" Joan called, descending her porch steps and making her way across the small side yard. "I wondered when you'd be by."

"Just checking on things," Caroline said, giving her dad's house a good look up and down. Between his hunting trips and fishing trips and trekking-through-the-wilderness trips, Caroline had seen less and less of her father over the years. That didn't keep her from checking on his house to make sure everything would be in order when he did return home.

"You're a good daughter," Joan said, following behind her as Caroline unlocked the front door and let herself inside. Caroline didn't feel like it. She felt like a daughter who was never measuring up, but it didn't do any good to dwell on such negative thoughts. She certainly wasn't going to start ruminating today when she had a big meeting in…

Caroline glanced at her cell phone. She only had a few minutes to check on the place before getting back to town. Though she usually enjoyed chatting with Joan, today's visit had to be brisk.

"Thanks for keeping an eye on the place," Caroline said before striding briskly into the kitchen, then living room and dining room. Everything looked just as she had left it.

"It's my pleasure!" Joan called, lingering politely in the entryway. "Have you heard anything from your dad?"

Caroline bolted up the stairs and quickly hurried down the hall, peeking inside each room before pulling the door shut with a satisfying slam.

"The last Trig heard," she called, "he was fishing somewhere out west."

"It's a shame he has this big old place when he doesn't spend any time here."

Caroline jogged back down the stairs. It didn't seem like a shame to her. It made perfect sense to keep the house habitable and clean and cozy for her dad's return. Trig also stayed here when he visited.

"Any chance he'll be home for Christmas?" Joan continued, admiring a photograph of Little Lake Roseley hanging on the wall.

Caroline sucked in a breath and plastered on her cheeriest grin. Her father hadn't been home for the last five Christmases.

"Too soon to tell," she said, aware that she should engage more to be polite. She adored Joan. It was just that she was so short on time this morning. "What are your plans?"

Joan's cheeks rounded in a proud smile. "I'm so glad you asked."

"Really?" Caroline said, finally stopping to study her. Joan stuck a thumb to her chest.

"I'm going to be a great-aunt."

"Paige and Charlie?" Caroline said with a gasp. "They're expecting?"

Joan nodded.

"They just told me. Paige and I are going to pick out fabric from Pleats and Patches and make a baby quilt together. It's a great winter project, don't you think?"

Caroline hugged Joan.

"It's a great *anytime* project."

Joan laughed. "Sweetheart, yes. It certainly is!"

Joan's eyes crinkled deeply with delight. Caroline thought of Paige and how good a fresh start in Roseley had seemed to be for her. A move, a wedding and now a baby on the way, things were certainly moving fast for her.

She was thrilled for Paige. Getting married and having a child sounded like wonderful things, but she wasn't really sure she wanted that for herself. She was determined not to repeat her mother's mistakes where those two commitments were concerned, and the best way to do that was to not pursue either. Instead, she was content to focus on starting a new business and landing the Behrs' Christmas gala.

"Joan," Caroline said, leading Joan outside so she could lock up again. "I'm so sorry to run but I have an important meeting. Give Paige and Charlie my congratulations, won't you? I'm so happy for them."

"Of course, of course. I'll tell them. Keep me posted about your dad."

"I will!"

Caroline slid into her car and closed the door. She would leave love and motherhood to women like Paige. In her experience, love didn't last and children were little people she didn't understand. She'd always felt like her parents had not worked very hard to understand her. And now that she was older, they were even more disengaged, especially her mom. The last meaningful conversation she'd had with her had been the day she'd reluctantly stood in her mother's wedding and—

Caroline punched the gas pedal, letting the reverberation of the car engine drown out her bad memories. She wouldn't worry about marriage or family when she had other exciting business adventures to attend to and the next step toward her goal was waiting for her on the other side of town.

CAROLINE SHIVERED AGAINST the wind and hustled through the front doors of The Nutmeg Cafe. She had expected to meet Bianca at her office or the hospital or anywhere besides the charming little restaurant, but when Bianca had suggested the cozy spot, she was happy to comply.

The place was immaculately clean, and vintage paintings and knickknacks covered the walls and adorned shelves that ran around the room's perimeter near the ceiling. The place looked like a charming flea market with most of the decorations on loan from the local antiques shops but available for purchase. Dozens of butter dishes were displayed in an early-twentieth-century hutch cabinet. A grand-father clock and half a dozen cuckoo clocks chimed the time on the hour. Various mirrors and paintings covered the walls.

Being almost Thanksgiving, crafted pumpkins decked out every inch of the room. Some were covered in orange, gold or purple crushed velvet, while others glittered with gold-sequined beads. They were stacked and tucked in every nook and cranny.

From a far table, Bianca waved to her. She was perched on the edge of her chair, dressed business casual, and sipping from a coffee cup. Caroline quickly crossed the room, savoring the aroma of turkey and gravy and hot buttered biscuits.

"Mrs. Behr, nice to see you again," Caroline said, clasping Bianca's hand in a firm shake before settling into the seat across from her. "Thanks for agreeing to meet with me."

"I'm always open to new things," Bianca said, offering a polite smile. "Are you hungry?"

Caroline shook her head though her stomach was growling. "I'll stick with water for now."

"It's not much of a working brunch, then."

Caroline was focused on things other than eating—like a signed contract.

They settled into polite chitchat for a few minutes before Caroline jumped in. "I hope you enjoyed the wedding the other night."

Bianca nodded. "It was lovely. I hear you served as assistant wedding coordinator and maid of honor."

"Coordinating weddings feels like old hat. I'm eager to tackle new things. Tell me about your vision for the Christmas gala."

Bianca's face smoothed into a patient smile. "If you're so eager, why don't you share your vision. I'm sure you're familiar with what we usually do every year."

Of course she was. She'd been familiar with it since she was a teenager. The hospital gala, unofficially dubbed the Behrs' gala, was one of the biggest splashes in town every holiday season.

"There are a number of directions we can go," Caroline began. "I know you typically do a theme every year—Old Hollywood, Arabian Nights, Masquerade—for example. We can select a new theme if you want, but I think your gala already has the best theme built in."

"Which is?"

"Christmas."

Bianca nodded with the roll of her eyes. "After last year's medieval theme debacle, Tex and I were leaning toward a simple Christmas concept."

Caroline had heard all about the gala from the previous year. The Behrs had brought in a big-city coordinator who hadn't had his finger on the pulse of what made Roseley, and its residents, tick. When actors, dressed as knights, had ridden into the ballroom, they hadn't planned on the music spooking the horses. The chaos hadn't struck the right chord for the Behrs, the hospital board or the donors who had been in attendance.

"There is nothing simple about Christmas," Caroline said. "In fact, we can mold Christmas into anything we want." Caroline flipped her planner open and turned it around to face Bianca. "I put together some images to express my vision for it. Imagine a *vintage* Christmas."

She watched with bated breath as Bianca flipped through the plastic sleeves of pictures Caroline had spent the last two days compiling. She'd visited Betty Jenkins at Grandma's Basement, a local antique shop, and had found a stack of beautifully illustrated vintage Christmas cards.

Heavily bundled, rosy-cheeked children raced sleds down a snowy farm hillside. Fawns nudged a star to the top of a woodsy Christmas tree. A family drove a horse-drawn sleigh through a snowy town as carolers sang and waved hello. And, of course, what Christmas card collection would be complete without a chuckling Santa Claus with his cherry cheeks and twinkling eyes.

"Everything from the invitations to the decorations to the menu could be inspired by the Christmas nostalgia you see here. The gala would be a throwback to a simpler time when garland was made of popcorn, homes smelled of pine trees and roasted chestnuts, and people gathered in the center of town to light candles and sing Christmas blessings." Caroline swallowed a lump in her throat as she recalled the last Christmas where the holiday had still had that kind of sparkle. It was the last Christmas before trouble in her parents' marriage had started to show. They'd taken her and Trig for an evening sleigh ride. All evening, while nestled under a heavy blanket, Caroline had followed every lift in her mother's expression, praying that things between her parents would be okay. "This gala wouldn't be about impressing or pushing your agenda," Caroline continued. "It would be an evening to invite guests to relax, take a breath and savor the magic of the season. It would be a time to come together like extended family. When you and I touch their hearts—"

"We touch their pocketbooks," Bianca said with a smirk. Caroline raised her brow. That was not quite what she was going to say, but

Bianca seemed pleased with her own conclusion and continued. "We want to renovate the children's wing of the hospital next year. In order to do that, we need guests to donate generously."

Caroline nodded and pulled a Christmas card out of its plastic sleeve. The aged cardboard felt fuzzy and worn against her fingers. The illustrated image painted on the front was one of her favorites. It was set at night with the dim lights of the Christmas tree glowing in the background. A little child, wearing red footed pajamas and a sleepy smile, was squatting down to offer one of Santa's cookies to a little Christmas mouse. Caroline passed the card to Bianca.

"We can use this gala to tell a story about love and generosity," she said. "The focus will be on the joy Christmas can bring when we focus on its simplicity, on family and community. I can throw you a gala that will inspire people, Ms. Behr. Make them feel like they are part of a greater family that cares for the children of Roseley. I have no doubt we can hit your fundraising goal for the hospital wing."

Bianca traced a finger over the card's image. After several moments, she looked up at Caroline.

"Ms. Waterson, I love it."

"That's wonderful," Caroline said. Her heart began thudding so hard, it felt like a bunny was thumping against the inside of her rib cage. "I'll draw up a contract and get it to you for review and—"

"Not so fast," Bianca said, setting the Christmas card on the table. "I want to leave the theme and planning in your hands. However, there is something important Tex and I want for the gala and it's nonnegotiable."

"Okay…" Caroline said hesitantly though she knew she'd promise Bianca the moon if she could just sign a contract with her. "Name it."

"We don't want to hold the gala at The Ballroom this year."

Caroline tipped her head forward, curious. The Ballroom, the largest reception hall in Roseley, was the only place big enough to hold the gala.

"Do you still want to hold the gala in Roseley?" Caroline asked.

"Yes, of course. But a new venue came onto our radar this year and we want it."

Caroline scrambled to think of any venue even half the size of The Ballroom. Other than holding it outside, a terrible idea during a Roseley winter, she was at a loss, although she hated to admit it. What sort of event planner didn't know about a new venue coming on the market? But after drawing a complete blank, she didn't have a choice but to ask.

"Where are you thinking?"

Bianca tipped her head thoughtfully to the side. "Tex and I dated during a different era." It was true. Tex and Bianca had at least forty years on Caroline. "We were coming of age when society norms were changing, but we still enjoyed a couple of teenage years meeting friends at dances. You know, the kind of dances where young people congregated in a beautiful hall with a big band and gentlemen asked ladies to dance."

Caroline hated that she still couldn't connect the dots. She visualized the Roseley streets, scanning past shops and restaurants in her mind, searching for someplace that would fit the bill. Desperation took hold, making her clench her fists tightly under the table as she strained to think.

Finally, her mind came to the old, broken-down marquee on Egleston Drive. It was a street on the far edge of town, a place she hadn't driven by in ages. No one ever did. There was nothing along the long, lonely street except a dilapidated dance hall that had sat vacant for all of Caroline's life and probably since Bianca and Tex had been teenagers. Over the years the dance hall would be mentioned in the newspaper when someone had started plans to purchase it and turn it into a movie theater or office building. But deals always fell through.

"The Egleston Drive dance hall?" Caroline said slowly. Bianca's eyes brightened.

"Yes, that's it. Although back in my day it was called The Starlight. The high ceiling was painted to look like the night sky. We learned recently that someone bought it and has been quietly renovating it for months."

Caroline struggled to suppress her confusion. "Renovating it to be what exactly? A dance hall again?"

"I very much doubt that. Kids don't go out dancing the way they used to."

Caroline knew kids still danced but certainly not in the way Bianca probably remembered.

"Mrs. Behr," Caroline continued, "I doubt the new owner will have it renovated in the next month. Renovations of that scale take a long time."

"It's worth a shot, isn't it? I remember it being so beautiful inside. I hope they keep the charm of the old place."

Caroline wondered if her contract truly hinged on securing The Starlight.

"I suppose I can look into it…" she said carefully. "If it's not a viable location, then we can keep your reservation with The Ballroom—"

"Oh, no no no," Bianca said, waving a hand in the air to waft Caroline's suggestion away. "You must do more than look into it. *We want The Starlight.* If you think I'm giving you an ultimatum to secure The Starlight or forget throwing our gala…" Caroline braced herself as Bianca's stare darkened in seriousness. "Then you'd be right."

Caroline refrained from slumping back in her chair. Bianca loved her theme and concept for the gala and because of that she was close to landing a job that could positively steer the direction of her life. If she landed the Christmas gala, she would have the commission and a high-profile reference to strike out on her own. She could be her own boss, do things the way she wanted, and best of all, she'd never have to plan another wedding for as long as she lived.

Fate was dangling the opportunity of a lifetime in front of her face and if she could figure out a way to not only secure The Starlight but throw a gala there in the midst of renovations, she would find a way to do it.

"I will contact the new owner and get back to you as soon as possible," Caroline said, struggling to exude every bit of confidence she could muster. "Hopefully they are willing to work with us."

Bianca sat back in her chair, studying Caroline as a pleased smirk spread over her face.

"And if they are not willing?"

Caroline didn't want to make promises she wasn't sure she could keep. For all she knew, The Starlight had been purchased by a land developer who planned to gut the building and erect a car wash or convenience store. He or she might not even live in Roseley.

"If I can find him or her," Caroline began, "I will do everything in my power to book The Starlight for your Christmas gala."

Bianca gathered her purse and peeled off some cash to leave for the bill.

"That's what I wanted to hear," she said, slipping into her coat. "I have to run, Caroline, but I'm excited about this. Excited about *you*. I know you're the right person for the job."

Caroline beamed, scrambling to follow Bianca out of the restaurant.

"Thank you, Mrs. Behr. That means a lot to me. I'll head over to The Starlight now and see what I can find out about the new owner."

Bianca cinched the collar of her coat tighter and flashed Caroline a wink before strutting to her car. Over her shoulder, she called, "You'll know him when you see him!"

CHAPTER FIVE

DYLAN PARKED IN front of The Sandwich Board and rolled his eyes. His ex-wife, Giana, had a way of turning every situation into something about her.

"You can't keep our daughter from me, Dylan," she huffed into the phone.

"That's not what I'm doing," Dylan said, trying for control. "All I said is that ten o'clock at night is too late for McKenna to talk. She has to stick to a schedule. Without a good night's sleep—"

"With your work, Dylan, I doubt you're keeping her on a strict schedule."

"I'm doing my best. I'm sure we can find a mutually convenient time for the two of you to talk. She misses you."

"And I miss her so much," Giana said, her voice breaking. "May I remind you that our situation is because of you, Dylan. *You're* the one who chose to move halfway across the country with our daughter."

Dylan grasped the back of his neck. He had

wanted desperately for Giana and McKenna to have a loving, supportive mother-daughter relationship in New York City, but Giana had always wanted to do parenthood and marriage on her own terms. He hadn't wanted to move back to Roseley, but when he'd prioritized what was in McKenna's best interest, he had decided it was the right thing to do.

"You may call McKenna at any time during the morning or evening," Dylan said. "But she needs to stick to a reasonable sleep schedule and ten o'clock is just too late."

"Fine. I'll do that," Giana said. He could hear her huffing as she walked. Wherever she was going, she was heading there fast. "I have to lead a meeting in two minutes. I'll call her later."

Dylan closed his eyes, wanting his words to convey nothing but sincerity. "She'll be happy to hear from you, Giana."

Giana sighed. "I know. Bye."

Dylan ended the call and slumped back against the headrest. Angelo, a retired-aged man with a mass of smiley wrinkles, emerged from the shop, a giant brown bag of sandwiches in tow. Dylan rolled down the window to greet him.

"Thank you, Angelo," he said, accepting the giant bag.

"No, thank *you*. We love bulk orders, especially when you call it in the night before. It makes things much easier on us, especially my CeCe."

"How's she doing today?"

Angelo beamed. "She's pretty excited. We're flying to Florida tomorrow to visit our daughter, Tracy. She has an ocean-view timeshare."

"That sounds fantastic."

"CeCe has been counting down the days for the last two months."

"What about you?"

"I can do some fun in the sun, but I'll be ready to get home after a week."

"You always struck me as someone who could be happy and content anywhere."

Angelo chuckled. "I love the buildup to the holidays. For me, nothing is better than Christmas in Roseley."

Dylan understood. It had been years since he'd been in Roseley for Christmas. He was looking forward to experiencing it this year with McKenna.

"I hear you. Safe travels and have fun."

"Thank you, thank you," Angelo said, patting the truck hood as he hurried back into his sandwich shop.

Dylan pulled away and made it halfway down the street when his cell phone rang again.

This time he bit his lip with delight when he saw the name on his caller ID.

"Well, if it isn't Roseley's up-and-coming event planner," he said in lieu of a hello. "When do you have your big meeting with Bianca?"

"It was this morning," Caroline said.

"Are congratulations in order?" From what he had seen at Tyler and Olivia's wedding, Bianca would be a fool to not hire Caroline on the spot. Although, in his experience with the Behrs, they didn't always see what was right in front of them.

"Not quite," Caroline said, the disappointment in her voice making him groan.

"Oh, boy," he said. "What hoops does she want you to jump through first?"

"What makes you think there are hoops?"

"Life experience."

"You know, Dylan," Caroline said, a playful jest to her tone, "nearly everyone in Roseley adores the Behrs. If you have some big beef with them, you might want to ask yourself why."

"Is that what I should do?" Dylan said, pulling up to the job site. He threw his truck into Park and grabbed the giant bag of sandwiches. By the time he had climbed out of his truck and had made it to the tailgate, his friend

Bobby had arrived to lend a hand. "You know I'm always open to advice."

Dylan opened the tailgate and motioned to the coolers of drinks. He handed the bag to Bobby, who headed off to pass out lunch.

"I very much doubt that."

"Is that anyway to talk to your mate?"

"Mate." Caroline snorted a laugh. "Before we fall down *that* rabbit hole again, I called to see if you were true to your word."

Dylan straightened. "Always."

"Bianca wants to hire me as her event planner, but she set a special condition."

Dylan grimaced. "Of course she did. Just drop the contract by the house and I'll review it tonight."

"Well, it's not as easy as that." Caroline cleared her throat as she continued. "My theme is a throwback to a vintage Christmas. You know, the kind of Christmas from when we were kids and life seemed so much simpler."

Dylan's mind drifted to Christmases of his childhood. If he had had a choice of a hundred adjectives to describe Christmas back then, he wouldn't have chosen *simpler*. Nothing about celebrating with his family, especially his workaholic father, had been simple.

The memories, battling to spring up uninvited, sent him striding faster across the parking lot and through the loading dock off the back of the building where Bobby and the other workers were unwrapping their sandwiches. He returned a friendly wave to his crew before continuing through the darkened building.

"What does that have to do with Bianca's special condition?"

"Landing this gala is the most important thing to me, Dylan, and I'm willing to work with any and all parties involved, no matter how much they antagonize me."

Dylan chuckled, running his hand over a worktable, as he wandered through a grand hall covered in a heavy coating of construction dust.

"I thought I was the only person who could really antagonize you, Red. Isn't that what you used to tell me?"

"It was true when we were kids," Caroline said. "And it is unfortunately still true today. For example, didn't I tell you to call me Caroline?"

"Old habits die hard."

"Look. I want to bury the hatchet and forge a better relationship with you."

Dylan slid an extension cord out of his path with his foot as he contemplated Caroline's words. As much as he liked the idea of getting along with her, he was confused why she was offering an olive branch at this moment, over the phone and without provocation.

He waved up to electricians who were walking on scaffolding nearly thirty feet off the ground.

Dylan covered the mouthpiece of his cell phone and called up to them.

"Lunch is at the loading dock!"

Exiting the hall, he made his way to the lobby and glanced around, checking on the progress his crew had made over the last few weeks. He had a ways to go, but he knew the project would be a success.

"Look, Caroline," he said. "You're going to have to be frank with me. I'm in the middle of work so unless you have a specific question that you need answered right this second, maybe we can talk later."

"That's the thing," Caroline said. "I do have a specific question for you."

"Can you get to it, then?"

"I think I need to ask it face-to-face."

Dylan scowled in confusion as he accepted a clipboard from his foreman and glanced over the checklist.

"I already said I'd review your contract."

"That's not what I need to talk to you about. In fact…"

Dylan passed the clipboard back to his foreman and grasped his hip as he waited.

"I think you'd better step outside," she said.

"I'm at work."

"Yeah," Caroline mumbled. "I know."

Dylan glanced at the front glass doors that led outside to the street. They were opaque from years of dirt and grime.

"Wait a minute," he said. "Are you...*here*?" No one, aside from his family and his crew, knew what he had planned to do for a living once he returned to Roseley. He'd managed to find investors, purchase a building and hire a crew very quietly. If a beautiful redhead was standing on the opposite side of the doors, it meant she knew he was no longer practicing law.

Dylan unlocked the dead bolt and pushed the front doors open into the chilly air. He stepped outside and glanced around before spotting Caroline on the sidewalk. She threw a single wave as he made his way to her.

She was wrapped in a cornflower blue winter coat with faux white fur around the collar. The cool blue against her peachy complexion made her clear eyes sparkle like sapphires.

"Hi," she chirped, abnormally enthusiastic. He raised a single brow.

"Hi..."

She glanced at the weathered marquee above their heads. The light bulbs had long been burned out and the paint had peeled and fallen away decades earlier. A large section of the sign had been dismantled and hauled away. But still, in the void where bright lights had once glimmered, Dylan could still see the spirit of the old building. It had been neglected for a long time but he knew its magic was still there, patiently waiting to be restored to its original greatness.

"You know," she said. "I remember your dad talking about this place when we were kids. He said it was spectacular back in the day."

Dylan's dad had regaled many stories of his evenings spent at The Starlight. When the topic of the dance hall came up, his dad had usually tipped his head back with a nostalgic sigh, recalling the razzle and dazzle of the place.

Dylan's grandparents had owned a dance studio and after Dylan's dad was born, they had brought him along for special occasions at The Starlight when they had taught lessons before big events and dances. The place had already started to go out of fashion by the time his dad was a teenager, but his dad's face rarely lit up the way it did when he was remembering his early years spent there.

"That's what he said." Dylan tried for nonchalant, not ready to divulge his secret, but when the corner of Caroline's mouth twisted, he knew his cover had already been blown.

"When you said you moved back to Roseley," she said, "I assumed it was to practice law. I never took you for a business owner."

Dylan frowned. "Who told you that?"

"I have my sources."

Dylan repressed a groan.

"Delia," he said flatly. His mother had never met a person she didn't want to help. He usually loved that about her, but under this circumstance not so much so.

Not that buying The Starlight was a monster secret. It had been a little secret, something he hadn't wanted to advertise around town until he'd had a chance to start renovations and get a sense that he could do it. Getting McKenna settled into their new life, away from New York City and sadly absent of Giana, would have been challenging enough. Also buying an old dance hall with a stigmatized past and finding a way to renovate it and positively market it to the people of Roseley was like climbing Everest—without oxygen.

Caroline winced. "Yeah. I've been asking around all morning to find the new owner. After a lot of dead ends, I talked to CeCe at The Sandwich Board. She told me she fills a large lunch order once a week to feed a renovation crew. Then Angelo said you are the one who always picks it up. It made me very curious why that would be. What would a bigwig, New York City lawyer like Dylan Metzger be doing with a remodeling crew in this town?"

"I'm not a bigwig—"

"I remembered that I saw you driving a truck the other night…"

"Leaving the wedding?" His eyes narrowed to feigned sultriness. "Were you stalking me?"

"At the time I noted how I didn't picture you as a truck guy. I figured you for some sort of luxury car with a bloated lease payment—"

"Get to the point, *Red*."

He had said her old nickname to get back on some equal footing with her. Something about her discovering his project, without him having any say about it, brought out his antagonistic side.

Caroline pressed her lips firmly together and he could tell she was tempted to correct him. She sucked a breath and continued.

"Delia said you bought The Starlight."

"Did she at least hem and haw before telling you?"

Caroline tipped her head, contemplative. "Nope. She also said she's making Italian meatballs for dinner and that I'm invited. She's sweet."

Dylan shrugged even though he agreed. Delia's invitation to move home had been a godsend when he had been at his lowest point. She could do whatever she wanted for the rest of his life, and he would refuse to get upset with her—for the most part.

"You obviously went through a lot of trouble," he said. "So, what do you want?"

"Well…" Caroline swayed on her feet and flashed him the most beautiful smile he'd ever seen. For a second, the brilliance of it made his stomach clench to keep from showing how much it affected him. Maybe he really was climbing Everest without oxygen because the sight of her left him light-headed. "The Behrs don't want to hold their gala at The Ballroom this year. Apparently, they think very fondly of this place. They used to attend dances here. Since I'm *mates* with the owner I thought you would be willing to…"

A grumble rose in Dylan's throat.

"Oh, no," he said, holding up his hands in objection. "No way. Nuh-uh."

"Dylan," Caroline pleaded, following as he turned and bolted for the doors. "Buddy, friend, comrade, just listen for a second."

Dylan slipped through the front doors of The Starlight and strode through the lobby with

Caroline hot on his heels. He lodged a pointer finger in each ear and shook his head.

"Nope, nope, nope," he mumbled. "La, la, la, la, la. Not going to happen."

"Dylan!" Caroline's cry warbled, muffled because of his childhood antics that for the first time in his life made perfect sense. He really did not want to hear what she would say next.

He caught sight of Bobby and a few other guys and even though they were watching with notable amusement, one guy elbowing Bobby as he broke into a chuckle, Dylan didn't care.

Caroline didn't understand what she was asking him to do. He had started very ambitious renovations this year, but he had the energy and excitement to do it because the goals he was reaching for were all his. He wasn't going to open himself up to anyone else's expectations or timelines, *especially* the Behrs.

When they'd made it to the dance floor, the room seemed dark and empty, but Dylan knew better. The electricians were still diligently, yet quietly, working on the scaffolding over the stage.

Caroline, obviously oblivious to them, tugged hard at his elbow. His finger popped out of his ear as her voice echoed against the staggered pillars around the perimeter of the room.

"Dylan, please! Would you just listen to me for a second?"

He slowed and crossed his arms across his chest as Caroline darted around to face him.

"We could really help each other," she continued. "I know it."

"Is that so?"

"Yes. I've given it a lot of thought."

"In the short time since you realized I bought this place? How long has it been? A full forty-five minutes?"

"Sometimes the best ideas don't need a lot of processing time. When you know it's right, you just *know*."

He huffed, not buying any of it.

"What do you think, guys?" he called, motioning to his crew on the scaffolding. Gerald, one of the electricians, hooted in agreement.

Slowly, Caroline turned, her face brightening, though he quickly realized it wasn't from embarrassment. She held a look of awe, much like he had the first time he'd sneaked into The Starlight.

When he'd seen the aged fresco paintings covering the walls and the long stretch of warped, wooden flooring leading to the band stage, he'd imagined, for the first time, a life trajectory that hadn't been unjustly dictated by his father. For the first time, he'd allowed himself to imagine doing something...else.

"Talk about a time capsule," Caroline said, spinning in a slow circle to admire it all.

"Right?" Dylan said, forgetting everything except how serene Caroline's face looked. "I want to keep the integrity of the place. We're stripping this floor and upgrading to a Marley floor that will look similar."

"When does that go in?"

"It's one of the last things. We have to finish painting first."

"You have to take pictures before you do that."

Dylan huffed in amusement. "I had a professional photographer come through as soon as I got the keys. Betty Jenkins had some framed photos of the place back in its glory days. Do you want to see?"

Caroline grinned. *"Yes."*

Dylan led Caroline to a small adjacent room he'd claimed as a makeshift office while his permanent office was under construction. He slid out a few poster-sized frames he had left leaning against the wall. Betty had kept large photographs of the original lobby and dance hall. She even had a few event posters of the big bands that had passed through town.

"Betty to the rescue," he said. "I'll hang these

up in the lobby once renovations are complete. Folks can see what it looked like when it first opened."

"Oh, my," Caroline breathed. "I had no idea how gorgeous this place was."

"Yeah. It's kind of sad, really. Culture changed and attending dances fell out of fashion quickly. From what I understand, the previous owners struggled to find a new market and then when The Ballroom opened, everything was modernized for parties, not dances. They couldn't compete."

"It's strange that it sat vacant for so long."

"It's almost been bulldozed half a dozen times. Luckily for me, it never was."

Caroline traced her fingers over a framed picture of a big band playing to a hall of beautifully dressed teenagers. It was a time when men gave women corsages.

"Why did you buy it?" She looked up, studying him carefully. The weight of her question and all that would be required to do his answer justice made him feel instantly exposed. He readjusted his hand positioning on the frame.

"Who wouldn't?" he managed, hoping the answer would appease her. "Check out that ceiling. It made people look up…" He turned to face her. "It will again one day."

Caroline sighed with satisfaction. "She'll be thrilled."

"Who?"

"Bianca. She was hoping you'd renovate to keep the original essence. She specifically mentioned the ceiling."

Dylan harrumphed and slid the frame back into place. The last thing he ever wanted to do was thrill the likes of Bianca Behr. "I already know what you and the Behrs want," he said. "But the answer is no."

"Dylan," Caroline said, following him out of the office and toward the back loading dock. "I don't know what your history with the Behrs is, and you don't have to tell me if you don't want to—"

"Gee, thanks."

"But if you want to change the public's perception of this place and, you know, eventually make money after you open, the Behrs' Christmas gala can put The Starlight on the map in a big way."

"I don't need the Behrs—"

"Of course you don't, but their money burns the same as anyone else's, doesn't it? Their gala could help get you out of the red from buying this place, couldn't it? No event in Roseley is bigger than theirs."

Dylan stopped and faced her. He was a long

way off from being out of the red, but she still had a point.

"Ninety percent of new businesses fail within the first year," Caroline continued. "And of the ones that succeed, ninety percent of those fail within the first five years. You can't afford to be choosy, Dylan. I am literally dropping the best Christmas gift in your lap. The Behrs will pay you handsomely to throw their gala here and if they love this place…"

"What?" Dylan said, frowning though interested. Caroline leaned in, delivering her next words with a dulcet tone and smile.

"You'll be golden."

Dylan released a groan out of concession. The Behrs' endorsement would go a long way in reframing how the residents of Roseley saw The Starlight. He wanted to hold weddings and galas and graduations here. He wanted it to be *the* Roseley destination for the biggest and brightest parties of each season. He wanted it to be a magical place he could share with McKenna. He just didn't want the Behrs involved in the opening. Not them. Not for his first event. He wanted to do the first one on his own.

"You make a great case, Caroline," he said. "But unfortunately, we won't be done by Christmas. Even if we expedited things, which we can't do, it wouldn't get the place finished by Christmas."

"Christmas Eve," Caroline corrected. "We need it good enough by Christmas Eve."

"Good enough?" Dylan said with a scowl. He wasn't going to debut The Starlight until it was perfect. It had to be impossible for anyone in town to criticize, because they wouldn't just be judging the building, they'd be criticizing why a successful lawyer like him had left his career and invested everything he had into a property his dad had once sadly called "the eyesore of Roseley." He had never thought himself a perfectionist—far from it—but he had a vision for The Starlight, and he wasn't going to settle for "good enough" just to accommodate the Behrs' timeline.

"This place already has charm and character," Caroline said with so much zeal he couldn't help but think she believed it. "My Vintage Christmas doesn't need a perfectly polished hall to be spectacular. Having things a little…undone—"

"Undone?" This time Dylan laughed so hard Caroline's face instantly went pink.

"Well," she said defensively, "people will love that it isn't finished. They'll feel like they got a sneak peek. They can say they saw it first, saw it when it was still a diamond in the rough. It's the same as finding a talented garage band before they become famous. They'll feel like they discovered The Starlight, and they'll love that, Dylan. I *know* it."

Her voice broke as tears filled her eyes. She spoke with such passion, such conviction, he couldn't help but wonder if *she* was the lawyer instead of him.

"What has gotten into you?" Dylan said, stepping closer. "You're far from the Caroline Waterson who clogged around in her dad's old muddy work boots while digging for worms with us. You're…"

Caroline's brows pinched together. "What?" she said, the word low and pointed.

"Hmm," Dylan said, truly unable to name it. "Something."

He wanted to say something special. He wanted to say that listening to her reignited his own passion for this place. But he couldn't find a way to say that without feeling exposed.

"Dylan, I've been doing things Sheila's way for years and not getting a lick of the credit. Come Christmas I'm either launching my new business with the Behrs' gala or I'm hitting the unemployment line and looking for a new job because there is no way I'm beginning the new year as someone's assistant again. I want to create something magical for myself. Haven't you ever dreamed of something no one else can imagine but you?"

A chill skittered up the back of Dylan's neck, partly because of the conviction in Caroline's voice and the mere fact that, yes, he had. He'd daydreamed of renovating The Starlight for a lot longer than he'd admitted to anyone. It had been safer to protect his dream from the judgment of others. Well, the judgment of two critical people in particular; one lived in his old New York City apartment but spent all her time at the office, while the other was a workaholic who had died a few years ago without really getting to know him or Isabel, his children.

But now that he had already started the process, the reality of doing something of his own, *on* his own, made him so darn scared and so darn excited at the same time, he sometimes didn't know which emotion would win the day. As he stared into Caroline's eyes, he recognized a kindred fierceness.

"Dylan?" she pressed, batting long black eyelashes up at him. "Dylan, do this for us."

"For us?" he said. After battling with Giana for the last two years, he was far from wanting to be a part of an "us" unless it was in reference to him and McKenna. Even in business, taking on an "us" felt dangerous. In his experience, the other half of any "us" he'd been a part of had eventually walked out without remorse.

"Listen…" he began. If he was even going to consider hosting the Behrs' party, he had plenty of ground rules to lay down first. "If we're throwing the gala here—"

Caroline bounced a half a step off her feet, a squeal escaping her throat. "I knew you'd see it my way! We will throw the most beautiful gala this town has ever seen!"

She shoved a file of paperwork into Dylan's hands and sprinted for the doors.

"Hey!" Dylan called after her. "I didn't agree to—where are you going?"

"We'll hammer out details later!" she called on her way out the doors. "I have to call Bianca right away. You made the right decision, Dylan!"

When the doors latched shut behind her, Dylan blinked, mouth agape. She had come in like a lamb and blown out of the room like a lion, and he felt woozy about what had transpired in between.

Dylan opened the file folder. An early-twentieth-century drawing of Santa Claus stared up at him.

"Big guy," Dylan breathed. "I don't know what just happened, but I think I'm in for a wild ride."

CHAPTER SIX

CAROLINE SLID ONTO a stool behind the front counter of The Lollipop, Roseley's charming candy shop, and grabbed Faith's root beer float. After taking a loud, giant slurp through the straw, she sat back and flashed her cousin a satisfied grin.

"Hey, leave some for me," Faith said. "What's gotten into you?"

"I just landed my first solo job."

"What?" Faith leaned closer, her eyes widening with excitement. "The Behrs?"

Caroline nodded excitedly. "Yep! Can you believe it? Dylan is looking over our contracts now."

"Dylan Metzger? Wait, now I'm confused."

"He bought The Starlight Dance Hall—"

"That crappy building on Egleston Drive?"

"That's the one!" Caroline sang. "But it looks different inside than what you can see from the road."

"Geesh, I sure hope so. For your sake."

"I'm going to deliver the contract to Bianca

in the morning and then give Sheila my two weeks' notice—"

"Two weeks? Yikes."

Caroline slumped on her seat. She'd been so excited about how quickly things were moving forward with the Christmas gala she hadn't given herself much time to think about delivering the bad news to her current boss. She had been warning Sheila for months that she had been taking steps to start her own event planning business, although where Sheila focused primarily on weddings, Caroline had plans to focus on other events. Sheila always promised that she would be happy to support Caroline when the time came, but she never took steps to find more help or a replacement, despite Caroline's warnings that she should.

"We have a wedding the day after Thanksgiving and another one that Sunday and after that she's on her own."

"Will she be able to find help for the Christmas weddings?"

"Honestly, I do most of everything for her. She wouldn't need to find my replacement right away if she just did the heavy lifting herself."

"Okay, enough about Sheila," Faith said, motioning to Mallory, the owner, that they would need two more root beer floats. "Tell me about the gala."

The gala.

Caroline grasped her hands tightly in her lap and tried to repress the nagging feeling that quitting her job and putting all of her career eggs in one basket prematurely was a dangerous risk. She'd been so averse to taking risks in the past, in nearly every area of her life, if anyone was shocked at her recent rush of enthusiasm, it was certainly her.

With a decisive nod she explained, "The commission will get my new business started real quick."

Outwardly, she was determined to appear bold. Inwardly, she was determined to ignore her modest bank account.

"Are you sure?"

Caroline gnawed at the inside of her cheek, subtly pinching it between her teeth in a way Faith couldn't see. She wasn't *completely* sure that a successful gala would help her establish her business, but being an entrepreneur meant taking risks, didn't it? If she wanted a life other than the one she had, she had to take some chances.

Caroline gave a toothy grin, hoping her over-enthusiasm would help keep her nerves in check.

"And you're going to be working with Dylan Metzger?" Faith waggled her eyebrows.

Caroline straightened her shoulders, determined not to think of Dylan as anything other than a means to a professional end. Letting her mind wander even a little bit ignited those nerves again, though a very, *very* different type.

"Unfortunately."

"Girl, more like fortunately. He's no John, mind you," Faith said, batting her eyelashes as she referenced her husband. "But he did nothing but turn heads at Olivia's wedding."

Caroline rolled her eyes. "If you like the tall, dark and handsome type, I guess."

"You don't?"

"He's not my type."

"Honey, he's everyone's type."

"He's annoying and antagonistic. I have no idea what he's doing throwing away his law degree to renovate an old dance hall, but frankly, I don't care. He and his dance hall are going to help me get my business off the ground."

"Then I'm glad you two reconnected."

"We were never close so I wouldn't say 'reconnected.'"

"That's not how I remember it. He and Trig were as thick as thieves back in the day and you were always in the picture somehow. Your little trio—"

"We were no trio," Caroline said, harrumphing. Just recalling the old days made her prior excitement wane quickly. "He and Trig were always off doing stuff with Dad and I was left behind."

"Didn't you keep up with them step for step? Fishing, shooting—"

"Nuh-uh," Caroline said, eager to set the record straight. "Dad didn't want to waste his time teaching *me* to shoot." She lowered her voice to mimic her father. "'Trig has the natural skill, honey. He has the eye of a marksman. Archery is a man's game.'"

Caroline's gut twisted as she tried to hide her hurt. She'd recalled her dad's words many times over the years and still found them hallow. Though he never said it, he apparently thought things like talking and visiting were activities best reserved for Trig too.

"Oh," Faith said. "Whenever I hung around, your dad was willing to teach us stuff too. Why do you think I like working on motorcycles? I learned how to fix a Harley-Davidson Shovelhead engine in your driveway."

"Yeah, I know." Mallory slid her a root beer with a wink. She gratefully accepted it and swirled the straw around the glass before continuing. "You remember him being around but in reality, spending time with us, you and me, didn't really happen that often. I lived with the guy and for the better part of my life he was either spending time with Trig or taking off with him to camp, hunt or fish. I was assigned to Mom and you know how that worked out."

Faith grimaced in empathy.

"How is she doing?"

Caroline bristled, not wanting to talk about her mother. Instead, she powered on.

"Trig was assigned to Dad. Even though I wanted things to be more balanced, they never were. In reality, Dylan probably spent more time with Dad than I ever did. Weird, right?"

"Super weird. Families are…"

"What?"

"Thorny."

Caroline raised her glass with a declarative nod. Faith had suffered her own thorny childhood. Their upbringings had been different, but a common theme of being overlooked felt eerily similar. *Thorny* was right. Caroline had spent years trying to squeeze her way into places she hadn't been invited. As a result, her heart had certainly been pricked and pierced.

They clinked their glasses together in a sign

of solidarity as Caroline's cell phone rang. A glance at the caller ID showed Sheila's name. Caroline held up the screen to show Faith before slipping off her stool. She grabbed her coat and hurried outside.

"Caroline, dear," Sheila said, launching into her latest crisis before Caroline could mutter a hello. "I need to speak to you right away."

"I can head back to the office—"

"No, no, no. The Burgenston wedding for this Sunday is canceled."

"Canceled? Why?"

"The bride realized she's in love with the best man and the groom realized he wants to move to Europe and study architecture. Love is strange."

Caroline thought love was too unpredictable for her. It was why she could never stomach wedding planning. People thought every aspect of their wedding was a reflection of their swelling love for each other. But with every detail she helped them plan, all she saw was how hurt they would eventually feel. The infatuation would wear off and they would realize they had made a horrible mistake.

Caroline snuggled down farther into her coat. Every wedding she worked on only reminded her of her mother's betrayal.

"I emailed you a to-do list," Sheila said,

powering on. "I'm sure I'll think of more. Cancel all the vendors and make sure you confirm things with the Flores wedding on Friday. We can't afford for two holiday weddings to fall through. That would be just my luck."

Caroline winced. It was really bad timing to put in her two weeks' notice when Sheila had just been dealt an ugly blow. Still, she had to rip off the Band-Aid sooner than later.

"Sheila," she said. "I need to talk to you when I get back to the office. It's important and—"

"Sorry, dear, but I'm getting a nail dip this afternoon. How's tomorrow?"

"It can't wait."

"Then meet me at Bellissima. You can talk and I can beautify."

"Sheila—"

"I'm getting another call. See you in a bit!"

Caroline shoved her cell phone into the front pocket of her coat. It looked like she'd be giving her two weeks' notice in front of an audience.

FOR MONTHS CAROLINE had practiced how to tender her resignation letter but as she arrived to Bellissima, a local beauty shop, she knew she had not visualized properly. After a quick glance about the shop, she found Sheila reclined in a lavender-colored chair while wearing a teal face mask and cucumbers over her eyes.

"I thought you were getting a nail dip," Caroline said, dropping her resignation letter lifelessly at her side. Harper, one of the technicians, grinned at her.

"She decided she wanted the works."

"The works, eh?"

"When life gives you lemons," Sheila said, mumbling through a small mouth slit, "you visit Harper."

Caroline blew away a curly hair strand, feeling relieved Sheila couldn't see the annoyance on her face. Harper, however, was quick to notice.

"Would you like to take the chair next to her?" Harper asked. "You have a little stress forming between your brows. We can soften that with a green tea formula I've been developing."

"No, thanks, Harper. I have a lot to do today."

It was the understatement of the century. First, deliver her two weeks' notice. Second, tackle everything on Sheila's extensive to-do list. Third, collect the contract from Dylan and hand-deliver it to Bianca. Sometime in there she needed to get started on gala plans, confirm items for the Flores wedding and, eventually, find something to eat.

"Hungry?" Harper said, as if reading her mind.

"Starving."

Harper smiled knowingly and led her to a cooler by the register, which was stocked with goodies from The Lollipop.

"Mallory delivered macaroons this morning. Help yourself."

Caroline snagged a few pastel-colored macaroons and perched on the edge of a recliner next to Sheila.

"Look, Sheila," she said. "I don't want to do this here, but I think the sooner you know, the better."

"Would you like me to step away?" Harper asked. "I don't mind."

"Nonsense, stay," Sheila said. "What happens at the beauty shop stays at the beauty shop. Right, Caroline?"

Harper looked to Caroline for direction. Caroline didn't want to make her uncomfortable but something about having her nearby helped calm her nerves.

Caroline relaxed her expression to imply Harper should stay as Sheila plucked the cucumbers off her eyes and glared at Caroline.

"Don't tell me," she said, her normally gregarious voice now as flat as roadkill. "You're leaving me."

"I wouldn't put it that way," Caroline said.

Things weren't meant to be personal. She was leaving Sheila's business, not her life. While she *was* looking forward to putting a lot of distance between the two of them, her decision to leave was mostly for business reasons. "But, yes. I'm giving you my notice."

Sheila's face contorted into disgust. Caroline gulped and braced for impact.

"How? *Why?*" Sheila cried, sitting up a little straighter in her chair. "Haven't I been good to you? Taught you everything I know?"

Caroline shoved a macaroon in her mouth to keep from delivering a rude retort. Sheila hadn't taught her much. Most of what Caroline had learned had been from figuring things out on her own. Sheila's coaching style was more sink or swim. She'd hired Caroline on, then left her with little guidance or preparation.

"I appreciate everything you've done for me, Sheila," Caroline managed after a few seconds. "As we discussed several times before, I have no intention of doing anything to infringe on your business. But I'm ready to strike out on my own. I always said it would happen. Today's the day."

"Today?" Sheila said in horror. *"Today?"*

"Well, I'm giving you my notice today. I will stay on for the next two weeks."

"Ha. No," Sheila scoffed. She tipped her

head back on her headrest again and placed the cucumbers back on her eyelids. "You will stay on until you find your replacement."

Caroline frowned.

"Sheila, I can't do that. You've known for months I was leaving."

"It's the busy season," Sheila said matter-of-factly. "I need a replacement."

Caroline sat, confused. It was certainly not the busy season for weddings. It wasn't slow but it certainly wasn't busy.

"Sheila—"

"Harper, dear," Sheila said with urgency. "Would you get me a sparkling water? This mask is dehydrating."

Harper winced.

"Sure," Harper said, making for the cooler again.

"Sheila, look…" Caroline began.

"Oh, Caroline, dear, are you still there?"

Caroline gritted her teeth.

"You know I am."

"Good. Dear, there is no way you can leave me high and dry without finding me a replacement. Have you canceled with the Burgenston vendors yet?"

"Not yet."

"End of day, then."

Caroline could feel anger bubbling up in her

throat. But instead of giving in to her temper, she dropped her resignation letter on Sheila's lap and slipped out without another word.

CHAPTER SEVEN

DYLAN TRUDGED THROUGH the back door of Delia's house, savoring the smell of homemade spaghetti sauce and meatballs. He'd no sooner kicked off his work boots when he heard the pitter-patter of bare feet against the linoleum. Crouching down just in time, he caught the full weight of McKenna as she sprang into his arms.

"Oof!" Dylan groaned, falling to his backside. McKenna squeezed his neck and squealed happily in his ear. "Hello, Little Mouse," he said, smacking a kiss to her temple. "Miss me, did ya?"

McKenna pulled away and pressed a hand to either side of Dylan's face.

"Daddy," she said. "I'm hungry."

"Me too. What's Grandma making us?"

Dylan had had strong anxiety about moving home. He'd begun living on his own when he was eighteen years old. Moving back home as a grown man to live with his mother and sister, all while bringing a child with him, had given him pause nearly a dozen times just on the drive from New York. There were plenty of ground rules to lay down with three adults living in the house and plenty of expectations to set when it came to parenting McKenna consistently among the three of them. But when he put in a long day of work and came home to the support of his family, he knew there were some sweet perks too.

"I told you I was making meatballs," Delia said, winking at her granddaughter. "McKenna, you like meatballs, don't you?"

McKenna stared up at Delia before shaking her head. Her mass of dark brown curls bounced in every direction.

"I'll eat yours," Dylan said, standing and scooping McKenna up into an arm crook. "Meatballs are Grandma's specialty. How'd you two do today?"

Delia lifted the lid on the saucepot for a quick check before wiping hands down her apron.

"We took a stroll outside."

"In this weather?" Dylan made a face. The wind whipping off Little Lake Roseley could redden your nose in three seconds flat.

"Ice formed on the puddles and we had fun cracking it with our boots."

"Simple joys," Isabel said, wandering in

from the living room. Even in blue jeans and a sweater, his sister was striking. McKenna had the same mass of brown hair and long, black eyelashes.

"Where are you going?" Dylan said as she collected her purse. "Aren't you staying for dinner?"

"I'm meeting friends to run lines." Isabel squatted to hug McKenna goodbye. "But we're hanging out tomorrow morning, Little Mouse. I don't have class until noon."

"You'll bring her by before class?" Dylan confirmed.

"Yep. Mom has to work till two."

Dylan nodded, calculating what his day would look like. He'd have McKenna for over two hours before Delia could watch her. She was old enough to attend preschool but enrolling her had its own set of challenges.

"We'll figure it out," Delia said, carrying a casserole dish of browned meatballs to the table. "Come on, McKenna. Climb up in your chair, please."

Dylan settled McKenna onto her chair and sneaked a sliced cucumber off the table. They all turned at the sound of the doorbell, followed by heaving knocking. Immediately, Dylan laid a reassuring hand to McKenna's shoulder. She had instantly covered her ears and scowled up at him.

"It's okay," Dylan whispered. "It's just someone at the door."

Delia stripped off her apron. "At this hour?"

"It's not even six o'clock, Mom," Isabel said with a laugh, already hurrying to answer it.

"True. When it gets dark early, I forget that."

He and his mom placed the rest of the food on the table while straining to hear the voices at the front door. Isabel was talking and laughing with someone.

Finally, as Dylan settled into a chair next to McKenna, Isabel made her way into the kitchen, an excited gleam in her eye.

"You know, Mom," she said, "I think I *will* stick around for a little while. It's been so long since I've talked to Caroline."

"Caroline?" Dylan said as the redhead trailed into the kitchen. She could have knocked him over with a feather, or better, the white fur collar framing her rosy face.

"Hi, Mrs. Metzger," Caroline said, her smile as wide as Little Lake Roseley. "Nice to see you again."

"Meatballs, see?" Delia said, motioning toward the table. "As promised."

"Yes, I see. I won't keep you." Caroline dangled a pen in the air. "Dylan, I stopped by to collect that contract."

He frowned. He had been so busy at work he hadn't had a spare moment to read it with a fine-toothed comb—twice—like he wanted to.

"I haven't gotten to it yet. I didn't think you were serious about moving so fast."

Caroline shrugged playfully. "Lots to do and I still haven't learned how to make more hours in the day."

"You and me both, girl," Isabel said, grabbing Caroline's coat by the shoulders. "Let me take that for you."

"Oh, no," Caroline said, trying to stop her, but Isabel would not be deterred. She had the coat off Caroline before she could say, "I really can't stay."

"Have you already eaten dinner?" Delia said.

"I—I had a big lunch."

Delia popped both hands to her hips. His mother could sniff out a lie faster than a bloodhound.

"Nonsense. Caroline, you take the chair next to McKenna. Isabel, grab the rolls." Delia settled herself on her own chair, wafting a hand of invitation toward the empty chair. He knew his mother would keep her hand extended until Caroline finally relented. For the sake of good manners, he hoped Caroline would just sit down.

Caroline glanced at Dylan before reluctantly making her way around the table to a chair on the other side of McKenna.

"I suppose I can stay for a few minutes if you can look at the contract after dinner."

Dylan nodded. He didn't want to read it while Caroline peered over his shoulder but nothing about the evening was going easily, especially when he could sense an explanation about McKenna, or better, an introduction, was needed.

"McKenna," Delia said. "Would you say grace, please?"

While everyone folded their hands and bowed their heads, Dylan gave a quick glance at Caroline. She was peeking at his daughter. When she spotted him watching her, she bowed her head too. McKenna spoke a few pieced-together lines of prayer that she had obviously heard many times and wrapped it up with "Amen."

"That was beautiful," Caroline said. "I couldn't have done better myself."

"McKenna," Dylan said, taking his daughter's pudgy little hand. "This is my friend Caroline." He kissed McKenna's hand. "McKenna is my daughter."

Caroline offered a humble wave. "It's nice to meet you, McKenna. How old are you?"

When the silence stretched a bit long, he held up three fingers to prompt her. McKenna glanced at him and then held up her own three fingers. She whispered, "Three."

"Three?" Caroline said, acting impressed. "You're so big."

McKenna seemed unfazed by the compliment, so Caroline continued. "I like your bib."

McKenna proudly patted the snowman picture on her bib. Then she pointed to Caroline as if reminding her that she forgot hers.

"Caroline doesn't need a bib," Dylan said but McKenna persisted.

"You need it," she said, shaking her extended finger at Caroline, "if you're gonna eat meatballs."

Dylan tapped on McKenna's plate, trying to redirect her attention to her own dinner. When he glanced back at Caroline, he discovered she had already opened her napkin and had tucked it into the collar of her blouse.

"I like to wear a bib when I eat meatballs," she said. "Thank you for reminding me, McKenna."

McKenna grinned up at Dylan. Then she pointed at his chest. "Daddy, you too. Come on."

"Me too?"

McKenna didn't wait for him to comply before pointing around the table at Delia and Isabel. After a pause, each adult opened a napkin and tucked it into their shirt collar.

"Aren't we a sight?" Delia said with a chuckle. "There's no doubt who's in charge around here."

"Yeah," Dylan mumbled. "Caroline."

Caroline took a bite of her dinner and flashed him a grin. "And don't you forget it," she said.

As McKenna fumbled up the stairs ahead of Delia, off to take a bath and put on her pajamas, Dylan washed dishes at the kitchen sink while Caroline dried them.

"Thanks for helping," he said. "You know you didn't have to."

"And skip out after eating two big helpings? Never."

Dylan rinsed a plate and placed it on the rack in front of her. She took it and dried it.

"You seemed to hit it off with McKenna," he said quietly. He couldn't think of a person in recent history who had done so so easily.

"She's beautiful."

"Thanks."

"And funny."

"Sometimes unintentionally..." Dylan said with a grin. "But yes, she is."

"Is she in preschool?"

"We're waiting another year."

"Gosh, I guess I'm not sure when kids are supposed to start that."

The truth was, he wasn't sure about it either.

"Have you seen that new preschool on Maplewood?" Caroline said. "It opened up this summer. I can't remember the name of it, but it was a play on Roseley, like Coming Up Roses or something like that."

"Huh," Dylan said, intensely studying the plate he was washing.

"They do a lot of nature play."

"Okay."

"Cutting-edge stuff, all the newest developments in education."

"Mmm-hmm."

Caroline leaned a hip against the counter. He could feel her eyes on him.

"You don't seem interested."

Dylan drew a breath. "I'm a long way from thinking about preschool. I've got a lot going on. McKenna does too." He was ready to get on to any other topic.

"What's the story with her mother?"

Any topic but that.

"Uh... Giana?" Dylan dried his hands on a

towel and turned for the table. He ran a kitchen cloth over it, wiping the smudged sauce smears off McKenna's place setting. "She stayed in New York."

"Are you two separated?"

Dylan gritted his teeth, irritated to utter the word that was now a way to describe him. "Divorced."

Caroline hummed a sad note. "I'm sorry to hear that."

Dylan knew she wasn't as sorry as he felt for saying it. He'd wanted nothing more than to make his marriage work, and most days, especially when McKenna asked about her mother, he still couldn't believe he was a divorcee. Sometimes the rejection made the familiar lump in his throat bob for the surface, but some days, like right now, he had to swat away the anger that swelled inside him.

Dylan straightened and gripped a kitchen chair for moral support.

"It's what Giana wanted. It became official after McKenna and I moved to Roseley. I didn't want to raise McKenna in the city without family to help us and Giana…"

He pressed his lips together as if he shouldn't say the next part. But one look at Caroline's expression, earnest with concern, propelled him to go on.

"She decided she wasn't cut out for motherhood."

"Oh." Caroline's face fell and he could only imagine that the pain he saw registered there reflected his own every time he remembered the truth: Giana didn't want to mother their child. "Did she say that?"

"Very clearly." He could tell Caroline was waiting for more explanation, but he didn't like to relive all the bitter arguments. McKenna was going to grow up without her mother around every day and it was a reality her mother chose.

"I'm sorry," Caroline said, gently. "It's a tender subject. I didn't mean to pry."

Everything about McKenna's world felt like a tender subject these days.

"You weren't prying," he said, walking back to the sink and letting the soapy water down the drain. "I should get used to answering questions about Giana. Heaven knows I still don't know how to explain things to McKenna."

"It'll come to you with time."

Dylan wanted to believe that was true, but a lot about the last year made him feel like he was always in over his head.

"Let's take a look at the contract, huh?" he said.

"Of course."

They sat at the table and spread the contracts in front of them.

"I usually like to read these things a few times," Dylan mumbled. "The devil is in the details."

"I understand, but the Behrs are good people," Caroline said. "They wouldn't try to sneak anything into the contract."

Dylan lifted a reprimanding eyebrow. "You would make a lousy lawyer."

"Well, the contract you sent me—the one for The Starlight—looked pretty standard. Basically, you're agreeing to host the gala on the evening of December 24. You'll allow us, mainly me, to decorate and have the event catered. The hospital, with Bianca as the contact person, will make the first deposit upon signing and the second payment the day of. I added a few notes for you to review."

Caroline sat silently as Dylan read every line twice. Finally, when he felt satisfied that everything still seemed up to par, he relaxed and signed.

"And what does your contract with Bianca look like?"

Caroline slid her contract to Dylan. After a few minutes, he looked up, pleased.

"Well done. It has nicely laid-out terms and you're going to earn a pretty penny."

"Thanks," she said beaming. "I still can't believe it's happening."

"You don't have a moment to lose though. I imagine you'll be pulling all-nighters from now until Christmas Eve."

Caroline rolled her eyes, collected both contracts and tucked them into her bag.

"I still have to put in at least two weeks with Sheila."

"At least?" Dylan said. Caroline's cheeks reddened and he could tell she didn't want to disclose the next part. "Did she refuse to accept your resignation?"

"Something like that."

"Something *like* that? Or exactly that?"

"I can't quit until I find her a replacement."

Dylan scratched his chin and relaxed back on his chair.

"Well," he said, "you absolutely cannot do that."

"I know. I have so much to do already."

"Tell her no."

"I already did."

"Apparently you didn't."

Caroline stood and put on her coat in a huff. "It's fine. I'll figure it out. I can find her a replacement quickly and still get everything done."

"I'm not saying you can't. I'm saying you shouldn't."

"It's fine." Caroline plastered on an over-the-top fake smile and responded in a rush. "I'll be by to look at the dance hall this week. I need to get measurements for decorations. When will the band stage be done?"

Dylan stood slowly, noticing every shade of red in her cheeks. "Not for another two weeks at least."

"Right. Very exciting stuff. I can't wait to see it."

Dylan walked Caroline to the door. "Do you want me to draft a formal letter for you? Sheila can't hold you to more than two weeks no matter what she says."

"Of course not. It's fine. I'll see you later." She patted her bag, contracts intact. "Thanks for these."

"You're welcome." He watched from the front porch as Caroline hurried to her car, slid in and tried to start it. The agitated screech the engine made as it tried to turn over was no match for what he imagined Caroline was mumbling at it. Illuminated by porch lights, her lips moved furiously as she repeatedly turned the ignition over. "Need some help?" he called.

Caroline glanced up before focusing her attention to her ignition again. Dylan was just about to grab his coat when the engine finally fired up. Caroline gave a hurried wave before backing out of the driveway and speeding down the street.

"Well, don't let me keep you," he said with a grin.

CHAPTER EIGHT

CAROLINE LIFTED HER head off her pillow, aware that her cell phone alarm was going off, though muffled, from somewhere in her bedding. Digging through covers, she finally located it.

"Oh, for Pete's Dragon!" she cried, leaping out of bed and running for the bathroom. She'd have to fly like the crow to make her first appointment, so a long hot shower was completely out of the question. She'd just finished splashing off and tugging on clean clothes when she thought she heard a knock on her front door. She paused and craned her neck, certain she must be mistaken. No one showed up at her home unexpectedly, especially at seven thirty in the—

Knock, knock, knock.

Caroline dashed down the stairs and peeked through the peephole, shocked to see Dylan on her front porch.

It had been a week since he'd reviewed the contracts, and in that time she'd thought of his strong jawline no less than a dozen times.

She opened the door, remaining partially behind it to shield herself from the frigid draft. "Hey," she said. "What are you doing here?"

"Are you going to let me in? I can't feel my toes."

Caroline waved him in, and Dylan slipped inside and shut the door behind him. In the entryway with the dim morning light, he looked taller than she remembered. It was all she could stand to not stare up into his gorgeous blue eyes.

The collar of his black Carhartt coat was flipped up. His hair looked a bit messy, like he'd run his hand through it several times, leaving a cool, natural-looking style. He looked as if he hadn't shaved in a few days but instead of making him look disheveled, it heightened his handsomeness. Then there were those blue eyes. Caroline fought a tingle of nerves as Dylan held up a brown bag.

"I brought you croissants and coffee," he said. She raised a brow.

"Why?"

She hadn't meant to sound ungrateful, but she had no idea what he was doing here. He gave her a careful look up and down, his eyes lingering a bit longer than she would have expected. It sent nervous tingles through her body.

"Are you still getting dressed?" he said.

She'd managed to tug on pants and a top but she was standing barefoot on the linoleum and her hair was—

Caroline ran fingers through her curly locks.

"Of course I am!" she called, dashing upstairs and into her room to grab some styling spray. She fixed her hair, fluffing and twisting it into a styled topknot. She grabbed her makeup bag and socks and started back down the stairs. "What are you doing here? Did we have a meeting scheduled?"

"Not quite," Dylan said, crinkling the bag open to snatch a croissant. He took a bite. "I was thinking about you last night—"

"Thinking about me?" She stopped on the bottom stair. She was on more even footing with him now and caught a flash of a blush on his face. It was quick, something she could have easily missed if she hadn't stopped short to look at him, but it had been there. She was sure of it.

She didn't mind the idea that Dylan Metzger had been thinking about her. What he'd been thinking about specifically didn't matter as much as the fact that she'd popped into his thoughts at all. Ever since she'd seen him at Tyler and Olivia's wedding, she had occasionally thought about him too, though she reminded herself to keep things professional. Her memory of his devilish grin that could make her throat go dry was always forced back into the recesses of her mind. Well, almost always.

"Well," Dylan said, clearing his throat, "I haven't seen you in several days. How was your Thanksgiving?"

"What?" Caroline said with a confused head jerk. "Busy. I had to work a wedding the day after."

"Oh."

Faith and John had invited her to dinner with John's family, but Caroline had had so many last-minute wedding details to attend to, she'd gratefully settled for a plate of leftovers that Faith had dropped by. She saw Faith and John all the time so what difference did it make if she didn't see them on Thanksgiving? Thanks to Faith, she'd gotten a slice of homemade pumpkin pie and she'd pulled off a gorgeous wedding with very little assistance from—

"How are things going with Sheila?" Dylan asked right on cue.

"Ugh," Caroline groaned. She grabbed her boots from the hall closet and quickly pulled them on as Dylan retrieved her coat and held it open for her. After slipping it on, she turned and found him genuinely interested. "I've turned into a certified headhunter."

"That explains why you haven't been by," he said. "We finally finished restoring the fresco on the east and southeast walls. I knew you'd want to come see it."

Caroline didn't want to get into the nitty-gritty details of all she had been doing since she'd last talked to Dylan. It wasn't that she hadn't wanted to see The Starlight again. It was that she had not had twenty solid minutes to do it. And she was so tired she had slept through her alarm—again.

"I do. I will. It's just my to-do list for Sheila is keeping me from getting my own work done."

"I will draft a letter and get her off your back by lunchtime," Dylan said. "Just say the word."

"Nonsense. I want to leave on good terms."

"You're leaving solely on her terms. There's a difference."

"I don't see it that way. Sheila will be lost when I leave. The least I can do is find her help."

Caroline zipped up her coat, trying to ignore the fact that she had caught a whiff of Dylan's aftershave and found it delicious. She might have secretly crushed on Dylan when she'd been a scrawny, freckle-faced kid and he'd been the cool, older friend of her brother.

Her irritation with him over the years had been a confusing mix of feeling left out of the fun he enjoyed with her dad and brother, and a desire to get his attention.

But now that he was her work colleague, she could catalog those old feelings in the past where they belonged. Thinking about how good he smelled and how nice he looked in his work jacket was stupid. She could shiver away the nerves that had risen on her skin with willpower—fierce, determined willpower.

She turned, ready to interrogate him about what he was doing at her house, when he moved a step closer. His masculine scent assaulted her senses, sending her thoughts unraveling. And those eyes... She bit the inside of her cheek to keep from showing how they affected her.

"What?" she mumbled through gritted teeth. She didn't have any makeup on and figured she looked a fright. She rubbed her hands to her cheeks. "Do I still have creases on my face? I woke up not ten minutes ago."

He shook his head, his eyes falling over her face. "Nope," he said with a soft blink. "No creases."

She peered back at him, momentarily mesmerized. He couldn't look at her that way without making her come completely unglued, and she could not afford to be anything other than put together this morning. If he didn't tuck those baby blues away, she'd have to bolt from her apartment and leave him standing there.

"Look, Dylan," she said. "I have to put on makeup and get to a meeting with Bianca at—"

"The Starlight in fifteen minutes."

"Uh…yeah."

As if resurfacing to work mode, he pulled a coffee from the bag and handed it to her. "Are two creams and a sugar okay?"

"Uh. Two sugars and a cream would be better but—"

"You put on your makeup, and I'll drive."

"Drive where?"

He opened the front door. "You don't think I'm going to let you and Bianca prance around The Starlight—"

"Prance?" she spat, irritated.

"—and let Bianca change whatever she wants just because she's the first one to throw an event there in forty years, do you?"

"I don't understand. She and I are just going over my decoration plans. What would she change?"

Dylan looked at her from beneath hooded

eyelids. "Trust me. When it comes to control freaks, Bianca Behr is ten times worse than Sheila."

THEY WERE ONLY a few minutes into the meeting with Bianca when Caroline realized what Dylan meant.

"These pictures are beautiful, Caroline," Bianca said, holding her sketch up against a stucco wall. "But I just don't think they are going to do for this gala."

"Pardon?"

Caroline had pulled several all-nighters compiling all the buyer sheets and sketches for what the gala would look like. She'd also put together the invitations and promo pieces and was ready to send them to the printer. That was, just as soon as Bianca signed off on everything.

"I was hoping things around here would be a little more…you know…" Bianca looked to Dylan. "Brighter."

"Brighter?" Caroline said, noticeably confused.

"Yes, brighter."

"Can you be a little more specific?"

Bianca strode to the center of the room. The echo of her high-heeled boots against the warped grain filled the space nearly as much as her disapproval.

"I know you said you're going to keep with the original paint here—"

"The original palette, yes," Dylan said.

"That was one of the things you said you had hoped for, Bianca," Caroline said. Bianca spun slowly, sizing up the walls.

"That's lovely in theory, but in reality, people love a modern adaptation too. A mesh of the two could be nice. Don't you think?"

Dylan crossed his arms. "A *mesh*?"

"You can always modernize a wee bit as you go. It's just a suggestion, of course," Bianca said, cloyingly sweet.

"I'm keeping the original palette, Ms. Behr," he said, his voice strained. "But thanks for the suggestion."

As Dylan and Bianca set eyes on each other, it made Caroline want to step between them like a referee in a boxing match, sending them to their respective corners.

"Bianca," Caroline began steadily. "If we're going to be realistic about the timeline, it's a good idea to keep in mind the *tone* of your gala, more than the details."

"The devil is in the details, dear," Bianca warned with a tsk-tsk. Caroline paused, recalling that Dylan had said something like that only a few nights earlier.

"Can we lock down the invitations and promotional pieces?" Caroline said. "Do you like the style I designed?" She had spent hours designing the invitation. It displayed an old-fashioned Santa Claus with a child sitting on each knee.

"Yes," Bianca said, clapping her hands together in resolve. "It's perfect since we're raising money for the children's wing."

Caroline nodded and checked her tablet for the next thing on her list.

"Because it's a vintage theme, the lighting really should be low and warm," Caroline said. "Antique lamps and strings of white lights will make this place feel like home. The gas fireplace will also make a beautiful conversation piece once it's decorated."

"Will it have a mantel?" Bianca asked, hopefully.

"It's projected to be done by Christmas Eve," Caroline said, glancing at Dylan. "Right?"

Dylan shrugged. "I don't know. I can't promise it."

"But we'll try," Caroline said eagerly. *"Right?"*

Dylan's stare set on her. "I said, *I don't know.*"

"Well, what do you know?" Bianca said pointedly, her lips thinning with fading patience. "What about the stage?"

"Of course the stage will be done," Caroline said, hurriedly. "Imagine half a dozen Christmas trees as bookends and the band front and center—"

"The Hometown Jamboree."

"Right."

"Very good." Bianca strolled around the dance hall, dragging a finger along the fresco to point out a layer of dust. "I suppose if this is as good as it can be..."

"We still have a few more weeks of construction," Dylan said, matter-of-factly. "But it will be in working order by Christmas Eve."

"Thank you, Dylan," Bianca said, turning to glance at him over her shoulder.

"Mr. Metzger."

Bianca turned slowly to face him, her eyes flashing at his correction. Caroline froze, unable to breathe. As Bianca and Dylan stared at each other, Caroline realized their looks might not kill, but they were certainly ready to maim.

After a beat, Bianca formed her mouth into a perfect line.

"I'll leave you both to it," she said. "Thank you, Caroline. It looks like you have everything under control. Check in with me again in a few days, won't you?"

"I will."

"Good. I'll see myself out. I have an appointment with the hospital board."

Bianca was no sooner out of the dance hall and cutting a line to the entrance doors when Caroline smacked Dylan hard against the shoulder.

"What was *that* all about?"

"What?" he said defensively.

Caroline lowered her voice to mock him.

"It's Mr. Metzger to you," she grumbled. "Rude, much?"

"I wasn't rude. I was setting a boundary. Boundaries are nice. Boundaries keep people in check."

"Whatever you say, *Mr. Metzger.*" Caroline gathered her belongings as Dylan watched. "Just make sure you don't set yourself on the wrong side of a moneymaking boundary."

Dylan widened his gait, settling firmly on his feet.

"Is that what you think was at risk back there?" he said, amused.

"I don't know what happened back there," Caroline huffed. She readjusted her heavy satchel on her shoulder with a groan. "All I know is that you were intentionally trying to tick off your first client—my first client—and lose us an end-of-the-year payday."

"Nothing like that was at risk," he said. He took Caroline's satchel from her shoulder and slung it over his own. "Bianca would hold her gala here even if the roof caved in and it started snowing on the dance floor." He raised his brows. "Now where to?"

"Where to?"

"You rode with me, remember? I'm prepared to drop you somewhere before I get back to work."

Caroline's cell phone rang. When she saw that it was her brother, Trig, she held up a finger to Dylan and answered.

"Hi, Trig," she said. It was highly unusual for Trig to call in the middle of the workday. In fact, he rarely called, preferring only to text.

"Hey," he said, out of breath. "I'm about to catch a train but wanted to let you know I heard from Dad."

"Dad?" Caroline said, a painful mix of surprise and hurt smacking her hard in the face. When she caught Dylan watching her closely, clearly concerned, she turned her back, trying to carve out a moment of privacy.

She hadn't heard from her father in months. As she was the one who consistently called and left him voice messages that were rarely returned, it stung that their dad had called Trig instead of her. At the least, she thought that taking care of his house was reason enough for him to check in once in a while.

"He said he's heading home in a couple weeks."

"Really?" Caroline said, brightening. "For Christmas?"

"I'm not sure. He wants a rest before his ice fishing trip mid-January, so he'll probably turn up the end of December."

"Oh," Caroline said, immediately annoyed with herself for feeling hopeful in the first place. "Are *you* coming home? I can fix Christmas dinner or brunch or—"

"I'll be home, sis," Trig said. "But I have to work Christmas Eve so don't expect me until the twenty-sixth. Sorry."

"No, that's fine," Caroline said, still eager to see both her dad and brother at some point. "You and I can celebrate a day late. I know Mom and Darren are flying to Florida so it'll just be us." Her mom and stepdad usually kept to themselves during the holidays—well, all year actually. Reluctantly agreeing to stand in her mom's wedding had, in retrospect, felt like she'd unknowingly complied with that. In some ways she still felt duped.

"Cool, sis. Whatever you plan for us is fine with me."

Caroline measured her next question, not wanting to appear too eager. She was much more concerned with how her father was than what their holiday plans should be. "How did Dad sound? You know, really sound?"

"Oh, you know," Trig said, noticeably distracted. In the background she thought she could hear the train doors jostling. "Fine."

"Fine?"

"Yep."

"Did you tell him the house is all ready for him? I check on it every few days and—"

"I'm sure he knows. Look, I gotta run. I'll talk to you later."

Caroline ended the call, dejected. Her father wouldn't be coming home for Christmas—again. True, not two minutes earlier she had assumed he wasn't coming home, but the sudden confirmation stung.

"Everything okay?" Dylan asked.

"Perfect," she said, forcing a smile. "My dad's coming home at the end of the month."

"Oh, yeah?" Dylan said, noticeably confused. "Doesn't he usually come home for Christmas?"

"Not for several years, no. This year won't be an exception." Caroline sucked in a breath, trying for optimism. "He won't be here in time, but it's better than nothing, right?"

Dylan frowned, signaling that he didn't agree. "If you say so."

As his cell phone rang, he signaled that it was Caroline's turn to wait. After answering and muttering only a few words, he shoved his phone in his pocket and motioned for Caroline to follow him out of the dance hall.

"Is everything okay?" she said, hurrying to keep up.

"I think so," he said. "But I've gotta get home quick so you'll have to make a stop with me."

CHAPTER NINE

DYLAN LED CAROLINE into the house as an urgent little voice cried for him.

"Daddy!" McKenna ran into the kitchen. Her eyes were red and swollen. Tears streaked her cheeks. She was dressed in a pajama sleeper and her hair looked like she'd just rolled out of bed.

"Hey, Little Mouse," Dylan said, catching McKenna just as she leaped into his embrace. He hoisted her up into the crook of his arm and carried her into the living room. Caroline hesitantly followed behind.

Isabel, already dressed in her winter coat and boots, laid McKenna's clothes out on the couch.

"I'm so sorry," she said, noticeably in a rush. "Mom left to run errands and I didn't think anything of it until I realized I'm supposed to meet with my theater adviser this morning. I tried calling but I think Mom's phone is turned off. I would take McKenna with me, Dylan, you know I would, but my meeting is to go over audition pieces—"

"No, no, I understand. That wouldn't be wise," Dylan said. Caroline mentally scratched her head. She could understand a three-year-old getting under foot during a meeting but the way Dylan and Isabel exchanged knowing glances with each other made her curious.

"Hi, Caroline." Isabel beamed at her. "It's so nice to see you. When are you coming to dinner again?"

"Uh…" Caroline managed, laughing uncomfortably. "Hard to say…"

Dylan shot Isabel a warning look. "She's got a lot on her plate, Izzy."

"A girl has still gotta eat," Isabel said in jest. She winked at her. "I'll text you. Or better yet, just drop by any night around six." Isabel leaned to place a gentle kiss to her niece's cheek but McKenna buried her face into Dylan's neck to avoid her. Isabel offered Dylan an apologetic wince. "I freaked her out when I realized my mistake. I might have shrieked."

"It's okay, sis."

"It's not, obviously, but…" She turned to McKenna. "I'm really sorry, kiddo. Aunt Izzy didn't mean to be so loud. I'll make it up to you tonight."

Dylan nudged her along. "Go on. I can tell you're running late."

Isabel rolled her eyes. "*So* late." She pointed at the clothes on the couch. "I didn't have time to get her dressed, but I laid out clothes. Ms. Callie will be here any minute. Bye!"

Caroline admired Dylan as he calmly stroked McKenna's back and whispered something only McKenna could hear. She figured they would have to hang out for a few minutes until Ms. Callie, whom she assumed was the babysitter, arrived.

"Caroline, may I show you our special nook?" Dylan said, grabbing McKenna's clothes off the couch. He was speaking to Caroline, but his paternal tone was for McKenna.

"I love special nooks," Caroline said, playing along.

Dylan stroked McKenna's back as he carried her to a far corner of the living room. It had a small purple tent covered in rainbow butterflies. "You might assume this is my office, Caroline, but the truth is, it's really McKenna's hideout."

Caroline leaned against the bookshelf. "I love the butterflies," she said.

Dylan smiled, his voice teasing. "Only rainbow butterflies will do."

McKenna peered out from Dylan's neck. "Only rainbow butterflies," she repeated.

"Why don't you show her?" Dylan said. He lowered McKenna slowly to the ground. She crept into the tent. After a few moments, she peeked out from behind a flap and grinned up at them. Her dark brown eyes twinkled with pride.

"May I try it?" Caroline said, squatting down. She pulled back a tent flap and peeked inside. The ground was covered with furry throw pillows and blankets. McKenna even had headphones and picture books in it. "What a great place to read books and listen to music."

McKenna shook her head. "No music."

"No?" Caroline said, surprised. "It's not a good place for that?"

McKenna shook her head harder, this time smiling. She pointed to Dylan.

"Daddy, you say it," she said.

"Doesn't every woman need a secret hideout with rainbow butterflies?" he said. He held up McKenna's shirt. "Little Mouse, we have to get you dressed." He turned to Caroline. "Would you mind giving us some privacy?"

"Of course." Caroline wandered back to the kitchen. Though she stayed out of view, she couldn't help but hear Dylan and McKenna chatting away. McKenna was talkative with her dad, and very giggly, but Caroline couldn't hear what they were saying. Finally, after a few minutes, McKenna scurried into the kitchen and waved for Caroline to join them. She was dressed in a bright red jumper, white collared shirt and ankle boots. Her curls were still wild.

Dylan stood nearby, a cell phone pressed to his ear. As he talked to someone on the phone, the conversation obviously about work, Caroline looked around for a brush.

"Would you like to brush your hair?" she said.

McKenna shook her head. "I don't like it," she said.

"I never liked it when I was your age either," Caroline said in full agreement. "How about a finger comb?" McKenna hesitated a moment before nodding.

She sat on the edge of the couch and gently combed fingers through McKenna's fine curls. After pulling two bobby pins from her own messy knot, she worked to smooth and secure McKenna's front locks back off her face with them.

"My mother always said," Caroline continued with a smile, "a woman could tackle the day if she had bobby pins, mascara and gold earrings, but I never adhered to that advice. Just give me some lip gloss any day. Right?"

She turned McKenna to face her.

"I can comb your hair too," McKenna offered. Caroline glanced at Dylan. He sounded engrossed in his conversation, but he was watching them. As she figured he might still be a minute, Caroline scooted to sit on the floor. She uncoiled her strawberry blond curls.

"Can you be gentle?" Caroline asked.

"I know how to be gentle," McKenna said, rubbing Caroline's shoulder softly. Caroline smiled to herself. The little girl certainly did understand the concept. Though her fingers snagged in Caroline's hair, she could tell McKenna was concentrating very hard to live up to her promise.

"Thank you," Caroline said softly when McKenna appeared to have finished. "Does it look good now?"

"Yes," McKenna said, hurrying to tug at Dylan's sleeve. "Daddy, look. She's boo-tiful."

Caroline smiled up at Dylan but still couldn't quite pinpoint the expression on his face. Finally, his stare softened as he nodded in agreement.

"Beautiful," he said.

DYLAN TRIED TO keep the stress of the morning from getting to him. His foreman, Bobby, had plenty of things that needed his attention back at The Starlight, but as he was needed at home for a while, he did his best to prepare for Ms. Callie's visit. Watching how Caroline interacted with McKenna, however, clouded his train of thought. She was a natural, her warmth emanating as she spoke to McKenna. The relaxed smile on McKenna's face as she interacted with Caroline intrigued him.

McKenna didn't take to new people very easily, but watching his daughter play with Caroline's hair, something both seemed to enjoy, he couldn't help but stare. Redheaded, freckle-faced little Caroline who used to throw his can of bait into the lake just for spite was a soft touch with his daughter.

"I'm sorry to make you wait here," he said once he ended his business call. "My mom should be back in a few and can drive you home."

"I don't mind," Caroline said. He figured she was just being polite, sweetly polite. If there was anyone in his life who had as much to do as he did, or more accurately, much more to do than him, it was her.

She turned to McKenna, who had sat down on the floor next to her.

"Is your babysitter nice?"

McKenna blinked up at her.

Dylan realized he should probably forewarn Caroline about what was coming next. They weren't waiting for a babysitter, far from it. But when Ms. Callie visited, the energy he displayed beforehand really helped set the tone for McKenna. If he could get Caroline alone to explain, he would, but Ms. Callie was scheduled to arrive at any moment—

Dylan's phone vibrated. He read the incoming text message before squatting to look McKenna in the eye.

"McKenna," he said softly. "Ms. Callie is here. She's going to ring the doorbell in a few seconds. Would you come with me and greet her?"

McKenna stayed planted on the floor next to Caroline. Dylan turned to face the door, keeping his tone steady.

"Okay," he continued calmly. "I hear her on the porch. She's going to ring the doorbell in one…two…"

Dylan winked at Caroline. For as quiet as she was, she seemed tense, as if sensing that something important was about to happen.

Finally, after a three…four…five…, the doorbell rang. McKenna let out a disgruntled yelp as Dylan meandered to the front door and welcomed Ms. Callie inside.

Ms. Callie, also known as Caldonia Garner, had been a foster placement for the Garner family thirty years earlier. The Garners were well known in Roseley for fostering many children over the years. They had also adopted several children, including Callie.

"Hello, Miss McKenna," Ms. Callie said, holding out her hand for a high five. "Did you hear me ring the doorbell?"

McKenna brightened and jumped to her feet. She ran and smacked Ms. Callie's hand. "We did our countdown."

"That's what I like to hear." Ms. Callie shook Dylan's hand. "How are we doing today, Dad?"

"Aunt Isabel and McKenna had a rough morning."

"Do we need a snack before we begin?" she asked.

Dylan winked. "A snack wouldn't hurt."

Ms. Callie opened her bag. "I'll give you a few minutes to make a snack while I get set up here."

Dylan motioned for McKenna and Caroline to follow him to the kitchen. He quickly pulled a container of freshly cut fruit from the refrigerator and scooped some into a bowl for McKenna, who had already climbed into a chair.

"I feel like I should go," Caroline said, wincing. She glanced into the living room where Callie was pulling some interesting toys out of her bag. "You and McKenna are obviously preparing for something important. I can call for a ride—"

"No. Please don't do that." Dylan ran a hand through his hair. The feeling of being pulled in several directions at once was something he had been used to in New York City. The fast pace of working at a law firm demanded that he get used to the pressure, and for several years he'd enjoyed it. But his life was different now. He could happily admit that McKenna had changed him for the better. He usually tried to focus on one thing at a time. It was just times like this morning when things cropped up unexpectedly and he couldn't. "I know my mom will be back shortly to drive you. When I picked you up this morning, this—" he motioned to McKenna "—was not on my agenda."

"I don't mind," Caroline said with a smirk. "As long as you dish me some fruit too."

Dylan hitched his shoulders and scooped fruit into bowls for Caroline and himself. Once he handed her a fork, she clinked her bowl against his and stabbed at some honeydew. Side by side, they leaned back against the kitchen counter, eating fruit and watching McKenna. For a few fleeting moments, it all felt easy. Too easy.

Ms. Callie peeked her head into the kitchen.

"Miss McKenna, are you ready to play some games with me?"

Dylan heaved a sigh of relief when McKenna slid off her chair and took Ms. Callie's hand, letting her lead her into the living room. Sometimes McKenna was in good spirits and ready for her session with Ms. Callie. Other days it took a lot of prodding and encouraging.

Just as Dylan was about to explain who Ms. Callie was and what she and McKenna were about to do, he heard Delia's car in the driveway. He breathed a second sigh of relief. He knew how busy Caroline was and he didn't want to keep her from her work any longer.

"Delia has great timing, huh?" Caroline said, buttoning up her coat.

"Truly. I gotta get back in there, but thanks for being so understanding, friend."

Caroline groaned. "I still don't know about this friend thing," she said. "I thought you were going to think of something else."

"It'll come to me eventually," he said with a wink.

Caroline popped a last piece of fruit in her mouth and flashed him a wide grin that radiated so warm, he felt like the sun was beaming on his face.

"Don't worry," she said as she ducked out the door. "I'll keep reminding you."

CHAPTER TEN

CAROLINE SHOOK HANDS with another applicant
and waved them out the front door of Sheila's
office before settling back behind the computer again. It had been a very long week, a
week that should have been the first of her two
weeks' notice. But as Sheila expected her to
stay on the job until she found a suitable replacement, the passage of time didn't mean
much to her anymore, aside from the fact that
she had a gala to throw in mere weeks and not
enough hours in the day to tackle it.

"How'd she do?" Sheila asked, sweeping
into the office. Caroline shrugged, unable to
feign excitement. As much as she wanted to
push her job off onto someone else, she felt
loyal enough to her boss to find a good worker.
So far, no one suitable for the job had applied.

"She used to be in catering," Caroline said,
reviewing the application. "But that's where
her strengths end."

"No good communication or organizational
skills?" Sheila said, sitting on the edge of her desk.

"Maybe you could train her," Caroline said, wondering what training from Sheila might look like if she really buckled down and tried it.

"I need someone ready to hit the ground running," Sheila said. "The Dingleman wedding is on Christmas Eve and as you won't help me…"

"*Can't* help you," Caroline retorted, glaring at her from over the top of her computer.

"To*may*to, to*mah*to," Sheila said. "Or in our line of work…wedding *en*-vuh-lohp or wedding *on*-vuh-lohp."

"That's not the same thing," Caroline said. "If I choose to help you with the Dingleman wedding, I'm choosing to not start my business."

Sheila opened a compact mirror and checked her lipstick. "Everyone thinks the grass is greener on the other side, Caroline, dear." The pretentiousness dripped from her red-stained lips as she continued. "But the truth is, you're going to learn how difficult it is to run your own business."

Caroline swallowed a snarky response and glared at her computer screen. From her perspective, *Sheila* didn't know how to run her own business.

"I'm heading out now," Sheila sang, snapping her compact shut and slipping into her coat. "The roads are getting bad. Make sure you head home early."

Caroline nodded. A winter storm had blown in over the course of the day and had been getting worse all afternoon. She had every intention of getting home to her warm, cozy apartment soon. As she closed down her computer, the image of Dylan's family sitting around their dinner table popped into her mind.

It had surprised her to learn that Dylan Metzger was not only a dad but a good one. Watching him interact with McKenna had been touching.

Caroline bit the inside of her cheek recalling the earnestness in Dylan's eyes when he had spoken to her too. It was enough to make a woman teeter on her feet a little.

She palmed her cell phone and was about to shove it into her purse when she stopped. Turning it on, she sent a quick text message to her dad.

Heard you're coming home at the end of the month. Want anything for the house?

She stared for a long time, waiting for the three little dots indicating Gus was responding. As per usual, there was nothing. Just as she was about to put it away, it rang.

"Hello?" Caroline said, answering, not recognizing the number. "This is Caroline Waterson. May I help you?"

"Hola!" a woman's voice sang cheerily on the other line. Caroline scrunched up her face in confusion. "I just got cast in a play for next semester so I need an event planner to help me celebrate!"

"Isabel?" Caroline said, tugging on her coat.

"Who else would it be? Do you know any other actresses?"

Caroline didn't. Faith's sister-in-law, Samantha, could certainly be lumped into the extroverted performer category. But when it came to actresses, Isabel was the only one she knew.

"Congratulations," Caroline said, locking the office and making her way to her car. It was buried under a couple of inches of snow. Fumbling to get inside, she immediately wished she had used her remote starter to warm it up first.

Isabel giggled into the phone. In some ways the college coed seemed like an adult, but in other ways, especially when it came to expressing herself, she had the exuberance of a kid.

"Thank you! I play a Spanish thief and the biggest female role in the show. But that's not the reason I called."

Caroline started her car engine, holding her breath as she waited for it to fire it up. As it was freezing cold outside, she could only assume the weather had something to do with the delay.

"I want you to come for dinner tonight," Isabel continued. "We can celebrate my new role and you can see McKenna. She's been asking about you."

"Has she?" Caroline said. McKenna was one of the sweetest children Caroline had encountered. As McKenna had mostly been shy around her, chatting freely with Dylan as soon as Caroline had left the room, it was flattering to know that their brief encounters had left a good impression.

"Dylan keeps saying that we'll see you again, but I hope it's tonight. I think he…"

"What?" Caroline said, perking. Did Dylan want to see her again too? The thought, she had to admit, kind of thrilled her.

"I'm on my way home from work," Caroline said, throwing the car into gear.

"Perfect!" Isabel said. "I'll whip up some…" Isabel giggled again. "I forgot I can't cook. How do scrambled eggs sound?"

Caroline chuckled. "If we're celebrating *you* tonight, then I'll pick up dinner. I already have an idea."

DYLAN GATHERED HIS blueprints for the new entryway and made his way out of The Starlight, ready to call it an evening. As he'd spent the better part of the day inside, he did a double take when he pushed through the back doors of the loading dock to the parking lot. The pavement was completely covered with several inches of fresh snow, and more was blowing in at a forty-five-degree angle.

He spotted Bobby packing up his truck and shuffled to greet him.

"Great job today," Dylan called. "Do you think we'll get it all done in time?"

Bobby tossed his toolbelt into the bed of his truck and slammed the tailgate.

"We don't have a choice now, do we?"

It was true. Now that they had to get The Starlight in working order within the next three weeks, there was no time to waste. Unfortunately, when it came to being a single dad, more of his day felt like he was managing McKenna instead of the job site.

"Take it easy out there," Dylan said. "This snow is coming in heavier than predicted."

"They're calling for ice now," Bobby said.

"Hey, in case I haven't said it… It's good to have you back in town. Working with you kind of reminds me of the old days."

"Yeah, I know what you mean." Dylan tossed blueprints into his truck cab. "You've come a long way since high school, buddy."

Bobby smiled wryly. "I know what you're alluding to and thanks for not bringing it up on the site."

"Never," Dylan said. "The past is the past."

Bobby harrumphed. "You don't actually believe that do you? The past is never just the past, my friend."

Dylan recalled the past ten years. He'd started dating Giana in college. He'd met her at a party she'd thrown for half the campus and he hadn't been able to take his eyes off her. She pulled focus in any room she entered and he'd loved that about her. Friends? Admirers? She'd had more than she could count, but she'd wanted to date *him*. He'd been so enamored with her he'd willingly adopted her work hard, play harder mentality. Before he'd known it, they'd graduated law school and had managed to get hired on at the same firm. Life was one big adventure for Giana, a nonstop adrenaline rush like skydiving from one brass ring and social event to another. He'd been happy to jump along with her, believing they were in it together. That's why it had been such a shock when Giana had deployed her parachute and had left him free-falling without warning—and with their child in his arms.

"People can improve though," Dylan said. Of this he was still certain. Bobby had been a bit of a troublemaker as a teenager and Dylan had once been a rising star in his law firm. Good friends, the supportive ones, saw your positive changes and encouraged you to keep going. Bobby had just needed a clean slate to prove himself and Dylan had needed a wife who cared enough to work on their marriage. At least one of them had gotten what he had needed.

Dylan was about to climb into his truck when Bobby trotted over to stop him.

"While we're speaking of the old days…" Bobby began. "What's going on with you and Caroline Waterson?"

Dylan jerked in surprise. They'd all graduated from Roseley High, though Caroline had been a couple of years behind him and Bobby.

"Caroline? She's throwing that big gala, but you already know that."

"Yeah, I know that's what's happening. But what's *going on* between you two? Gerald and a couple other guys seem to think you two were getting on pretty well."

Dylan scratched his chin. He hated to admit that he'd actually been thinking the same thing recently, though he would never admit to thinking of Caroline as anything other than a friend—at least to another living soul. He hadn't been able to get Caroline out of his head since she had stormed up to him and Micah at the wedding reception.

"She's a great gal…" he began.

"A *gorgeous* gal."

Dylan couldn't argue with that. Caroline was one of the most beautiful women in town. But what he liked best was the way she'd talked to McKenna. His daughter was skittish with most people, sometimes even his mother and sister. When McKenna had talked to Caroline and had even let her do her hair, he'd taken notice. Caroline was gorgeous all right, but anyone could see that it was her kindness that made her a true gem.

"Yeah, she's a sweetheart," Dylan replied. "But we're just working together. It's strictly professional."

"Well, just so you know—" Dylan cocked his head closer "—she's been turning heads the last few days."

"Here? On the job?"

"Yep. She's given the guys plenty to talk

about." Bobby grinned. "I would ask her out myself if I thought you truly weren't interested."

Dylan had more important things on his mind than getting romantically involved with anyone. He also wasn't a glutton for punishment. He'd been badly burnt once before, and his heart still carried the scars. Now that he was a dad to a little girl who needed a lot of support, risking love with anyone, especially someone he was working with, seemed like a very bad idea. An exciting idea when his thoughts turned to Caroline, but a bad one all the same.

"I'm not…we're not…whatever you want to do, man. It's a free country."

Bobby now laughed, slapping Dylan on the shoulder. "Yeah, right. I know better than to believe that, but nice try." Bobby returned to his truck before Dylan could muster up more of a protest.

As he watched Bobby fishtail out of the parking lot, he couldn't help but admit that he had spent the afternoon looking forward to seeing Caroline again—whenever that would be.

Dylan fired up the engine to get the heater started, then began scraping the snow off his windshield. After a minute, he hopped into the warmth of the cab and heard his cell phone vibrating in the center console where he'd left it.

"Giana," he said, answering. "Can you call back in twenty minutes? I'm on my way home and I know McKenna is looking forward to talking to you."

"Heading home from where?"

"The Starlight."

"I keep hoping you'll change your mind about that dumpy place. It sounds like a nightmare."

Dylan swallowed a retort. The Starlight was more like a dream. When he'd listened to his dad share stories about the dance hall, he'd secretly daydreamed about buying it and fixing it up, making it the prominent Roseley destination it had once been. His father had always said it would never amount to a thing ever again. His dad had always been quick with a sharp critique, but there was something in his criticism of The Starlight that almost sounded like a challenge, and one Dylan had always wanted to tackle.

It was when his marriage was ending and he'd decided to move McKenna to Roseley that his fascination with The Starlight resurfaced. Giana had told him he'd never be able to build a law practice in such a small town, at least not one that could even glimpse the career he had in New York City. In her opinion, he was wasting his time moving to the small town and he'd never amount to anything there. In her criticism, he heard a familiar challenge, and it reawakened his old daydream about renovating The Starlight. If he was going to rebuild his life in a new place, he had thought, he'd pursue a new dream—make that an old dream—too.

"Do you really think you can make money renting it out?" Giana pressed.

"Of course. I'm sure you've already heard news about my first contract."

News in Roseley had a way of winding quickly through town and even finding its way to places like New York City.

"You're going to have a very busy Christmas, Dylan." She released a long, labored, groan of disapproval. "Are you really satisfied working with that place? Of not using your law degree so you can play—" she scoffed into the phone "—*party planner*?"

"I'm running a business and filling a need in town. And yes, I think that will make me feel satisfied, purposeful. I'm also raising our little girl and she wants to talk to you tonight."

"I only had a minute. I'm about to walk into a dinner meeting."

"Can you talk after?"

There was a long pause before Giana replied, "I'll try to call tonight."

"Good," Dylan said, satisfied. "That's good, Giana. She misses you."

"You know," she said, the sudden sultriness in her tone making his skin prick with longing, "the apartment feels so empty without you, Dylan."

He imagined Giana didn't spend too much time in the home they'd once shared. She preferred to work all day and socialize every night. She always had some event to attend, some place where she could network. If she didn't, she was always looking for a last-minute write-in. There was a time, before McKenna, when he'd enjoyed that fast-paced rhythm too. When he thought of the good times they'd once shared, his gut twisted, making him wonder if moving to Roseley had been a terrible mistake.

"I miss you," she whispered. "Things aren't right without you."

Dylan had ached to hear such words from her for the last three years. When Giana had turned her full attention to him, he'd felt like he could sprout wings and soar. Unfortunately, she'd never turned that full attention to her role as a mother. After watching her reject McKenna so many times, he had realized that McKenna was never going to be good enough for her mother. And once he'd started prioritizing McKenna over their social life, Giana's attention quickly shifted. He felt as if he'd never been a priority to her.

"McKenna misses you," he said. "Please promise me you'll call tonight."

"I promise," Giana said before hanging up. "I'll call later."

Dylan couldn't help but pray that Giana would live up to her promise. But he also knew better than to pass that promise to McKenna.

By the time he navigated the snow-covered streets and returned home, he found Caroline's car in the driveway. Inside, Caroline and Delia were busy transferring food from take-out boxes and onto plates.

"What's this?" he said, kicking off his snowy work boots. Delia was visibly pleased.

"Caroline was kind enough to bring us all dinner."

"It was the least I could do considering you let me crash meatball night. It's not as good as your cooking, Delia," Caroline said, "But I hope you all like Thai food."

"Love it," Dylan said. "But I don't think McKenna will try it. You know how three-year-olds can be."

"That's why I got her macaroni from The

Bayshore Bar. Isabel clued me in on her favorite."

"Wow," Dylan said, fumbling through his amazement. "But you really didn't have to pick up food from two different restaurants, especially in this weather."

"It was my pleasure." Caroline pulled several water glasses from the cupboard and began filling them with ice and water.

"McKenna likes plain water, no ice," Dylan offered. She nodded and filled a plastic cup for McKenna.

Just as they had finished setting the table, McKenna bounded into the kitchen, with Isabel right behind her, and climbed up into her seat as if having Caroline over for dinner was old hat.

"It smells delish," Isabel said, dropping a noodle into her mouth. She'd taken the seat next to McKenna.

Caroline pulled a dessert box out of the refrigerator and lifted the lid just enough to show Isabel. "Just wait until your celebratory dessert." When Isabel spotted the contents, she beamed. "Only the best for the Spanish thief."

"The Spanish what?" Dylan said as he and the others sat. "Izzy, did you get the role?"

Isabel held out her arms with pride.

"First stop—Roseley. Next stop—Broadway! I'm thief number one."

"Number one, huh?" Dylan bit back a smile. Apparently, there were several thieves.

"Do you have a lot of lines?" Delia asked. Isabel nodded happily.

"Twenty-seven."

Dylan laughed. "But who's counting, right?"

Isabel squared her shoulders. "*I am.* I play a thief who steals men's hearts and makes off with their fortunes."

Dylan smirked. "Sounds…dangerous."

Isabel scowled at him.

"By dangerous you mean *theatrical.*"

"I know what I mean," Dylan said, noticing that McKenna was fumbling to tuck her napkin into her shirt as a bib. "Heart stealing sounds like a risky business."

As Isabel and Delia chatted about the production, Dylan couldn't tear his eyes from Caroline, who moved to help McKenna. He smiled to himself as he watched her care for his daughter. It was certainly more interesting than anything he could watch in a show.

After Caroline returned to her dinner, she caught Dylan's gaze. They stared at each other for several moments, the chatter of his mother and sister fading to his ears. It was in the silence, the quiet, he felt completely at home, and for the moment, that coziness included Caroline. She was good at stealing McKenna's affections, all right, but he couldn't help but wonder if she was getting away with his heart too.

CHAPTER ELEVEN

CAROLINE CURLED UP on the sofa as Dylan sprawled out on the living room floor. McKenna took a few hurried steps into the living room before springing onto her dad, landing square on his chest.

"Go easy on Daddy," he groaned, but McKenna heard none of it. She was already enjoying herself, flopping from one side of her dad to the other and back again like he was her personal jungle gym. "Please no dirty socks in the face," he whimpered. At his cue, McKenna sat on his chest and kicked a gray-soled sock under his nose, dissolving into hysterics when he made an exaggerated horrified expression.

Isabel watched from the doorway. "Oh, boy. The nighttime ritual," she said. "I can almost set my watch to it."

"You do this every night?" Caroline asked him.

"Nearly," Dylan said.

"It looks like a workout."

Dylan grabbed McKenna midclimb and tickled her as she flailed to get away.

Isabel nodded. "It is. It's also good practice for her."

"Oh?" Caroline said, lifting a brow. She wondered if she was missing Isabel's meaning.

Gus had occasionally let her tag along when he'd taken Trig out to do things. But from as far back as she could remember, it had always been the Gus and Trig show. She'd always felt more like the spectator in their world than a principal character.

By the cherished look on McKenna's face, she was used to having her dad's unbridled attention and affection. It plucked at a sad heart, making her aware of all she'd missed.

Still, she couldn't exactly say Gus had been unloving toward her. They'd shared a few sweet moments over the years. But they'd never shared the kind of warm relationship that Dylan had with McKenna. Dylan was affectionate, and it captivated her. Whether her longing was for her father or for Dylan, who seemed gentler and kinder than she remembered, she wasn't sure. All she knew was that she wanted to settle onto his couch and wear out her welcome.

"You're bruising my ribs, kiddo," Dylan said, sitting up. He raised his voice a few notches to make a bear roar. McKenna startled back and frowned at him, wagging a finger.

"No, no, no, Daddy," she said. *"No."*

"Roar," Dylan said, though much softer. He continued in a mischievous voice. "You should jump on Aunt Izzy."

McKenna shook her head and poked Dylan in the chest. "No. *You.*"

"What about your friend Caroline?" he countered. "She's all alone on the sofa."

Though McKenna had been warming to her, Caroline didn't think they were getting along well enough for horseplay.

"I like this," McKenna insisted, landing another jump on Dylan's chest. Dylan wrapped McKenna in his arms, giving her a giant squeeze until she squealed with delight.

Isabel turned her attention to Caroline. "Did you happen to bring any of your samples for the gala? Dylan said the plans are beautiful."

"Did you really say that?" Caroline said, brightening.

Dylan nodded. "Bianca is lucky to have you working on it."

Caroline glowed as she turned to Isabel. "I left them at home but I'll bring them next time." She paused. Would there be a next time? A next family dinner? A next evening where she was lounging on Dylan's sofa watching him play with his daughter? For as much as she worked and focused on starting her business, it felt odd that she was also assuming she'd be back at the Metzger home again. Inviting herself over with take-out boxes, even after Isabel's invitation, still felt uncharacteristic for her. If she was honest, it also felt like a slippery slope, one where she finally crashed into a wall of rejection and heartache. Wisdom told her that she should visit for a few more minutes out of courtesy and then put some distance between herself and the Metzgers, especially her work associate who was tumbling on the floor with his daughter.

"Let me know if you need any help," Isabel offered. "I can hang a garland with the best of them." She turned to McKenna and curled a finger to beckon her over. "Come on, McKenna. Let's get you ready for bed."

"No, sis, I can do that." Dylan scrambled to his feet.

"Nah, you two probably need to talk Starlight stuff. Besides, I need some more girl time with McKenna before evening rehearsals start."

"How'd she do this morning?" Dylan asked. Isabel mouthed something to him. All Caroline could catch was the word *meltdown*. Dylan nodded knowingly as he explained, "Ms. Callie said that's okay. This week will just be the photograph. I taped one up in the bathroom and her bedroom and—" He turned to McKenna. "Can you show Aunt Izzy the photo of the vacuum cleaner in your tent?"

McKenna screwed up her face as if she might begin to cry. "I don't wanna do that now, Daddy," she said, scooting around Dylan to put him between her and the tent. *"Not now."*

"Oh, it's okay," he said reassuringly as he squeezed her hand. "We won't do that tonight." He turned to Isabel. "She's getting tired. We'll start fresh tomorrow."

Caroline had been around children often enough to know that they frequently had meltdowns or cried when they got tired. In high school and college she'd babysat kids who threw temper tantrums simply because they didn't want to put on pants before leaving the house.

But the dialogue going on between Dylan and McKenna had a subtext she couldn't decipher. If she hadn't been paying close attention to them, she might have completely missed the moment when McKenna shifted from a happy kid to one who was about to cry at the mention of a vacuum cleaner.

Caroline waited until McKenna had scrambled up the stairs ahead of Isabel before turning to Dylan.

"McKenna is a sweetie. It's easy to see she adores you."

Dylan joined Caroline, sitting on the opposite side of the couch.

"Thanks. The feeling is mutual."

"I get the sense that she has some…extra needs?"

Dylan's eyes seemed to search hers as if trying to read any underlying judgment in her question.

"You picked up on that?" he said, cautiously.

She softened her expression to imply that she had.

Dylan ran a hand down the length of his face and drew a deep breath before explaining. "It's still early to officially diagnose anything, but Ms. Callie is helping us in the meantime."

"Is she McKenna's counselor?"

"Occupational therapist," Dylan said. "She confirmed my suspicions that McKenna needs extra, specific support. She suggested McKenna might have a sensory processing disorder."

Caroline readjusted on the couch, curious. "I've never heard of that."

"Most people haven't. It's not yet an official standalone medical diagnosis, and truthfully, you don't diagnose it unless it is very severe. But how Callie described it made a lot of sense, at least to me."

He glanced around the room as if searching for a way to explain.

"People with SPD have a hard time processing information through their senses. Some children have trouble being touched. For example, the lightest brush of a shirt on their skin might feel like steel wool. Other children can't stop being touched. They like being squeezed. Bright lights might bother them or certain food textures. For some children it can affect several senses, but for McKenna, it seems to mainly affect her hearing. Loud sounds disturb her *a lot*."

Caroline wondered what constituted as a loud sound as she thought back to Isabel's comment about musical rehearsals.

"So…" she said. "When Isabel shrieked the other morning—"

"A typical response for my sister," Dylan said with an eye roll. "She can be pretty dramatic."

"It bothered McKenna."

"More than bothered. It would have been completely overwhelming. It's an annoying shriek to you and me but to McKenna…" Dylan paused as if considering. "The truth is,

I don't know what it must sound like to her. All I know is that she goes berserk crying. Worse, she doesn't have the vocabulary yet to better describe when something is bothering her. Can you imagine how frustrating, how scary that might be?"

Caroline couldn't, but by the way Dylan's demeanor had softened, his empathy for his daughter reverberating in his voice, she knew McKenna was fortunate to have a dad who wanted to find out.

"Your nightly ritual?" Caroline said slowly. "Is it some sort of therapy?"

"Sort of. We're playing because we love each other. I would do that every night with her no matter what." He grinned a smile so rich, Caroline thought she might be catching the first real glimpse of Dylan Metzger. "McKenna doesn't have trouble being touched," he continued. "So when we play on the floor, I use that time to practice sensory integration. I didn't do it much tonight because you're visiting, but I normally try to make different volumes of noises. It's a safe way for her to get used to some sounds that bother her."

Caroline considered how all of this sounded foreign to her. Sensory integration had certainly never been on her radar when she'd been growing up and she'd never heard of anyone speak of it before. But it was fascinating. Not fascinating because it existed but because Dylan had sought out an explanation for what had been bothering his daughter so he could better help her.

Dylan continued slowly as if gauging the value of every word to better explain.

"For louder, scarier noises like road construction or the hair dryer or something, our goal is to be quiet in the moment. I don't want to add to the chaos she might feel. Instead, I want to invite her into my calm."

Caroline glanced at the tent. "The headphones? They're not for listening to music, are they?"

"Ms. Callie is teaching us a lot of new techniques. McKenna wears headphones sometimes when we go out. The tent is a quiet place for her to escape to when she's feeling overstimulated. At home we count down quietly when we anticipate there's going to be a loud noise."

Caroline remembered how Dylan had counted down to Ms. Callie's arrival.

"You were integrating her to the sound of the doorbell."

"Right. Small steps. She hates the sound of the vacuum cleaner so we hung up pictures of vacuum cleaners in different places around the house. When she's ready, we'll run the vacuum cleaner upstairs while she sits safely in her tent with her headphones on. Eventually we want her on the same floor as the vacuum cleaner and then even turning it on herself—"

"To control the sound."

"You catch on quicker than most adults. Professional opinions keep changing so who knows what they'll suggest tomorrow, but for now, sensory integration is the best way I know how to help her."

Caroline hummed in understanding, but not just from what he explained. He had changed so much since childhood, and she couldn't help but think McKenna had been a big reason. Being around him felt different, felt… easy. "You're good with her."

"Not always. Sometimes I get overwhelmed. It's easy to get short or feel frustrated."

"I think they call that parenthood."

"Not everyone is cut out for it," he said sadly.

Caroline knew there was a lot more to his story with McKenna's mother. It spoke volumes that he chose to move to Roseley with a child who had extra challenges.

"What about Giana?" she asked.

Dylan lowered his eyes and sat quietly for several moments. When he looked up, Caroline could sense the weight of the world on his shoulders. She wondered why she hadn't noticed it before. All at once his face looked longer, like gravity had dragged it half an inch toward the ground.

"She wasn't cut out for it, was she?" Caroline supplied.

Dylan blinked in agreement. "Looking back I should have seen the warning signs. There were many but the biggest was the one that didn't change after McKenna was born—she didn't like kids. I foolishly thought she would change. I mean, how could a person not like spending time with their own kid?"

Caroline winced. When it came to her father, she'd had the same thought a time or two.

"She didn't want McKenna?" Caroline asked.

Dylan rolled his eyes. "I know it sounds like I was the one who changed the playbook after we got married, but I didn't. That's what was so confusing to me. Before we got married she had said she wanted a child. But after we had McKenna, even before McKenna's extra needs were apparent, she admitted she didn't realize what having a child would entail and…" He shifted uncomfortably, readjusting his body as he offered a vague explanation. "She wasn't cut out for it," he said.

Caroline wanted to erase all his bad memories that made the lines around his eyes deepen.

"McKenna is fortunate to have you. You seem like you really try to understand her."

Dylan huffed. "Nah, you should see me on a bad day."

"You're trying your best, Dylan. Just showing up is ninety percent of it. Trust me, I should know." When she realized she'd admitted more than she cared to explain, she readjusted awkwardly. "I mean…anyone can see…"

Dylan's expression perked. "You should know, huh? There's a loaded statement if I've ever heard one."

Unable to find a more comfortable position, Caroline rose from the couch and began collecting the throw blankets McKenna and Dylan had tossed around while playing. With careful precision she began to fold them, feeling Dylan's eyes on her.

"Don't we all have daddy issues?" she said with a chuckle.

Dylan motioned for her to give him a blanket end. "That doesn't mean we should dismiss yours. Lay it on me."

"Ah," Caroline said with a scoff. "You know how my dad was. You were there for a lot of it." The truth was, she didn't like to think about her dad. But since she'd reunited with Dylan, she hadn't been able to stop thinking about

Gus or the emotional divide that had always existed between them.

They brought the ends of the blanket together, folding it into a perfect bundle.

"He taught me a lot," Dylan said, picking up the next blanket. "Fishing, shooting…"

"Look, he was a good dad," Caroline rushed to say. She didn't want a pity party where she berated her father for every tiny mistake he made raising her. He and her mom had done their best and she'd grown up to be capable and hardworking and self-reliant because of their straightforward lessons. "He showed me how to do stuff too."

"But…"

She knew Dylan was waiting for her to explain how her father had been there physically when she'd been a girl but not emotionally. And now, he was neither. The hurt propelled her off in a different direction, eager to feel something else, something more hopeful.

"I looked up that preschool I was telling you about," she said as she placed the folded blanket on the recliner. "It is called Growing Roses. Cute, right? I can reach out to my friend there and ask about their preschool programs. We can see if—"

"Red," Dylan said. She turned, expecting him to balk at another mention of the pre-

school. Instead she found his expression tender. "In order for us to be friends, this needs to be a back-and-forth. Don't you think?"

Caroline swallowed hard. He *was* becoming a friend, wasn't he? Somehow, in such a short period of time, she'd gone from scowling whenever she thought of him to counting the hours until she could talk to him again. It was the strangest thing. He hadn't been a stranger when she'd seen him at Tyler and Olivia's wedding, but still, she hadn't really known him either. Since the wedding she'd been getting to know him better than some people she'd known for years. Certainly better than she knew some people in her own family.

Caroline drew a heavy breath and released it in concession.

"I wouldn't know where to begin, Dylan. Really."

He nodded and she could tell he was scrambling to help her.

"Well," he said. "I haven't seen him in years, certainly not since I got back to town last spring. Is he well?"

Caroline sighed in annoyance. "It beats me."

"Aha." A knowing smile breached Dylan's lips. "Then I think we found our starting place. Follow me."

CHAPTER TWELVE

CAROLINE COULD RECALL being in the Metzgers' basement once before. She'd still been just a girl when Delia had been expecting Isabel. She and her mother had attended Delia's baby shower. While she'd been thrilled at first to see her name on the invitation, the excitement of being included as one of the girls had worn off after the first hour. Her frilly dress had scratched at the collar and her fancy dress shoes had jabbed into her ankles. She had spent the day sitting among a basement of women who had chatted about their husbands and children, and, of course, babies. As she sipped several cups of pink punch, and listened to her mother complain about her father, she had daydreamed about kicking off her shoes and sneaking off to Dylan's room to play video games with him and Trig.

But where pink crepe paper once hung were now Christmas lights.

"I had no idea you were such a Christmas enthusiast," she said. Dylan flipped off the basement overhead light, bringing the multi-colored lights into full glow.

"Isabel just strung these. She started coming down here to rehearse lines." Dylan fluttered his fingers playfully like he was explaining something mystical. "She says creative people have to set the right *mood.*"

Caroline giggled. "She's right, though in our business we call it ambience."

"Well," Dylan said, hoisting a few heavy record cases up onto a table, along with a dusty record player, "I'll take your word for it." He flipped through the first case, selected a record of big-band songs and put it on. His face relaxed into satisfaction when it began to play. "Ah. Don't you just love that old-timey feel from the record player?"

Caroline nodded, picturing the musicians who had recorded the song, as Dylan continued on to another case.

"I wanted to show you this." He patted the second record case. "It's my grandmother's Christmas collection. It occurred to me," he said while selecting a new record, "if you're going to throw a vintage Christmas gala, you'll need vintage-sounding music."

"We hired The Hometown Jamboree, remember?"

The Hometown Jamboree was one of the

most popular bands in Roseley. Folks followed them to different venues in town. They played The Bayshore Bar every other Thursday and were always invited to the parades and festivals. They also had a long-standing gig to play the Behrs' Christmas gala every year.

"Of course," Dylan said. "The Hometown Jamboree will be playing in the dance hall on the stage. But that old-timey feel of having the records crackle could be a nice accent. You could have Christmas records playing when people first arrive and are milling about the lobby."

The music swelled. A saxophonist began to wail just as the record jumped. The sound was too dated for what Bianca would have enjoyed back when she and Ted were going to dances at The Starlight. Still, the guests may enjoy it.

"It's a great idea, Dylan," Caroline said.

His brows lifted. "Do you like it? Really?"

"I do." She smiled. She was pleased that he was looking out for her. She could live on a thoughtful gesture like this for a month. "I can't believe I didn't think of it."

"You can't be responsible for everything, Red."

She hip-checked him. "I don't try to be, you know."

"But you take notice when someone needs something. Don't you?"

Caroline drummed her fingers over the stack of records. "Sure. Doesn't everybody?"

Dylan chuckled. "The world would be a much better place if everyone did."

"I pay close attention, yes," Caroline said. It was a trait that made her a great event planner. She remembered all the details, but more than that, she remembered the little things people said and she always found a way to help make their small wishes a reality. "I can't turn that off."

"Nor should you. Getting macaroni for McKenna, and from an entirely different restaurant, was more than thoughtful. It helped us to have a pleasant dinner. I appreciated that."

"You're welcome," Caroline said as a giddy feeling of pride and delight skittered through her. "But you thought of the Christmas records. Maybe you're good at noticing too."

Dylan's gaze lingered. His blue eyes twinkled under the Christmas lights. It made the heat rise in her cheeks.

"I notice how you take care of everything for Bianca."

Caroline nodded. "That's my job now."

"What about with Sheila?"

"Ugh, don't get me started," Caroline said. "Unfortunately, Sheila's still my boss."

"Okay," Dylan said. "What about with your dad?"

Caroline opened her mouth to explain when Dylan held up a hand.

"Wait," he said. "Ambience."

He gingerly flipped through the stacks, frowning as he searched. Caroline stared at the lines that formed between his eyebrows as he concentrated. The longer he searched, the deeper the lines ran. They made him look distinguished. She liked the look. Although, she thought as she wiped her palms down the front of her jeans, maybe that was because she liked him.

Finally, after a quick side-glance at her, he slipped a Christmas record from its cover and replaced the one on the record player. Soon, a rich baritone voice began to croon a melancholy tune about not being home for Christmas. Caroline fluffed stray hairs off her face as she forced a smile. She knew she looked as uncomfortable as she felt, but the song hit a little too close to home where her dad was concerned. She couldn't ignore the fact that Dylan had thought to play it.

"You're trying to make me cry," she said, playfully pointing a finger at him.

"Nope," he said gently. "But I'll listen if you want to tell me about your dad."

"Who says I want to talk about him?"

Dylan shrugged. "You can if you want."

She didn't like to talk about him with anyone, except Faith on occasion and even that was just surface discussions.

But now she felt something...different. Maybe it was the scent of the Metzger basement, which had instantly taken her back to a time when her parents had still been married and her dad had still been living year-round in Roseley. The music made her reminisce about the past, even if some parts of it were not so nice and shiny.

But even more so, the compassionate timbre of Dylan's voice instantly lulled her. He relaxed back against the table, giving her his full, undivided attention. Having someone, anyone, just do that might have been healing enough. But when Dylan did it, there was something intentional in the way he quietly waited. The lines around his eyes crinkled with interest and empathy and made her lean in to share, just this once.

"Dad's somewhere between here and Montana," she said. "When I try to call or text to find out how he's doing, I either don't hear back from him or I hear an update through Trig."

Dylan nodded. "Is that why you were surprised when Trig called you?"

Caroline recalled the hurt when she'd learned that Dad had, once again, connected with Trig instead of her. A lump, as if waiting on standby, surfaced in her throat. She swallowed hard, trying to force it back down.

"Dad and I have a strange relationship," she muttered. She thought of the text message she'd sent just that evening. She wondered why she ever texted at all since he rarely responded. She'd probably get a better return rate with messages in a bottle. Tossing them into the ocean would probably be more fun too. "I'm always hoping for something different, but I suspect he doesn't think about me often."

"Why do you say that?"

"I mean, think about it. If he cared at all, he'd call or text or..." She fumbled at the record stack again. "Come home for Christmas."

"Have you asked him to?"

Caroline shook her head furiously as the door to the basement opened. She straightened, momentarily relieved to be interrupted from their conversation. But as Dylan turned off the record player, she regretted the disconnect.

Delia trotted down the first couple of stairs and peeked down at them.

"Dylan?" she said, her normally sweet voice now sounding like a harsh intrusion. "It's Giana."

"On my cell?" he said, instinctively smacking at his hip for a phone that wasn't there. He turned to Caroline, his eyes pleading an apology.

"I'm so sorry to interrupt you when you were just starting to share—"

"It's fine," Caroline said, shaking him off as she bolted for the stairs. What more was there to share about her dad anyway? Nothing had changed since she was a kid and no amount of talking about it would change things now. "I was done talking."

Dylan flipped off the Christmas lights before following her. When they reached the top of the steps, Delia handed him his cell phone.

"It's on mute." Delia winced and glanced between the two of them as if recognizing what terrible timing Giana's call had.

"She promised to call McKenna," he explained. "Caroline, let me run the phone upstairs and then we can continue talking—"

"No, no, no. Go ahead and take care of McKenna." Caroline hurried to the front window. Digging her keys from her pocket, she pointed her fob at her car, starting the engine remotely. Then she quickly grabbed her coat from the hall closet and stepped into her boots.

"I know how important that is. Plus, I really need to get home. The snow is piling up by the minute."

"Caroline," Dylan said. "Please, wait. I'd like to help you dig your car out. Just give me a few minutes and I'll—"

"Nonsense. Go. I'll talk to you later." She flashed a bright smile to him and Delia before slinging her purse over her shoulder and yanking open the front door. The powdery snow that had accumulated since she'd arrived fell into the entryway. Flakes blew and swirled, the cold air lashing at her face.

Nobody wanted to listen to her bemoan how her dad didn't like spending time with her.

"Honey," Delia called as Caroline's boots crunched into the first step of snow. "It's a blizzard out there. Don't you want to wait in here while your car warms up?"

"I'm fine. By the time I get the windshield and windows cleared the car will be piping hot."

"Well, for heaven's sake," Delia said with a gasp. "At least zip up your coat."

"I will! Don't worry about me," Caroline sang. "Thanks for everything!"

She was ready to go. While Dylan was becoming something of a good friend, Giana's phone call reminded her that he had other things, more important things, to do than listen to her lament.

She waved, catching a glimpse of Dylan, his mouth agape in confusion. He wanted her to stay, that much was clear.

It felt like the story of her life, getting pulled in several directions at once. When she wasn't helping Sheila, she was pandering to Bianca. When she wasn't working through dinner and took time to talk to a lovely friend who actually wanted to listen to her, she felt the pull to escape. What could she say? Fending for herself while buttoning up her heart had become natural over the years. Changing things now felt nearly impossible.

With the palm of her hand, Caroline pounded at the snow and ice covering her door and fiddled with the door handle until she managed to pry it open. She grabbed an ice scraper from the passenger seat and got to work, brushing the snow and scraping the ice blanketing her car, hoping to be long gone before Dylan was able to pull attention away from McKenna.

She worked her way around the car quickly, building up a little sweat before finally collapsing onto the driver's seat. After stripping the hat from her head and unzipping her coat, she held her fingers to the vents, letting the heat warm them. She thought about how good it would feel to finally get home. Between the safe confines of her cozy little apartment walls, she could relax without having to recall the past. Sharing those details just reminded her of how alone she'd felt for so long, and what good did that do her? People, even kind people like Dylan, typically didn't stick around in her life for very long so it was better to keep from getting used to his attentiveness.

The car had just finally started to warm up when she shifted into Reverse. Instead of moving, the car conked out. The dashboard instantly went dark.

She shifted in her seat, wondering what had happened. After waiting a moment, she tried the ignition, praying the car engine would fire up.

Nothing.

She waited a few more seconds, trying a second time, then a third. When the driveway went dark, the motion detector light over the Metzger garage finally timing out, she was ready to face the cold, hard truth.

Her car was officially dead.

CHAPTER THIRTEEN

DYLAN HAD MADE it up the stairs just in time for McKenna to peek out of the bathroom.

"She just put her pajamas on," he said to Giana as he motioned for McKenna to follow him to the bedroom.

"I can talk to her tomorrow," Giana said in her typical hurried response.

"No, no, no. She's ready." He sat on the edge of the bed and pulled McKenna onto his lap. "Here, sweetie," he whispered to McKenna. "Mommy is on the phone."

McKenna pulled the bottom of her pajama shirt up over her face and peeked out smiling. Her cheeks were pink from the steamy bathroom and her wet eyelashes stuck together, looking even more prominent. She giggled and hid again, as if it was all a game.

"She's a little shy," said Dylan, holding the phone screen so Giana could see their daughter. He whispered into McKenna's ear. "Say, 'Hi, Mommy.'"

Isabel, watching from the doorway, stood

behind the phone to help coach. She waved, trying to get McKenna to mimic her. It didn't work.

"Hi, sweetheart!" Giana blew a loud kiss toward the screen. "How's my beautiful girl?"

McKenna recoiled into the crook of Dylan's arm and stared at Giana for a moment before looking up at him for guidance.

"Can you blow Mommy a kiss?" he whispered.

Isabel pantomimed how to blow a kiss, but McKenna just stared, deadpan.

"Blow me a kiss," Giana said. "Come on. I want a big one." After a few moments, her insistence intensified. "Don't you want to blow me a kiss, McKenna? Do you know how?"

"She knows," Dylan said, patiently. "Just talk, Giana. It's good for her to hear your voice. Just try speaking softly and—"

Giana rolled her eyes. "I *am* speaking softly. She doesn't want to talk back. I can't make her talk if she doesn't want to."

Dylan smiled reassuringly at McKenna, trying to stay positive amid Giana's irritated tone.

"Is it snowing in New York?" he asked. If McKenna and Giana couldn't connect with each other directly, perhaps they could get there in a roundabout way. "We're getting hit with a storm at the moment."

"Yeah," Giana said, waving to someone off camera. He could tell she was in a restaurant lobby. It was quiet enough for her to talk, but she looked distracted.

Dylan continued on. "McKenna ate snow today, didn't you, Little Mouse?"

"Ugh," Giana said. "Are you still calling her that? I thought we discussed nicknames before you moved."

"It's a term of endearment," Dylan said, trying for calm. "Tell McKenna what it looks like in the city. They would have started decorating for Christmas by now."

"It's the city," Giana said, her voice emotionless. "Look, Dylan. If she doesn't want to talk tonight, we don't have to press it, okay?"

Dylan could feel Isabel glaring at him. It was all he could do to not make eye contact with her. He didn't want McKenna to pick up on his sister's anger or his frustration, not when she finally had her mother's attention for a few minutes.

"I'll be quiet," he said, swallowing his pride. He didn't need to argue with Giana. After all, she was a pro at it. What he needed was for cool heads to prevail, his included.

Their daughter was too young to converse with anyone in real life, let alone on a cell phone. But he couldn't let the time slip away while he waited for McKenna to hold up her end of any conversation with her mother. He wanted to do whatever he could to help the two of them along, to facilitate a good mother-daughter relationship.

"McKenna," Giana said, shifting to a playful tone. "I'm going Christmas shopping next week and I'm going to buy you a giant present. If you think of something you really want, tell Daddy so he can text me. Okay?"

McKenna stuck her thumb in her mouth in lieu of a reply. With her one little comforting action, Dylan knew their conversation with Giana had run its course, and not just for McKenna.

Giana scowled, her delivery strained. "Put Daddy on the phone, please."

Isabel helped McKenna under the bedcovers as Dylan slipped into the hallway. Once he was obviously out of earshot, pulling the bedroom door shut, Giana made a gagging noise into the phone.

"McKenna is *still* sucking her thumb?" she said. "You haven't stopped any of the stuff we talked about before you left. Talk about a breach of contract, Dylan."

Dylan pinched the bridge of his nose. "I've had my hands full getting our daughter adjusted to Roseley."

"That's why you moved in with your mom and sister," Giana said. "Family support, wasn't it?"

Dylan recalled the many conversations he and Giana had had late into the night arguing about how to best help McKenna. He couldn't count the number of counseling sessions Giana had reluctantly agreed to go to only to complain about them later. In the beginning he had thought of counseling as a way to help protect their marriage, their family, but in the end it had better helped him transition to the divorce—to his new role as a single dad.

"She's still just a little girl, Giana," Dylan said. "We're taking it one step at a time."

"Whatever you say, Dylan." Giana waved again to someone off camera. "I have to get back to my colleagues. Give McKenna kisses from Mommy."

"Of course," Dylan said, ending the call. He rolled out his shoulders before returning to the bedroom. McKenna was selecting a storybook from the nightstand.

"She has a lot of nerve," Isabel whispered.

"Not now, okay?" Dylan said. He valued how much his sister, and his mother too, loved McKenna and supported him, but he knew no good would come from speaking poorly about Giana in front of McKenna. That had been something his mother had modeled well for him after her own divorce. Delia rarely mentioned his and Isabel's father. When he'd asked her about it, a year after his funeral, she'd shrugged and explained, "You're half him. What good could come from complaining about that? I let his actions speak for themselves."

His dad's actions certainly had. He'd put all his time and attention into his law career and had died just after Dylan had gotten married.

"I'll take it from here, sis," Dylan said, sitting on the edge of McKenna's bed. "Thanks for helping tonight."

"You got it." Isabel flipped on McKenna's night-light before pulling the door shut behind her.

Storybook in hand, McKenna scooted close.

"Did you pick a good one?" he said, as McKenna held up her book. She stuck her thumb in her mouth, an implication that she had. "Good," he said, recognizing the familiar story.

TWENTY MINUTES LATER, Dylan eased McKenna's bedroom door shut. The house was quiet, as both his mom and sister had retreated to her own bedroom for the night. He trotted downstairs and made his rounds through the house, pulling curtains shut and checking the locks on the doors. As he checked the front door, he noticed someone trudging up the front walk to the house. It was Caroline.

Dylan pulled open the door, grimacing against the wind. It raged, nearly sucking the breath from him.

"My car died," she explained. "And I can't get a hold of the towing company."

Dylan knew that even if she got through, it would be a long wait for a tow truck. The roads wouldn't be cleared until the storm stopped and there was no telling how much longer from now that would be.

"You've got to be freezing," he said, shutting the front door behind her. "Have you been sitting in a cold car all this time?"

"More or less." She removed her boots and coat and settled in on the couch, pulling the throw blankets over her.

Dylan immediately set about making her a cup of hot chocolate, throwing in an extra serving for himself.

Returning to the living room, he handed Caroline a warm mug.

"I can't feel my toes," she whimpered, taking a sip.

"I'll bet."

"It figures too. I have so much work to do tonight. I can't afford to get behind."

Dylan grabbed a heavier blanket from the hall closet and laid it over Caroline as she sipped her drink. Then he settled on the opposite end of the couch.

"What do you need to do?"

Caroline tipped her head.

"Review the menu so Bianca and I can finalize it with the caterer. Order decorations before stores sell out. I'm interviewing two people for my job this week and helping Sheila with the next wedding…"

"Oh, just that?" he chuckled.

"That's just the tip of the iceberg, not that I have to explain that concept to you. You know how it feels to have a start-up. What's it going to take to have The Starlight ready by Christmas Eve?"

"A ton." His to-do list was long. "But I always make time for the good stuff."

"Such as?" Caroline peeked at him from over the rim of her mug. "I'm all ears."

He puckered a face as he thought.

"Getting a business off the ground takes a lot of work," he said. "It'll take all I have to offer and then some. But my first priority is McKenna. I want to run a business and someday bring her in to be a part of it. In the meantime, I like being home for dinner and bedtime stories and early-morning snuggles. You know, the good stuff."

"The way you talk about her…" she said. "I didn't… I had no idea…"

"What?" he said, bracing for a dig. "You had no idea the Dylan Metzger of your youth had a heart?"

She shook her head and stared into her hot chocolate. "I had no idea fathers could feel that way about their daughters."

Dylan recalled what they had been talking about before Giana had called and how Caroline had practically flown out of the house given the first chance. As much as he sensed he should ask her about her dad again, he didn't want her fleeing into the storm.

"What's your good stuff?" he said. She glanced up from her mug.

"Running my own business for starters." Caroline glanced up with a dreamy look on her face. "I've wanted to do it for so long, I can almost taste it. Once Bianca sees what a great gala I throw, she'll hire me every Christmas, and probably tell her friends about me. I can plan all sorts of parties and events and…" She groaned in exasperation. "I just have to get over this first hurdle, this next month. Then it will be smoother sailing. Next year is going to be my year."

Dylan smiled. "You've got optimism, I've got to hand it to you. You're putting a lot of your eggs in the Bianca Behr basket."

"Bianca and Tex are very influential in this town. That's why I can't mess up anything with this gala. The stakes are too high."

Dylan knew all about high stakes, especially where the Behrs were concerned. He didn't like bringing up bad blood, especially when he now had to do business with them. But Tex and Bianca had almost destroyed his life with their meddling, so he didn't want to see Caroline fall victim to them anytime soon.

"You can't be everything to everyone, Caroline. Bianca is going to take and take and I…" He set his mug on the coffee table. "I just want you to protect yourself. Set some healthy boundaries."

Caroline held out her mug for him to place on the table too. "You're a lot more protective than I remember."

"I always take care of my friends."

"Ah, yes, that's right. *Friends.*" The words dripped with sarcasm, but he thought it was a defense mechanism. The way she set her eyes on him, her lips puckering in a feisty pout, reminded him of the girl he and Trig used to torment.

"We are, aren't we?" He sat back on the couch, this time settling closer. She slid her feet near his lap and nudged his thigh.

"If we must." Her eyes, her voice, were a playful challenge and it made his insides skitter about.

"Don't do me any favors," he said, reaching for her foot. She pulled it back before flicking another playful kick. "You're borrowing trouble," he warned. "The last time a person tried something like that—"

"You what?" she said, kicking him harder.

Dylan lifted a reprimanding eyebrow. "I tackled them on the playground."

"You wouldn't dare," she breathed.

He set his stare on her, determined to convey that he absolutely would. It felt like old times for a minute—he and Trig had never pulled punches with her. When she was around, she'd been one of the guys. But when she grinned and bit the bottom edge of her lip, his breath caught. He wondered if she had even realized she'd done it, nibbling her perfect pink bottom lip. It drew his gaze in a flash. For a moment he was completely captivated by it, by her. If she had done it as a subconscious reflex, he could no sooner ignore it than he could ignore the adrenaline coursing through his veins.

"Try me," he whispered. The seconds ticked as he debated if he wanted her to. He was a man who always kept his promises, even when they didn't make much sense. And actively flirting with a woman in his living room while his daughter slept upstairs seemed like the least logical thing he had done in a very long time.

But when her eyes darkened and she flicked her foot at his thigh again, he wanted to touch her. In a split second, he snatched her foot from under the blanket.

"Hey," she gasped, failing to pull away in time.

"Ticklish, are we?"

"No." Her defiance reminded him of the Caroline he remembered, the girl who used to instigate a fight for fun. He clamped a hand around her ankle and tickled the sole of her foot. Caroline's face reddened as she tried to repress her laughter.

"I'm not ticklish," she protested but she wriggled to break free all the same. When she finally gave in to her laughter, it was so guttural, it emboldened him to yank the blankets off her and dig his fingers into her sides. She giggled and squirmed and it only spurred him on. She was still a lot of fun.

As she gasped for breaths, she attempted to escape by struggling to the floor.

"You can't get away that easily," he said, following her over the side of the couch. They hit the ground with a *thud*, Caroline sprawled on her back and Dylan bracing himself on his side. Repositioning himself, he loosely pinned her between his body and the couch.

Though he had a hand free to tickle her, he paused as she gasped for air. He had to gauge if she was really having as much fun as he was.

"Time-out," he said.

Dylan didn't want to further cross any physical line with Caroline, as he recognized they were now both sprawled on the floor.

Her jewel-toned eyes were wild and searching, as if she was trying to anticipate his next move. Her full curls were splayed around her, like a holy, strawberry blonde aura, and her cheeks had flushed, looking hot to the touch. A lot had happened in the span of twenty seconds and it left him trying to decipher what she was thinking, feeling.

"Have you had enough?" he said, relaxing his grip on her. He felt very aware that his hand was palming her side, something he normally wouldn't do to any woman, without invitation.

She blinked up at him. "Have you?"

He hadn't. He wanted to cup her face in his

hand and take a reckless leap from friendship to something…more. For most of his life he'd seen Caroline as something of a kid sister, but since returning to Roseley he'd found her to be something new, something special.

He eased his hand carefully from her side and held it up defensively. She flinched as if expecting him to tickle-dive again with doubled ferocity. Eyes wide like a barn owl's, she watched him, and he knew his next move was the most important one.

"Truce?" he mumbled, struggling to recalibrate his feelings. He knew he was perfectly capable of ruining what they had. All he had to do was touch her again or, worse, kiss her. If sharing her feelings had made her bolt from the house earlier, initiating an unwanted kiss might have her fleeing into the night never to return.

She clasped his wrist firmly as if she had the strength to keep him from tickling her. He stared into her eyes and couldn't see the girl he'd once known. All he could see was the woman he'd been getting to know over the last week. She was mesmerizing and having her so close electrified every nerve ending.

"You know I can't do that," she said, her mouth twisting in a determined smirk.

What a treasure she truly was. She was

a kind, thoughtful, spunky treasure that he wanted to gather up into his arms. The way she looked at him, the way she squeezed his wrist as if upping the ante, made him think she might want him to.

But when he thought about the consequences, mistaking her signals and getting rejected and hurt for a second time, he knew his heart couldn't handle it. For the better part of adulthood, Giana had been his best friend and wife and partner in everything. For her to give up on their marriage so easily stung so deeply, he hadn't thought he'd be able to find his way back to normal.

As much as he wanted to kiss the smirk clear off Caroline's pretty mouth, he cared enough about her, about their friendship, to not do it without invitation. He didn't want to risk losing her.

"Why not?" he said.

"Because we're not even yet."

"No?" This wasn't the smartest move on his part, playing along with her, wanting to get involved with her, when he was still carrying around the emotional baggage of a newly minted divorce. But all the same, he rolled to his back and stretched his arms over his head, needing to know his feelings were reciprocated. "I'm not ticklish," he said. "But you can do your worst."

The floor above them creaked. Someone was moving about upstairs. When he opened his eyes, he found Caroline staring at him, sobered. The spell had been broken.

Playing now, as an adult and as a father who had an impressionable little girl sleeping upstairs, meant playing for keeps. He had to keep his wits about him and guard his heart.

Dylan found his way to his feet. He clasped Caroline's hands in his and pulled her up. She smoothed the hair out of her face and flashed him a sheepish smile. She looked a little shell-shocked, or perhaps just confused. By the pounding in his chest, he knew he certainly was.

"About your car…" he began. Caroline's expression dimmed as if suddenly remembering. "I can jump-start it, but I'd prefer to do that tomorrow morning after the storm dies down."

She fumbled for her cell phone. "You don't have to do that. I'll try the towing company again."

"You won't get through to them until tomorrow. It's getting late and the roads are getting bad." He knew she wouldn't like his next idea, but in light of the present circumstances, he also knew she didn't have much of a choice. "You should stay here tonight."

"Oh, no, I couldn't," she said. "I have an early meeting tomorrow morning that I need to prepare for and I need to shower and—"

"Nonsense. I'll fix you a bed on the couch and then we'll start out in the morning, crack of dawn. I promise."

"I don't know…" Caroline shifted her weight from one foot to the other and he sensed just how difficult it was for her to accept his offer. She might be used to being self-reliant, but she needed his help now, even if she didn't want to admit it. "I don't want to put you out."

Dylan motioned toward the couch. "I'm putting *you* out. I wish I had a bed to offer but, unfortunately, it's the couch for you."

"It's a lot warmer than my car, I guess."

Dylan flashed her a supportive wink. "I'll grab you some sheets."

He retrieved a pillow, sheets and a heavier blanket from the upstairs closet. Delia always had a stocked closet of mini toiletries in case of overnight company. He collected everything he thought Caroline might need to feel comfortable, including some of Isabel's clean pajamas.

"I'm glad she's staying," Isabel said as she piled the clothes on top of the bedsheets. "Not just because the roads are really bad either. I like her."

He shrugged. "Okay…"

"You know what I mean," his sister continued on, peeking past him into the hallway to make sure no one could hear. "You should bring her around more."

"I forget that you don't really remember her."

"I don't remember most of your friends. That's what happens when your brother is a decade older than you."

"I was mostly friends with Caroline's brother, not her. She and I are just working together now."

Isabel shot Dylan an incredulous look. "From what I saw this evening, you could have fooled me."

"When?"

"When you were playing with McKenna. Caroline was watching you so…"

"What?"

Isabel frowned as if searching for the right word. "She likes you."

Dylan would only admit to himself that he had hoped for such a thing. He and Caroline had certainly been developing a closeness, but if that meant something more than friendship, it both scared and excited him.

"I have other things on my mind right now, sis."

"I get it," she said. "You're running a new business and raising the best kid in the world."

"Right."

"But a word of advice?" Isabel waggled her eyebrows up at him. "Don't let the grass grow under your feet. Nighty-night."

Dylan headed for the living room, pondering how his sister was the second person to nudge him toward making a move with Caroline. But as much as he wanted to, being more than friends felt way too fast, way too risky. His divorce papers had been inked not six months ago and everything that had transpired with Giana leading up to that had left him feeling very vulnerable. By day he was in charge, capable and responsible—he had all the answers. But by night, when he was alone with his thoughts, he was still just a person who had had his heart broken.

Then there was McKenna. Even though he'd brought Caroline around to meet her, he had done so within the context that Caroline was just his friend. He didn't want to introduce his daughter to a significant other until things were serious. If the relationship didn't work out, McKenna would feel the loss of another important woman in her life. He couldn't subject his daughter to that, couldn't risk that kind of heartache. She still felt the pain caused by Giana's neglect.

"Thanks," Caroline said as he spread the bedsheets over the couch. "I appreciate it."

"No problem. I'll see you in the morning."

He made his way toward the stairs and reminded himself that he was doing his duty as a friend and father. The sooner he put thoughts of anything more with Caroline out of his mind, the better.

"Hey, Dylan?" Caroline called after him. He turned. "I'm—I'm glad we're friends."

He perked. "How did it feel to finally admit that?"

Caroline cocked a finger at him. "I'm tired and not thinking clearly. I fully reserve the right to take it back in the morning."

He grinned. "That's the Caroline I remember."

"And one more thing," she said, turning toward the couch before calling back over her shoulder. "We're still not even."

CHAPTER FOURTEEN

CAROLINE STARTLED AWAKE the next morning. She had tossed and turned for most of the night trying to get comfortable on the couch. All the while she'd tried to repress thoughts of pulling off the gala and hiring Sheila's replacement and, of course…

Dylan.

Every time she stirred awake and readjusted her pillow, she remembered the look in his eye before he'd tickled her over the edge of the couch. As kids she'd always been prepared for whatever he instigated. She would come back swinging and as he was older, faster and stronger than her, she'd usually end up mad that she couldn't best him. He'd usually laugh his head off, thrilled to get a rise out of her, and then they'd tear off on another round of it.

On the living room floor, with Dylan cozied against her, he'd certainly gotten a rise out of her again. And she was pretty sure she'd gotten one out of him.

Caroline blinked fully awake. She hoped

that no one, especially McKenna, was wandering around the house in the dark. While spending the night was completely innocent, she still didn't want to face a three-year-old's innocent interrogation.

After a quick glance around the room, she breathed a sigh of relief that it was empty.

It was still dark, the early winter sunrise still a long way off. She figured it was still a bit early to wake Dylan, but with so much to do that day, she was desperate to get her car running.

Snagging her phone off the coffee table to check the time, she discovered that Dylan had already texted her.

I'm awake. Ready when you are.

Caroline grabbed her purse and toiletry bag and sneaked into the bathroom as she sent a reply.

Thanks. Be ready in a few.

Once freshened up, Caroline went out to the kitchen and found the coffee already percolating. Dylan stood against the counter. In old Levi's and a navy flannel shirt, he looked like the perfect wake-up call. He grinned and offered her a cup.

"Two sugars and a cream," he said. Caroline accepted it, pretending that she wasn't completely impressed he had remembered.

"You're good at keeping me hydrated."

"I'm good at a lot of things," he said. His response was unexpected, and she knew the surprise flashed on her face because he faltered before powering on to explain. "I got your car started."

"Already?"

"You said you wanted an early start."

"Yeah, I did. I didn't hear you open the front door," she said, now wondering if he had seen her sleeping after all. The thought caused her to flush. Why was she suddenly so self-conscious around him?

"I went out the back door so I could clear the walkway."

"Oh." She sipped her coffee. "How responsible of you."

"Eh. I grew up."

Caroline couldn't help but agree. He had grown into a dedicated father who took good care of his daughter. He also seemed interested in taking care of her. That kind of attention was certainly a first for her. She wasn't sure what to do with it.

History had taught her that people weren't reliable enough to count on when she needed them. Trig and her dad were rarely around, and after her mom remarried, she'd turned her doting attention to her new family as if trying to redo her shot at motherhood. Being self-reliant was the only way Caroline knew how to navigate life, so to let down her guard now felt more than foreign. It felt dangerous.

"Did it just need a jump start?" she asked, ready to hit the road and put some much-needed distance between them.

"Yep. The main road looks clear, but I'd prefer to follow you home, just in case."

"No, no, no. You don't need to do that—"

"Let's not do this," he said, holding up a hand. Caroline's eyes widened as she watched him place his mug in the sink in one graceful motion before turning to face her.

"Do what?" she said.

"Go back and forth, you protesting and me insisting until you finally realize that my offer is something any good friend would do for another. With your car being unreliable right now, it's smart for me to follow you."

"Uh, okay," she said "Thank you for the offer. I accept."

The set of his jaw made her inwardly grin. As much as she wanted to protest, she secretly appreciated his concern for her, although she did have other friends she could depend on.

But there was something in the way Dylan offered help that made her take notice. His delivery didn't come across as if he was just doing her a favor; he gave the impression that taking care of her was his highest priority in the moment. She'd never experienced that kind of status in anyone's life before, and even though history warned her that it would be fleeting, she couldn't keep from enjoying it.

Without another hesitation, he pulled on his coat and hat and ducked out the back door. Caroline huffed a laugh before hurrying to the hall closet for her winter gear. After dressing, she trudged out into the snow.

CHAPTER FIFTEEN

DYLAN SAT AT his desk and flipped the plans for the main entrance. The marquee he had ordered was already being rushed but after talking to the company, he wasn't sure it would arrive in time to be hung before the gala. Having "The Starlight" written out in bright lights as guests arrived was one of the things he had been daydreaming about since he'd decided to buy it. He wasn't carefully wading into his new life in Roseley; he was staking a claim to the kind of life he wanted—one where family and purpose were the priority. The marquee was a concrete symbol he could use to brightly declare that to everyone, including himself. Without it, the soft opening of his new hall seemed anticlimactic.

"Chandeliers are on track to arrive next Monday, boss," Bobby said, poking his head around the doorway. Dylan stood and stretched.

"At least those will be on time."

"That's what happens when you rush."

"Yeah, something I didn't want to do in the first place."

It was going to be the tightest timeline getting the new floor laid, chandeliers hung, marquee and lobby completed and furniture moved in before Christmas Eve. Add to that all the decorating Caroline and her crew needed to do and it was enough to give Dylan a raging headache.

He rubbed his temples as his phone vibrated. One quick glance told him that the second brightest spot in his day had just arrived. It was a text from Caroline.

Hi! I'm out front.

Meet you there.

Dylan slapped Bobby on the shoulder, pulled up his mask and sauntered across the dance floor, the atmosphere thick with dust and debris from the reno.

Once he slipped past the hall doors and through the heavy plastic sheeting, he emerged to the lobby to find Caroline's bright smile waiting for him.

"Mornin'," she piped, overly chipper.

He lowered his mask. It had been several days since he'd followed her home after the snowstorm. The numerous text messages they'd exchanged about work since then had done little to dampen his desire to spend more time with her. He had been looking forward to her visit all morning.

He often found himself hoping that she'd drop in at the job site. But he sensed that her distance, preferring instead to text, had less to do with how busy she was and more to do with what happened the night she slept over. As much as he'd replayed that night over in his mind, imagining a scenario where he'd parlayed tickling into a kiss, he was grateful he had restrained himself, especially when she'd been distant for days and now seemed to be overcompensating with friendly enthusiasm.

"Mornin'," he said, holding up a dust mask. "I brought you a mask."

She held up one. "I come prepared."

He smiled. "No surprise there." He wanted to ask her what she'd been doing in the days since they'd seen each other. Had she been thinking about him? Instead, he held up his measuring tape.

"I know you said you wanted to get measurements inside the hall, but it's a live construction site at the moment, so you'll have to stick to the lobby for now."

Caroline pulled a measuring tape out of her

handbag and held it up, a proud smirk on her face. Dylan couldn't help but grin.

"You know I have the measurements of this room in blueprints."

"Not the kind of measurements I need," Caroline said, pulling her tablet out of her handbag and consulting her list. "We want trees in the lobby, a table for place cards, the record player, Santa…"

"Ah, Santa," Dylan said, dipping his hands into the front pockets of his Levi's. "How on earth did you book him on Christmas Eve?"

"He is a busy guy," Caroline said with a smile as she measured a space where Dylan assumed Santa's chair would go. "But he agreed to send one of his helpers, considering we're raising money for the children's wing."

Caroline brushed the toe of her boot over the flooring, moving a thick film of dust. As much as they'd tried to confine the sanding dust to the hall, the lobby was covered in it.

"Too bad it isn't white," Dylan said, moving to take the measuring tape. Caroline walked the end several steps, pulling it taut. "We could pass it off for a snow dusting."

She smiled and released the tape back to him before logging the measurement into her tablet.

"Are you keeping those doors?" Caroline pointed to the doors leading into the dance hall, which were hidden behind the plastic sheeting.

He nodded. "They're original and too beautiful to replace."

"Oh, I agree. I guess I can get those measurements last. How about the entry ones?"

"What are you planning?"

"Wreaths, three feet in diameter, and Christmas trees—several."

Caroline pointed for Dylan to root himself next to an entry door. Then she took the end of the tape and walked back, logging another measurement.

"Are you going to Willoughby's for the trees?"

Caroline's brow puckered as if she'd never considered such a thing until just now.

"I haven't decided yet," she said. "Bianca's crew handles all the transport and setup. We were just planning on using the collection of artificial trees they keep on hand for the gala every year but…"

"What?" Dylan anticipated her next words, watching as she seemed to piece together a thought in her mind.

"There really is nothing more vintage than using a real Christmas tree."

Dylan nodded in agreement. "I was planning on checking out Willoughby's when we get a little closer to Christmas. I've heard good things about their pop-up lot."

"Thanks for the tip." Caroline motioned for Dylan to follow her to another spot. "I might swing by and look tonight after I check on my dad's house."

"How often do you do that?"

"Not often," she said, after a moment of hesitation. "But his neighbor called and said the street lost power last night for the second time this week. It came back on, but I like to check and make sure everything is up and running. He doesn't need any more reason to sell the place and live out of his camper like a traveling vagabond."

She stopped short and blinked at him, as if realizing that she had said more than intended. Dylan took a few steps forward, cinching the measuring tape back into the reel until he'd reached her.

"Do you need help?" He didn't know why he was making the offer to do something personal with her. There was nothing she would need his help with, per se. She could easily scout out some nice trees at Willoughby's and check on her dad's place all on her own. But he hadn't seen her all week and just having her near made him happy, and there was no harm in that.

"You want to help me check on my dad's place?"

"Well," Dylan said, scrambling for a response that wouldn't scare her away. "Isabel is sitting with McKenna until seven, so I have a couple of hours after work. If you want…"

"To borrow your truck?" Caroline said, hopefully. Dylan's eyes widened, grateful she had supplied an answer that made more sense than just him keeping her company.

"Right. Borrow my truck. If you find a few trees you like, you won't want to wait. We can store them here until it's time to decorate."

"That's a great idea," Caroline said. "As long as McKenna doesn't mind giving you up for an evening." She thoughtfully glanced around the lobby before setting her gaze on him again. "Is it hard not seeing her all day?"

"Yes," Dylan said, glancing at his phone. "When I got your text I thought you might be Isabel. She's bringing McKenna by for a few minutes while the crew is on coffee break."

"It'll be quiet then," Caroline said.

"Right. No air compressors, nail guns, miter saws, sanders…"

"Your family is great, supporting you and McKenna in the way you need."

"They help me out more than you know."

"Anyone home?" an unfamiliar voice called

from behind them. Dylan turned just in time to see Bianca and Tex emerge from behind the plastic coverings, coughing. Tex had his nose buried in the crook of his elbow, as Bobby helped Bianca navigate the torn-up flooring in her high-heeled boots.

"I found them wandering in from the loading dock," Bobby said, noticeably frustrated. "I told them they weren't allowed through but—"

"Yes, thank you for showing us the way," Bianca said. "We didn't mean to intrude, but I wanted to show Tex the progress you've made."

Dylan's jaw tightened at the sight of them. No one was permitted in the active construction zone until it was cleared and safe. Bobby was an excellent foreman who put safety first. He would have certainly gone to great lengths, short of tackling them, to keep them out of the hall. The Behrs had ignored all the warning signs and did what they wanted anyway. Unfortunately, it wasn't his first time at this rodeo. Growing up in Roseley, he'd known all about the Behrs and their stronghold on the town. Their reputation for influence certainly preceded them, but Dylan hadn't gotten a taste of it until he had wanted to move back to Roseley. They didn't like his plans, and he could only imagine they still didn't, despite their facade for playing nice.

"Looks like you got the floor up," Tex said. "When does the new one go down?"

"Two weeks, isn't it?" Bianca said. "Do you have any pictures of what it will look like?"

Dylan clasped his jaw, struggling to hide his irritation. The Behrs had intruded without apology. Just because he was hosting their gala didn't mean they could pop by, unannounced, whenever they chose and disregard protocol and his foreman.

"This is an active construction site," Dylan said. "Visitors are not permitted back there."

"It's just a little dusty," Bianca said with a huff. "But it didn't look dangerous."

"People wandering around when my crew is working is always dangerous." He pointed a reprimanding finger square in Bianca's direction. *"Don't do that again."*

Bianca's face contorted, obviously taken aback by his reaction. He knew very few people in town spoke to her that way, but The Starlight was his business, and safety his responsibility. She controlled a lot, but not that.

From behind the Behrs' backs, Bobby nodded in a sign of moral support.

"You can leave the way you came," Dylan said, turning to Caroline, whose face had gone pale. He knew she would probably feel stuck in the middle, but he refused to give the Behrs another inch.

"How about if I pick you up?" he said to Caroline, trying to clear his thoughts. "Does four thirty work?"

Caroline glanced uncomfortably between him and the Behrs when Tex jutted in.

"Dylan," he said, clearing his throat. "We didn't mean to offend you."

"You didn't," Dylan replied, glancing back at him. They had never offended him. They had only tried to completely alter the course of his life without consulting him first.

"It looks like you're doing a great job around here," Tex continued, exchanging a look with Bianca. "Wouldn't you say, B?"

"Why, yes. We can't wait to see the finished product," Bianca said, nodding. "We know things between you and us haven't been the best recently..."

Dylan lifted a brow at Bianca. When he'd first returned home, he'd initiated a meeting with the Behrs. If he was going to build any kind of life in Roseley, he knew it was easiest to have them on his side. Tex had seemed willing to talk, but Bianca hadn't been very receptive to anything he'd had to say. After she hadn't let him get more than a few words in, he had decided to save his breath until she

224   HIS DAUGHTER'S MISTLETOE MOM

chose to come around to more neutral ground. From what he had just witnessed with Bianca powering through his construction zone, he wondered if she still needed time to accept his position.

Before Dylan could respond, the front doors to the main entrance swung open and Isabel and McKenna hurried in from the cold. Dylan swallowed a groan. His baby sister had the absolute worst timing.

"Daddy!" McKenna cried when she spotted him. She sprinted toward his outstretched arms. But when she spotted Bobby and the Behrs staring, she turned and dived to hide behind Isabel's legs.

"This must be McKenna," Bianca said, kneeling down to get level with her. "McKenna, dear, I've heard so much about you. Let me get a look at you."

"She's shy around strangers," Isabel explained, widening her gait as if by protective instinct.

"I understand," Bianca said. She rummaged into her purse before pulling out a peppermint. She winked at Dylan like they were somehow in on an inside joke at McKenna's expense. Considering how tense the air had been between them not a minute earlier, she'd rebounded pretty quickly. It's what had made any conversation between them so irritating. Bianca had treated every exchange with him like it was just business when things had felt very personal to him. "May I give this to her?" she asked.

Dylan was about to refuse, about to tell Bianca that McKenna didn't like peppermints or interacting with strangers, but he held his tongue.

As he tried to decide on a response, Bianca, still at eye level with McKenna, began to creep half a step at a time in McKenna's direction.

Dylan couldn't help but stare. Bianca Behr was one of the most powerful, prominent women in Roseley, and she was doing something that looked just short of a crab walk, in dress slacks and high-heeled boots no less, across his torn-up lobby floor. He glanced back at Tex, who was happily grinning like a fool.

If she didn't look so out of character, he could find his words fast enough to tell her that McKenna wouldn't like her encroaching on her personal space. But he couldn't. Something about the sight of Bianca, who appeared quite spry for seventy, had him at a loss for words.

McKenna peeked around his sister's legs, looking genuinely curious. When Bianca was almost within arm's reach, she slowly extended her hand and offered the peppermint. McKenna's eyes shifted from Bianca to the peppermint several times.

Finally, Bianca held it up to Isabel. "Perhaps you can give it to her," she said.

"Thank you," Isabel said, accepting it. His sister looked to him for direction, and he couldn't help but relax his face to indicate she could offer it to McKenna, or at least try.

Bianca watched, eyes twinkling, as Isabel offered the peppermint to McKenna. McKenna, as expected, buried her face into Isabel's backside.

"What a shy little nugget she is," Bianca said. She turned back and grinned at Tex as if wanting him to share in a beautiful new discovery.

Dylan worked the muscles in his jaw trying to decide how he felt about their interaction. Everything about this situation felt weird. He didn't like feeling manipulated by anybody, but every interaction with the Behrs irked him into feeling like he somehow was. Finally, his protective instincts propelled him to end things.

He addressed Isabel. "They're going to start sanding again so you need to take McKenna home."

Isabel nodded. "That'll be loud, won't it?"

It would be and though he knew they still

had some time before that happened, he was ready for his visitors to leave now.

He looked at Caroline. Normally talkative, she was all ears. Any fool could pick up on the fact that he had an intense history with the Behrs. He knew he would soon need to explain.

"Dylan," Isabel said, scooping up McKenna, who buried her face into Isabel's neck. "We'll see you at home."

"We'll see you at the gala though, won't we?" Bianca said, straightening. "You are all invited, Dylan. Your entire family, McKenna especially. Tex and I would love for all of you to join us, wouldn't we, Tex?"

Tex stepped forward. "Absolutely. You all need to come. After all, Santa Claus will be there." He grinned at McKenna. "It'll be your last chance to tell him what you want for Christmas."

McKenna peeked out from Isabel's shoulder. He knew his daughter well enough to know that the mention of Santa Claus had gotten her attention. Bianca laughed giddily, taking notice too.

"That's right," she said. "Have you visited Santa yet this year?"

"The gala will be too late for McKenna," Dylan said. If he had his way, he wouldn't attend it himself, but he had to be there. It was the first event in The Starlight in almost forty years. He'd worked too hard to miss its opening—and it would be the launch of his new venture in town. But McKenna was a different story. The music, the hustle and bustle of hundreds of people talking and dancing—it would be too much.

"Oh, please," Bianca said. "We would love to see her there. And the more the merrier." She turned to Caroline. "Caroline, dear. You're bringing your family, aren't you?"

Caroline glanced at Dylan. "I hadn't thought it through that far. If they were in town I would ask them but—"

"If their circumstances change, consider them invited," Bianca said. "Just give the right numbers to the caterer. I'll leave it up to you."

"Everything is coming along nicely, Dylan," Tex said, taking Bianca's hand and tugging her toward the door. Tex could at least appreciate that their presence was not wanted. Dylan suspected that even if Bianca was aware, she wasn't the type of person who let it discourage her from doing exactly what she wanted to do.

Bianca twinkled a wave to McKenna, who buried her nose back into Isabel's neck. She and Tex exited as Dylan motioned for McKenna to come into his arms.

"I'm happy to see you," he said, pecking a kiss to her cheek. "Are you going to spend the evening with Aunt Isabel?"

McKenna patted either side of his cheeks. "She's gonna buy me pizza and ice cream."

"Pizza *and* ice cream?" Dylan said, raising a brow at his sister.

Isabel hitched her shoulders. "Aren't aunts supposed to spoil their nieces rotten?"

After a few minutes of chatting and saying goodbye, Isabel took McKenna's hand and led her out of the building. When he turned to Caroline, she shoved her hands into her coat pockets, studying the floor for a moment. The silence stretched out between them, as he struggled with how to broach the topic on both of their minds.

"I already know what you're wondering," he finally said. He hadn't wanted to mention anything about his tie to the Behrs, but after the spectacle Bianca had made over McKenna, he knew that hope was gone. It was clear the Behrs wanted a relationship with his daughter. That was never the question, though—it was that they thought they knew what was best for her, and they didn't. As McKenna's father, *he* did.

"By the way you talked about them, I figured you had some sort of history. But after what I just saw…" She frowned in discernment. "Do you want to explain?"

He didn't. But, if he was going to be friends with Caroline, she deserved to understand some of the history.

"Tex and Bianca are McKenna's great-aunt and -uncle."

Caroline shook her head in disbelief. "I had no idea."

"Why would you?" he said. "It's a matter of coincidence. Giana didn't grow up in Roseley. She and I met in college. No one in town knows, except my mom and sister…and now you."

"Why didn't you tell me before?"

He shrugged. "I didn't feel like bringing up the baggage. I tried to grease the wheels with them when I first moved back to town, but it didn't go well. I was coming off of a custody battle that they had inserted themselves into so it was a bit naive of me to think our meeting would be anything productive. When it went south, it felt better to not think of them at all. Then they came calling with the gala…"

"And you were forced into working with them," Caroline said slowly, as if recalling how she'd worked to persuade him into a contract with the Behrs. "Do they ever get to see McKenna?"

Dylan smirked. "They just did." When Caroline's expression set, Dylan drew a breath to answer honestly. "Giana sends them pictures of McKenna. I've considered trying to bridge the gap again since we're living in Roseley, but navigating that..." Dylan rolled his eyes.

Caroline nodded slowly. "Families are thorny."

He huffed. It was the understatement of the year.

Finally, as if finding his reasoning solid, she winked. "Your secret is safe with me."

"Thanks, Red."

"*Caroline.*"

"Oh, at least give me this one thing. After the day I've had?"

When Bobby returned and motioned for Dylan to follow him, Caroline waved him goodbye.

"You're pressing your luck," she said on her way out the door. "See you tonight!"

CHAPTER SIXTEEN

CAROLINE HURRIED ABOUT Sheila's office, organizing invoices, tearing through the mail and updating the calendar. Sheila watched her from the doorway as she slipped on her coat.

"Do you have the final checks for the Kraft wedding?" she asked. Caroline put her hands on the file and handed it to Sheila before her eyes had even landed on it. Sheila sighed, pleased. "What would I do without you, Caroline, dear?"

"You'll find out soon enough."

"Ugh, stop reminding me. How's the progress going on finding your replacement?"

She braced herself before sharing, "Very few people responded to the job postings, Sheila." Caroline had no idea how she would find a replacement with the small applicant pool. Every morning she prayed that some perfect person appeared, gift wrapped on the office steps, ready to hit the ground running. Every morning she wound up disappointed.

"What about that woman who used to be

an administrative assistant?" Sheila said, flipping through the file. "She seemed friendly. Remind me."

Caroline shrugged. She had been lovely enough, but she hadn't seemed like a go-getter. "I can set up a second interview for her if you'd like to give her another look."

"That's fine," Sheila said. "We can discuss the other applicants tomorrow night at the Kraft rehearsal dinner."

Caroline sighed. She could count the weddings she still had to help coordinate on one hand and it was one hand too many. If she had followed Dylan's advice, the Kraft wedding would represent the end of her two weeks' notice and she could conclude her business relationship with Sheila in one final wedding. Instead, she was grasping the reality that a perfect replacement would never come and she'd be tied to Sheila for much too long.

Once Caroline locked up for the night and had made it to her car, she heard a phone chime. It was a text message from Faith.

Look what John brought home.

Caroline cooed when she saw Faith's photo text. It was a picture of a freshly cut Christmas tree strung with lights.

I love it! Caroline texted. Where did you get it?

The pop-up lot at Willoughby's.

Faith was the second person to mention the local nursery that day and it only fueled her growing desire to go pick out a Christmas tree, not for the gala, but for herself.

She stared longingly at Faith's beautiful tree. She had always loved decorating her family's Christmas tree every year. After her parents had divorced, the appeal had faded. Then once she moved into her small apartment, she couldn't justify getting a big, fancy tree. She had settled for an artificial tabletop tree next to her television, but the magic of admiring it at night just wasn't the same.

Caroline stared out the car window. It was silly to reminisce about Christmases past. She was trying for a future she could be excited about, so why spend time thinking about the past when it only made her sad?

She stared at her phone for several minutes before giving in and dialing the one person she wanted to talk to. He was one of the few reminders that her past wasn't all bad.

"Hey," she said, once Dylan answered his phone. "I know it's a little earlier than we said, but is there any chance you're already done for the day?"

"As a matter of fact," he said, "I'm just finishing up. Are you ready to swing by Willoughby's?"

Caroline bit her lip, processing what she wanted to do next.

"Great. I think there's a Christmas tree with my name on it."

PARKED OUTSIDE PERK'S PIZZA, Caroline and Dylan sat in the cab of Dylan's truck, sharing a small pizza with extra cheese.

"You're a purist, Red," he said. "A plain cheese pizza. You didn't even want dipping sauce?"

"I like what I like." She took a bite, letting the melted cheese stretch from her mouth.

"Next time I'm introducing you to pineapple and bacon."

"Ugh," Caroline groaned. "On a pizza?"

"It's sweet and salty, kind of like you."

"Is that supposed to be some kind of compliment?"

It was. He fluttered his brows at her. He certainly liked what he liked too.

"So what's the deal with this Christmas tree?" he said, thumbing toward the tree from Willoughby's that was still in the bed of his truck. "Why are you getting one for your dad when he won't be home for Christmas?"

"I don't know," Caroline said, nonchalant. "It seemed like a fun idea."

"And?"

"And what?" She flashed him a puzzled look.

"I think there's more. You shelled out a lot of money for a tree that won't sit in your own home."

"Sometimes a tree is just a tree, Dylan."

Yet she had paid a lot for a tree she wouldn't get to enjoy much. There had to be something to it. "And sometimes a tree is a pricey symbol of…what?"

Caroline lowered her eyes to her lap. He knew he was wandering onto touchy territory.

"I guess I miss the way things were."

"When you were a kid?"

"When we were still a family."

"Oh," Dylan said, releasing an empathetic sigh. "Now we're getting somewhere. Aren't you still a family?"

When he'd been a kid, he'd loved hanging out at the Waterson house. The time playing with Trig had been a lot of fun, and Gus had always taught him so much. He didn't think a family dissolved just because the parents divorced. After all, he still had his mother and

Isabel after his dad had moved out of state and he was thankful every day for them.

Caroline, however, seemed to see things differently.

"Still a family?" she countered. "I guess so, if you define family as a group of people who rarely talk and even more rarely see each other."

"What about your mom?"

Caroline took another bite of pizza and pointed to the clock on the dash.

"We'd better get moving if we're going to drop this tree off and get you home by seven."

"Okay," Dylan said, readjusting in his seat to put the car in gear. Caroline's demeanor had shifted quicker than a Lake Roseley wind and he was content to let the topic go for the moment. "McKenna's bath and bedtime story are waiting. Good thing I can eat and drive."

DYLAN SLOWED THE truck as they approached Gus's house. By the look on Caroline's face, he could tell the evening was about to get a lot more interesting.

A class B motor home was parked in the driveway, and nearly every light in the house was on too.

"What is he doing here?" Caroline gasped as

Dylan swung his truck around and backed into the driveway so they could unload the tree.

"Gus?"

"Yeah," Caroline said, bolting out the door before Dylan had even cut the engine. He hesitated, wondering if he should wait in the truck to give Caroline a few minutes alone with her dad. But then he decided she could probably use the moral support.

He hustled toward the house and made it through the back door just in time to hear Caroline exclaim, "But I would have stocked the fridge."

"No need to do that, honey," Gus said, rising from a weathered recliner. "I've been living on fresh trout and canned sardines for weeks."

"All the more reason. If you had texted, I would have at least turned the heat up for you."

"The cold don't bother me." Gus turned and spotted Dylan. "Is that you, Dylan? You're all grown up, son."

Dylan extended his hand and Gus gave it a hearty shake. "Good to see you again, sir."

"*Gus*. You're old enough to call me by my name." Gus studied Dylan for a moment before shifting his gaze to Caroline. A realization fell over his face. "What are you two…uh…"

He could tell Gus was connecting dots that

weren't there. He suspected something was going on, but he didn't ask.

"I'm checking on your house," Caroline supplied. "And borrowing Dylan's truck. I bought you a Christmas tree."

"A what?" Gus said. "Oh, no, no, no, honey. I don't need a Christmas tree. What would I do with it?"

"Admire it," Caroline said. "I'll decorate it for you. Remember how pretty it used to look in the window?"

"No, no, no," Gus said again, squeezing Caroline at the shoulder. "I'm too old for a tree."

"You're never too old for a tree." She shook her head. "I don't even know what that means."

"It means no, thank you." Gus's face was impassive as he added, "I don't want it. I don't want it at all."

"But I already bought it for you, Dad," she said. Her face fell as Gus patted her on the cheek. "It's outside and I can decorate it and…" Gus shuffled into the kitchen, leaving her slack-jawed in the living room. After listening to her talk about what the tree meant to her, Dylan knew Gus's refusal was a hard blow. "Dad?"

From the kitchen Dylan could hear Gus rustling around in the cabinet. He returned a minute later with an oilcan. When he proceeded to oil the hinges on the front door without responding to her, Caroline pantomimed to Dylan that she couldn't believe what was happening.

"Do you have to do that now?" she asked. "You've been gone for months. Why don't I make us some tea and we can catch up?"

"It sounded a bit squeaky when you came in. I should take care of it now," Gus said, lubricating each hinge. Dylan could tell Caroline was upset, probably more than she was even letting on, but nothing about Gus was mean-spirited or unkind. He was, perhaps, a little dense or unobservant, but he was a heck of a lot nicer than his own father had ever been.

"Did you catch anything, Gus?" Dylan asked, trying to keep things pleasant.

"Oh, enough to keep me happy," Gus said, squatting to reach the bottom hinge. "I've got some friends in Beaverhead County. We get along just grand, you know, shooting the breeze and fishing. Good times."

"Lucky them," Caroline said through gritted teeth.

"I'm not familiar with Beaverhead," he said casually.

"East of Yellowstone. After that I wound my way north—"

"Dad," Caroline interrupted. "Are you staying for Christmas or just passing through?"

"I had a breakdown in North Dakota and decided to head home and get it properly checked out."

"A breakdown?" Caroline gasped. "Why didn't you call me?"

Gus stood straight and chuckled, his belly jiggling enough that he had to hold it.

"Would you have come to help me?" he said. He grinned at Dylan. "I wouldn't put it past my Caroline."

By the look on Caroline's face, Dylan figured she probably would have. Nothing he had observed since returning to Roseley led him to believe she was the type of woman to let an eighteen-hour drive stop her from helping someone she cared about.

"Dad," Caroline said, ignoring his question. "I didn't know Trig was operating on outdated information. As of our last conversation, he said you were in Montana."

"Was. But I had a hankering for Perk's Pizza."

"Really?" Caroline said, brightening. "We actually have some in the truck. I can warm it up for you."

He shook his head, chuckling again. "I'm only playing with you, honey," Gus said. He held the oilcan to her elbow, then armpit, pretending to apply a little oil. With a smile he said, "I can smell it on you."

"Oh," Caroline said, instantly crestfallen. "Are you sure you don't want some?"

"When I got in I grabbed a take-out order from The Bayshore Bar."

Her brow furrowed. "Why didn't you call me first? I would have met you there."

"Oh, honey," Gus chuckled. "You're always worrying about me but I'm fine." He turned to Dylan. "Does your mother have a Christmas tree yet?"

Out of the corner of his eye, Dylan saw Caroline's mouth drop like a falling brick. They both knew what Gus's next words would be, but Dylan couldn't come up with a way to divert the conversation back to safer ground.

"Dad."

"What? I don't want a tree but Delia might. Why don't you take it to her? Little Isabel is home for Christmas, ain't she?"

Dylan could see Caroline working the muscles in her jaw. Gus was such a sweet-tempered man and always had been. When he was growing up he'd always gotten along great with the guy.

But Gus and Caroline did not see eye to eye on much of anything. By the time Caroline muttered a "fine" and Gus blew them a kiss before settling back into his recliner, Dylan knew that Caroline's good deed was about to be gifted to his mother.

CHAPTER SEVENTEEN

CAROLINE HAD GONE through the motions Friday night, doing her best to coordinate a rehearsal dinner with a smile plastered on her face. The Saturday night wedding had been a very small affair, a dinner with only thirty guests.

Caroline had always preferred small, intimate ceremonies. She didn't like when couples put on a big show in front of three hundred people. If someone insisted on getting married, she thought exchanging vows in front of a handful of guests was preferable. That was, if eloping was completely off the table.

Her life trajectory was finally leading her toward owning the business of her dreams and it was one where she would never have to think about another wedding again, unless she chose to. And not since she was a girl had she ever chosen to. Standing up in her mother's wedding and symbolically waving her goodbye had been enough to put anyone off weddings or the idea of a happily-ever-after.

Still, when she awoke Sunday morning,

several days after the debacle with her dad's Christmas tree, she couldn't help but remember how kind Dylan had been through it all.

Caroline lay in bed and squeezed her eyes shut, recalling how hard the interaction with her dad had been for her. After her encounter with her dad, she was confused and her emotions so jumbled, she hadn't talked much to Dylan afterward. He'd seemed to sense that she was upset and had driven her home in mostly silence. She'd tried to put on a brave, chipper face and had insisted that Dylan take the Christmas tree home. He hadn't wanted to, instead suggesting that he could carry it into her apartment for her. Even after he'd promised that he could make it fit or he'd carry it back out again, she'd painfully declined. The tree, unfortunately, was much too large for her living room and she didn't need to see it in there to realize it.

Dylan, she also thought, had been much kinder than she could have anticipated. He'd even offered to take the tree back to The Starlight and lop off the top of it so she could have a tree that fit. With each solution he presented, his persistence to make her happy with the tree came barreling through. She was finding it hard to keep her distance.

When her cell phone rang, Caroline scrambled to sit up, hoping that her thoughts of Dylan had manifested into him calling. But once she saw Olivia's name on the screen, she relaxed back onto her pillow.

"Well, if it isn't Mrs. Tyler Elderman," Caroline said. "How does it feel to be married to Roseley's finest veterinarian?"

Olivia sighed happily. "Splendid, but the honeymoon was not long enough."

"I've never seen a couple kiss so much on their wedding day. Have you come up for air yet?"

Olivia giggled, bringing a smile to Caroline's face. With Faith happily married and now Olivia finding Tyler, Caroline was starting to believe forever love was possible. Almost.

"I had to see how you're doing," Olivia said. "One of your texts came through after we landed in the Caribbean, but I haven't heard any updates since. You're trying to throw a Christmas Eve gala on your own?"

"Uh-huh," Caroline said, straightening. There had been a lot of developments in the last couple of weeks, so many that Caroline wasn't sure where to begin. "I've been busy."

"I'll say. That's fantastic news, Caroline. We're doing Christmas Eve with Hattie this year so you have to take a ton of pictures for me. I'm so proud of you, honey."

"Thanks. I actually have a lot to tell you…" Her heart was bursting to finally talk to her friend. She wanted to tell her that she was kind of crushing on Dylan and it confused her so much sometimes she couldn't think of much else.

"Come over for lunch," Olivia said. Her friend's voice was steady and calm because her life hadn't recently been turned upside down like Caroline's had.

"Oh, no. You're still on your honeymoon," Caroline said, though she desperately wanted to crash into Olivia's house and blurt all about how confused she felt about Dylan. "I wouldn't want to intrude—"

"Nonsense. Micah and Tyler are at the clinic for a few hours. Tyler loves me, but I know he also missed hanging out with his number one assistant." Caroline bit down hard on her lip, trying for control as Olivia continued to fill her in. "I'm getting caught up on laundry and then I have to grocery shop. By the stack of take-out boxes in the trash, it looks like Micah and Gary ate out the entire time we were—"

"Bianca Behr hired me to throw her Christmas Eve gala but only if we held it at The Starlight dance hall!" Caroline couldn't stop herself from blurting. "Which Dylan Metzger bought and is renovating to be open by Christmas Eve. And we've been spending all our free time together and I met his daughter, and I can't stop thinking about him and I'm so confused that what I feel for him is something more than friendship." Caroline slapped a hand over her mouth, collapsed back on the bed and exhaled in relief.

The silence lasted so long, Caroline checked to see if her cell phone was still connected.

"Liv?" Caroline said. "*Liv?* Did you hear all that?"

"Don't move," Olivia ordered. "I'll be over in fifteen minutes."

A little while later when Caroline opened her front door, Olivia stuck a fake tropical flower behind Caroline's ear and shook a box of chocolates in the air.

"Here's your souvenir," she said, taking Caroline by the wrist and pulling her to the couch. Once both women plopped down, Olivia tore into the chocolates and motioned for her to explain. "Dylan…feelings….go!"

"It's all been happening since we started working together," Caroline said. "He's not at all how I remember him. He's a great listener and an amazing dad and when I'm with him I feel…" Caroline took a chocolate and popped it into her mouth. She closed her eyes, savoring not just the sweetness but also the cozy feeling that came over her every time she thought of Dylan.

"Oh, mama," Olivia gasped. "I've never seen you like this before."

Caroline collapsed against the couch. "I know! Who am I?"

"A woman who had never met the right guy before."

Caroline hadn't expected to ever meet the right guy. In her experience, love looked like a chocolate truffle on the outside and a cooked brussels sprout on the inside. Eventually the sweetness dissolved away and the love you once believed in ended up wounding you. She didn't want to open herself up to that kind of pain. She had seen enough of it. She could be completely happy and content pursuing her goals and professional dreams. She didn't need love to be happy, right?

Before she could respond, her cell phone began to ring. Olivia grabbed it from the coffee table and held up the screen so they could both see the caller ID. "Speak of the devil," she said, fluttering her eyebrows. Caroline snatched the phone from her and bolted to her bedroom.

"Hi, Dylan," she said steadily, as she closed the door and pretended that she had not just been gushing about him to one of her best friends.

"Hey. I know you've been busy with the rehearsal dinner and wedding last night, but I wanted to call and see how you were doing after what happened on Thursday."

"Thursday?"

"With your dad."

"I'm fine," she said quickly, not wanting to let on that she'd been playing their interaction over and over again in her mind for the last three days. "Did you set the tree up?"

"Yeah. It took a day for the branches to settle. My mom was delighted."

"I'm glad," Caroline said. She really was glad for Delia. It felt nice to offer her a gift she would appreciate. She just wished her dad appreciated things too, like *her* for starters. "I'm sorry I was so grumpy afterward—"

"You had every reason to be," Dylan said. "You don't have to explain anything to me. That's not why I called. I…uh…"

Caroline pressed the phone to her ear, biting the inside of her cheek with anticipation.

"What?" she said, softly. "Is something wrong?"

"No, nothing. I was just thinking about the construction timeline. The crew is going to start putting in overtime tomorrow morning. If you want to get measurements of the hall during waking hours, tonight might be your best bet. I'm available after dinner."

"Oh," Caroline said, quickly calculating how a trip to The Starlight would change her plans for the day. "I *do* need to get measurements. Are you sure you don't mind heading over there today?"

There was a pause, which only made Caroline's heart quicken in anticipation. Finally, when Dylan replied, she swore she could hear him smiling into the phone.

"I'd be happy to," he said.

Caroline was giddy with the anticipation of seeing him again.

"I will meet you there." Despite her joy at seeing him again, she was determined to keep things professional. "Thanks for suggesting it."

"My pleasure," he said. "I'll text with a time later this afternoon."

Caroline chided herself for her enthusiasm.

"Great. Thanks, Dylan," she said. "See you later."

She disconnected the call and covered her cheeks with her hands. *Get a grip.*

Caroline floated into the living room, where Olivia was sitting on the edge of the couch, waiting for an update.

"Well?" her friend said. "Is everything okay?"

"Fine," Caroline muttered as casually as she

could. "I need to take some measurements of the hall later so he was just calling to pick a time."

Olivia shook her head. "Yeah, right."

"What?" Caroline said, defensively.

"You should see your face right now," she said. "It's obvious that was more than a work call."

AFTER CHATTING WITH OLIVIA, Caroline set to work going over plans for the gala. She didn't have time to take a full day off and everything she needed to get prepped before Monday now needed to get done before she met Dylan at The Starlight. She was just going over the music selection to send to The Hometown Jamboree when her cell phone rang.

"Honey," Gus said. "Who's been plowing the driveway since I've been gone?"

"Harold Pickens. He lives about five houses down."

"I can plow my own driveway while I'm home."

"I'll get you his number—"

"Just give him a call and tell him to hold off until mid-January."

"Uh, okay," Caroline said, scrambling to make a note to do just that. Once she hung up, her phone rang again. It was Sheila.

"Hello, dear. I was just sipping a mimosa and thinking about the *Roseley Courier*. Try rewriting the job posting to include some extra perks. Maybe search online for optimal keywords. What do young people want in a job these days?"

"Uh…" Caroline tried to clear her head to recall all the complaints she'd had with her job over the years. She'd had more than enough reasons to leave, but once she'd gotten settled in as Sheila's assistant, her loyalty and concern grew. She and Sheila had been a two-person show and as much as she wanted to leave, she knew how difficult it would be for Sheila. "Better pay, supportive managers, flexibility in schedule, respect—"

"What about petty cash for occasional lunches out?"

Caroline pinched the bridge of her nose. "I can't put that in a job posting, Sheila. Why don't you write up what you want it to say. Then I will take a look at it."

"Nonsense. I'm sure you'll do a better job than I would. You're so clever at writing these things. See if you can get something out in tomorrow's newspaper, won't you?"

Caroline hung up the phone, jotting another note on her to-do list when Bianca called.

"Hello?" Caroline sang, trying her best to sound positive.

"I hope you're enjoying a lazy Sunday, Caroline," she said. Caroline rolled her eyes. Nothing could be further from the truth. "Tex and I were discussing the guest list and how we wish your family could attend."

"Actually," Caroline said, "my dad just returned to town. I'd love to bring him as a plus-one."

"Of course. He's more than welcome."

"Thank you, Bianca." Having that time with her dad would be the perfect gift. And Trig would be home the next day. The thought made her chest swell—maybe this year would be a little like their old family Christmases.

"Tex and I were also discussing Dylan's family," Bianca said. "It's important to us that they attend too."

Caroline's throat began to tighten. She could feel another one of Bianca's ultimatums coming on. Giving her the gala contract once she secured The Starlight was one thing. That was professional and, for the most part, a reasonable request. But expecting her to convince Dylan to bring his family was not appropriate. She could sense she'd have to set some—what was Dylan always calling it?—boundaries.

"The gala is on Christmas Eve and his family

might already have plans, family traditions," she said smoothly.

"I understand," Bianca said. "But Tex and I are making a big announcement at the gala and we'd really like McKenna to be there."

"You'd have to talk to Dylan," Caroline said. She really did not want to be in the middle of Dylan and the Behrs' relationship. It was probably awkward for Dylan to even work with the Behrs, considering they were his ex-wife's family.

Caroline caught a glance at the clock. She needed to wrap up this conversation.

"I ran over the table placements today," Caroline said, hoping her avoidance didn't come across a rude. "We can go over them this week."

"Working on Sunday. I knew I hired the right person for the job. Thanks, Caroline!"

Caroline's phone vibrated immediately after she hung up. It was her dad again.

"Hey, honey," Gus said. "I carried those ornaments out of the basement for you."

Caroline frowned. "Why? I gave the tree to Delia like you asked."

"Right but I thought if you wanted to, you know…"

Caroline didn't know. She hoped her dad wasn't about to offer all their family ornaments to Delia as well. Even though her family didn't care about being together at Christmas, it didn't mean she was emotionally prepared to give all the family heirlooms away.

"What do you want, Dad?"

"Trig always liked when the mantel was done up, remember? I thought you might want to set it up before he gets here."

Caroline pressed her eyes shut. She adored her brother. The two of them had always gotten along as kids and though Trig didn't come home to visit as much as she would like, she always looked forward to seeing him. But sometimes she just didn't get her dad's fascination with pleasing him when he rarely took the time to understand her. It was nice to hear that her dad wanted to decorate for Christmas—she wanted to recapture some of their old traditions this year too—but why couldn't they have kept the tree, then?

As she replayed her conversation with Bianca, she figured today was as good a time as any to talk to her dad about what would please her. The gala. But an invitation to the gala needed to be done in person.

"You know what," she said, packing up her planner and notes for the day. "I'll be over in a few minutes."

Caroline arrived to Gus's house excited to tell him about the gala and even more excited to officially invite him to come as her date. She knew that getting dressed up and going to a fancy event wasn't something Gus would enjoy. However, if he saw how important it was to her, she hoped he'd agree to join her.

"I remember those galas," he said once she'd let herself into the house and he'd shown her the decorations. After she'd sifted through them, she followed him into the kitchen. "One year they did an Arabian Nights party, wasn't it?"

Caroline nodded, holding out one of the invitations. "This year it's Vintage Christmas. I picked the theme."

"Is that so?" Gus opened a can of soup and warmed it on the stove, taking a quick glance at the invitation. "Looks like those old Christmas cards we used to send."

"Exactly," Caroline said, pleased he made the correlation. "Bianca Behr has been really happy with my work. I have every reason to believe that she'll hire me next year too."

Gus smiled, actually looking a bit proud of her. "My Caroline, the wedding planner."

"*Event* planner," Caroline corrected. "I'm striking out on my own, yes, but no weddings. I never want to plan weddings."

"Can you make a living without them?" Gus asked. He wasn't the first person to ask her this. In a town as small as Roseley, it was difficult for most folks to see an event planning business that didn't include one of the biggest events in a person's life. Caroline, however, had every confidence she could still be successful. She was staking her entire business model on it.

"I can do galas and parties and all sorts of other things."

"You were always such a good wedding planner though," he said. "At least that's what Trig said about…you know."

Caroline squeezed her eyes shut, wanting to get back on track.

"That's in the past. The future is galas, Dad."

"I understand," Gus said, patting her affectionately on the cheek. "I'm happy for you, honey."

"You haven't heard the best part. You can come along as my guest, my plus-one."

"On Christmas Eve?" Gus scratched his chin. "Hmm, I don't know about that. We'll see."

Caroline shifted her weight to her opposite foot, his noncommitment digging at her.

"What's there to see? We could spend Christmas Eve together for the first time in years. They'll have food and dancing. You have to make sure your suit still fits, but I can help you with that. Maybe get a haircut."

Gus ran his hand through his sparse hair and chuckled.

"I thought I was in fashion."

Caroline smiled. "Yes, you're always one for being trendy, Dad."

Gus poured his soup into a bowl and grabbed a spoon. Caroline followed him as he made his way back to his recliner and settled in. It looked like an early dinner in front of the TV.

"There's plenty of soup, if you want some," he said.

"No, thanks." Caroline remained standing, repositioning herself in his line of sight. "Can I put you down as my date?"

"Oh, I don't know," Gus said. "Don't you have one of your girlfriends or someone you'd rather take?"

Caroline shifted uncomfortably on her feet, her forced smile waning. "But then you won't get to see my gala."

It was the first event she was throwing all on her own and it was happening on Christmas Eve. All that hard work… He had to see it.

"Okay, I'll think about it," he said, turning up the volume of the TV and returning his attention to his program.

"I kind of need a yes or no, Dad. I have to give the caterer a head count."

Gus's eyes darted from Caroline to the TV. "What was that? Do I have to decide now?"

Caroline bit the inside of her cheek, willing back tears of frustration. She clutched a box of her parents' decorations to her side.

"I gotta go," she managed. "I have to get back to work."

"Okay, honey," Gus replied, but he was already consumed with his television program. "Will you be by this week to decorate the mantel for Trig?"

Caroline let herself out of the house without a reply. She doubted her dad had even noticed.

CHAPTER EIGHTEEN

DYLAN HAD JUST left to meet Caroline at The Starlight when his cell phone rang. He'd spent the day anticipating their meeting and now that the minutes until he saw her again were dwindling, he found himself walking a little lighter on his feet, pressing the gas pedal a little harder.

He had just sent her a text message, letting her know that he was on his way. He assumed she was calling him with a response. Instead, he saw that it was Giana.

"Hey," he said. "I can't talk right now."

"Are you with McKenna?" Giana asked.

"No. She's with my mom for the evening."

"Why? Where are you?"

Dylan and Giana had started talking divorce eighteen months earlier. To be completely accurate, Giana had started talking divorce while Dylan continued to go to counseling, looking for a way to get their marriage back on track. When Giana made it clear she was done and that they should go their separate ways, aside from co-parenting McKenna, he'd begun plans to move to Roseley. Their divorce had been finalized months ago, and he'd been living in Roseley for months before that, so he knew he shouldn't have to hide the fact that he was going to meet a friend, and a work colleague at that. Still, his friendship with Caroline felt like it was deepening into something more and if he was honest, he found himself wanting it to more and more.

"I'm running to The Starlight. What's up?"

"I'm just sitting here thinking about Christmas. What are your plans?"

Dylan's gut clenched. He had heard the same tone in Giana's voice many times before. On the surface it sounded like she was thinking out loud, asking a simple question. But all at once, he knew she had a plan. Figuring out what it was so he could safeguard his and McKenna's Christmas was the challenge.

"Just what you would expect, Giana. A quiet, cozy Christmas in Roseley. Why?"

"Well, I was thinking," Giana said, her tone teasing. "Several friends of mine are flying to Colorado with their children for a ski trip. I thought it would be fun to stop off in Michigan and pick up McKenna."

"Pick up McKenna for what?" Dylan said,

his tone dropping from polite to horrified. *"Skiing in Colorado?"*

Their daughter sometimes couldn't handle eating a meal at a restaurant. She sometimes had to wear headphones to tolerate the noise at the grocery store. Giana wanting to take her skiing, something she was too young to even do, sounded ludicrous.

"The other children love it," Giana continued. "Taylor and Rod are bringing their babysitter so McKenna could play and have fun with the other children while I hit the slopes during the day. She'll have a blast."

Dylan grasped the top of the steering wheel, struggling to not snap at her. In recent months, he had stopped explaining details to Giana about McKenna's condition, but he felt like that decision had mainly been driven by Giana. She rarely had more than a few minutes to talk and usually wouldn't commit to a time, choosing instead to call him, like this, right out of the blue. He also sensed that when it came to discussing McKenna's sensory processing disorder, Giana was only interested in quick sound bites. That left little time to help her really understand just how challenging McKenna's struggles were.

"McKenna isn't like other kids, Giana," he

said, struggling for control. "She wouldn't *have a blast*. We've talked about this."

"It was just a thought, Dylan," Giana laughed. "Don't get so bent out of shape."

He couldn't decide how else to respond. Giana was the one talking in absurdities. "I think you should go on your ski trip solo, Giana. McKenna wouldn't enjoy anything like that."

"Maybe in a couple years," Giana suggested.

"Yeah," he grumbled. "Maybe."

"Well," she said, shifting gears seamlessly, "if Colorado is out of the question, then I think New York City for Christmas is a good compromise, don't you think?"

New York City? Compromise?

Dylan sensed that the phone call was about to get a bit more harried, just by the way Giana's voice was picking up steam. When she got an idea in her head, she had a way of talking louder and with perfect diction. He'd seen her do it thousands of times in the courtroom. She could really sway a jury, and in the past, had successfully swayed him more times than he cared to remember.

He pulled off the road and onto the shoulder. He didn't want to talk about what he sensed was coming next while parked in front of The Starlight. He didn't want to continue his conversation with Giana in front of any audience, especially Caroline.

Dylan parked the car and sucked in a deep breath. Arguing with his ex-wife wasn't what he wanted to do right now, but he had to quickly manage Giana's expectations before they raged out of control.

"McKenna hasn't experienced Christmas in the city before," Giana continued.

"We were in New York City last year. All of her Christmases have been in New York."

"But she was still so little. She didn't get to appreciate all the festivities. Now that she's older, she would love it."

As much as he had tried to explain to her just how McKenna's brain worked, he never felt like she heard him. She agreed with what he said one minute and then the next, proceeded to do just the opposite of what was in McKenna's best interest.

"You're welcome to come visit McKenna anytime," Dylan said. "Especially at Christmas. You're also welcome to stay at the house so you can spend more time with her in person."

He cringed at his offer but was fully prepared to back it up if Giana agreed. He knew his mother and sister would politely accommodate Giana if he asked them to, even though both women harbored a lot of bitter feelings since the divorce. He couldn't blame them. He knew they would take his side no matter what. They were his family and they would support him even if he was making a mistake. Over the past several years he'd certainly made plenty, but when it came to raising McKenna, he was determined to do his best. They saw that, and unfortunately, they saw all the phone calls he facilitated between Giana and McKenna. His ex-wife just didn't seem interested in connecting with their daughter and it infuriated his family as much as it did him.

"Christmas in Roseley?" Giana groaned. "That may work for you, Dylan, but I'm a city girl. The only Christmas tree I need is seventy-five feet tall and standing in Rockefeller Center."

Dylan couldn't think of a polite way to point out that flying to Roseley had nothing to do with the festivities and everything to do with spending time with their daughter. Instead, he tried to be helpful. "What about a visit in January? Or February for her birthday?"

"Well, which is it?"

"Whenever you want to come, Giana. We'll always do our best to accommodate your schedule if you—"

"You're the one who moved her halfway

across the country, Dylan. I can't be hopping a plane to Michigan every time I want to see my daughter."

Dylan knew his choice to move McKenna to Michigan came off as selfish to some people. Unfortunately, some of those people happened to live in Roseley and were throwing a gala at his venue.

But after a lot of careful consideration, and soliciting the advice of some trusted friends, he really thought it had been the best option for McKenna. Maybe not the best option for Giana, but certainly she could see it had been a good one for their daughter. In New York City she would have spent her days in day care while he and Giana worked long hours to support their expensive lifestyle. In Roseley she was being raised in a home with three adults who loved and understood her. He couldn't put a price value on family, but it was more important than anything New York had to offer.

"We can come visit you in January," Dylan said, fighting for calm. "I offered several times to bring her for a visit this fall, but you were the one who couldn't find the time."

"No," Giana said. "You're the one who threw a hissy fit because I hired a babysitter."

Dylan gripped the steering wheel tighter. He had flown McKenna to see her mother, crashed at a hotel for the weekend and had reluctantly, very reluctantly, let Giana take McKenna for the day. He had reminded himself that Giana loved their daughter and would keep her safe, but he also knew she would do things McKenna wouldn't like. She'd take her to places that were too loud and, therefore, scary. She'd get irritated and angry when McKenna cried and then blame their daughter for ruining their outing together.

What he had not expected was that Giana would tire of McKenna's fits and drop her with friends for a few hours while she ran errands. When he'd called to check in and discovered the news, he had outlined a few more boundaries for their future visits.

Dylan drew in and then released a deep breath and then another. When he felt himself getting angry with Giana, he worked overtime to keep his temper in check.

"Christmas is less than two weeks away," he said. "And I have a lot to do during that time to get ready for The Starlight's first event. Why don't we talk about the next visit after the holidays?"

"That sounds great, honey," Giana said, her voice dripping with sarcasm. "I'll be the only partner without their kid at the holiday party, but I hope *your* holiday is good."

And there it was.

Dylan knew Giana had had an ulterior motive for wanting McKenna. She wanted him to fly her to New York City for Christmas so she could show her off to the partners. Once again, things were not about what was in McKenna's best interest.

He couldn't understand it, couldn't wrap his brain around the selfishness. McKenna was the sweetest child in the world. She was bright and funny and affectionate. If Giana would just try to see the world through McKenna's eyes, to love their daughter the way she needed to be loved, her heart would burst open with gratitude like his did every day.

A wound in Dylan's heart that hadn't been poked at in weeks, or at least not since he'd met Caroline again, now began to fester. For how long had he hoped he could improve the relationship between Giana and McKenna? For how long had he done everything in his power to fix his family? Consistently failing to do that reminded him how dangerous love could be. How could you trust it when it deteriorated into a fight about how to celebrate Christmas with their child?

Trouble in their marriage had begun long before McKenna had been born. At parties, she'd been more fully engaged with talking to everyone, heck, anyone, instead of him. The time they'd spent alone together had dwindled as Giana focused outwardly on every shiny, exciting thing that came her way. At times, he'd started to feel like an accessory on her arm, more than her friend and husband. If he'd thought talking to her back then had been tough, it was nothing compared with getting her to listen now that the conversation was usually something she never seemed to have time for—McKenna. Foolishly, he had thought that if he gave her his best, he could make her happy. Being wrong about that had taught him a lot of things. Most of which was how to set better boundaries.

"Don't you have anything to say?" she snapped.

Dylan shook his head. When Giana started to get mean with him, he stopped talking. It was one of the first boundaries he'd learned. "Goodbye," Dylan said, ending the call.

He dropped the phone in the center console and slammed his hand against the steering wheel. Giana had a way of pushing his buttons, and as much as he tried not to get emotionally drawn in by her, sometimes he felt powerless to rise above it.

He leaned his head back against the headrest and shut his eyes, trying to calibrate his breathing, his thoughts, his heart. He didn't want to meet Caroline feeling so unraveled. She deserved the best of him and he deserved a night off from worrying about Giana's shenanigans or whether he was doing a good enough job raising McKenna.

He reminded himself that he was doing a good job. He was working hard to build a business that could financially support McKenna and himself. He was building a lifestyle that would bring calm and peace to their household. Once McKenna was in preschool full-time next year, he had plans to move into a house in Delia's neighborhood so his mother and sister could continue to provide them with support. He was doing his best.

When his cell phone rang, he expected it to be Giana, calling to continue the argument. Instead, it was Caroline.

"Hello?" he said. "I'm only a few minutes away. I got caught on a phone call."

"Oh, great. I figured something had come up."

Dylan glanced at the clock. He was twenty minutes late!

"I'm so sorry," he said, immediately pulling out onto the road. "I'll be right there."

Dylan couldn't believe he had been ruminating about Giana for so long without realizing it. But as she never seemed to listen, or worse, hear what he was trying to say, it took a while afterward to return his blood pressure back to normal.

Dylan accelerated and steered for The Starlight. He looked forward to a nice evening with Caroline.

CHAPTER NINETEEN

CAROLINE HAD GOTTEN most of her large measurements from his blueprints weeks earlier. But he patiently assisted her as she gathered dozens of smaller measurements of all the nooks and crannies that gave the old building character.

"These are perfect," she said after a half hour of measuring and logging the details in her tablet. "I ordered some decorations based on my best guesses, but with these exact measurements, I have a couple other things in mind I can get now."

"I'm sure you'll make it beautiful," he said, shoving his hands in his pockets. "But you know, you're kind of overlooking the most important feature."

Caroline scanned the notes on her tablet. "Short of measuring the electrical outlets, I'd say I'm covered."

"Do you think so?" he said, hinting that he had something surprising up his sleeve. He led her across the hall and up the steps to the rear of the band stage. "You may have spent plenty of time here over the last few weeks," he said as he stopped and faced her. "But you've never seen this before. Wait right here, okay?"

Caroline settled back on her feet, glancing around.

"You haven't brought me here to help with renovations, have you? Because I've got to tell you, I have enough on my plate."

Dylan chuckled. "No hard-core construction plans for tonight. Promise. Wait right here, okay?"

Caroline blinked up at him and reluctantly let him take her tablet from her hands. He darted off the stage to set it on a table and then disappeared for a few moments. He cut all the lights in the hall, aside from the emergency runners. When he returned, he knew her eyes were adjusting to the dark, just as his were adjusting to capture the perfect contours of her face.

She looked around on either side of her, then spun in a complete rotation.

"What am I supposed to see?" she said.

He motioned for her to look up. Against the dark of the hall, there was just enough light from the exit signs to make out the catwalk hanging above their heads. She looked at it and then back at him again.

"The…catwalk?" she said hesitantly.

He grinned. "Do we dare?"

She glared at him through hooded eyelids and delivered her best sarcasm. "It looks like a great place to get murdered. Thanks."

He burst out laughing.

"Only the best for you, Caroline."

"You're not serious about climbing all the way up there, are you? How high is it?"

"Almost thirty feet. And I am serious, unless you've developed a fear of heights in the last twenty years." He winked at her. "As I recall, you challenged and beat Dickey Arterbury to a cliff-jumping contest when you were too young to understand the risk involved."

"He thought boys were braver than girls," Caroline huffed. "I had to set him straight."

Dylan led her to the steps and patted one. "It's a good thing you wore boots."

Caroline popped a hip as if considering. At the motion, Dylan couldn't help but skim his eyes over her figure. As he'd watched her work, carefully focused on gathering measurements, he'd been admiring the way the fabric of her sweater and the denim of her blue jeans hugged her curves as if they had been hand tailored for her. She was dressed modestly but watching her move still sent his heart fluttering.

"I will climb up first," he explained. "Your modesty is safe with me. Besides, it's a safe climb. I had alternating-tread stairs installed. See?"

The steep ladders had been replaced with alternating stairs, sturdier vertical bars and railings. They made it easier to climb and descend and provided a couple of platforms to rest on along the way. The top stair was also large enough for them to comfortably sit on, stern protection from falling.

"And what is the plan once we get up there?" she asked. "Exactly."

"We're going to admire the view."

Caroline glanced around the dark dance hall again.

"What view?"

While he could explain that she was all the view he needed, he instead motioned for her to stay put for one moment. He again jogged off the band stage, disappearing into the dark of the wings this time.

"I sure hope you're not getting a bungee cord!" Caroline called.

Dylan hummed an amused note as he navigated the light board. Being with Caroline sometimes gave him the same topsy-turvy feeling he imagined bungee jumping to have.

"Look up!" he called as he brought up the

ceiling lights. From his vantage point, he could see Caroline standing, completely transfixed, beneath his newly installed illuminated ceiling. He returned to her side feeling equal parts pride and satisfaction.

"Dylan," she breathed. "I had no idea."

"I know."

Growing up he'd heard stories of how beautiful The Starlight ceiling had looked back in its day. His father, who was seldom impressed with anything, had described it more times than he could count. In fact, Dylan couldn't recall his dad being impressed with anything the way he'd been impressed with The Starlight's ceiling. The sky Dylan had installed was even grander than that. He and his dad had never been close, but if his dad was still alive, Dylan knew he'd be impressed.

"People never look up, Dylan," his father would say while explaining how the photoluminescent filaments worked. "If you can make them look up, you're really doing something spectacular."

Dylan assumed that the historical photographs he'd found of the dance hall ceiling, hadn't done the lights justice. When he'd finally purchased the theater and began meeting with his designers and construction crew, the number one priority, outside of upgrading the hall to the twenty-first century, had been to fully upgrade the lights and lightboard to an electronic system. His designers helped him add creative subtleties that would entice people to look up. He knew that if his dad could see it, he'd agree that what Dylan had installed was nothing short of spectacular.

"They'll love it," Caroline said.

"Who?"

A chuckle rose slowly in her throat. *"Everyone."*

The ceiling looked like the night sky. Thousands of twinkling lights formed the vast constellations. A cloud machine gave the illusion of clouds roaming. The ceiling was painted in perfect dark blue and violet hues.

"The design includes a shooting star," he said, resting his hands on his hips with pride. "But it only happens once or twice a night."

"Dylan it's…it's…"

He waited patiently as Caroline struggled to put words to the sight. He understood the feeling. When he'd finally seen the finished product, he had had the same mix of awe and amazement. He'd wanted to share the experience with Caroline before everyone else saw it. He wanted to see it through her eyes.

"Heavenly?" he supplied. She broke her gaze from the celestial sight.

"You created something I've never seen before," she said. "It's extraordinary, Dylan."

He wavered on his feet. He could tell by the charmed look on her face she fully appreciated his Starlight, seeing it the way he had always hoped people would. And when she said his name, it was as if she really saw him too.

"Come on," he said, jerking his head toward the stairs. "Wait till you see it from up there."

CAROLINE APPRECIATED HOW many times Dylan had glanced down to make sure she was okay on their climb. Once they had both reached the top stair, which was covered in a thick blanket, Dylan sat and invited her to join him. Caroline held on to the railing and stared down at him.

"Darn," she joked. "I was hoping to dangle my legs off the ledge." Dylan offered her his hand.

"Just relax," he said as she clasped it and maneuvered to sit beside him.

"You know," she said as she spread a hand over the blanket. "I doubt your crew left this big, cozy blanket up here. This is proof of premeditation."

"Guilty," he said, shifting the humor in her observation to something more sincere. "But the gala isn't just a big first for me. It's a big first for you too. I couldn't let anyone see my night sky before you did."

She bit the inside of her cheek, trying to keep herself from swooning at his words. It meant a lot that he had thought about that, prioritized her above anyone else. She couldn't remember a time before when anyone else had.

As she admired the way the lights cast eyelash shadows on the tops of his cheeks, she realized how comfortable she felt. Even though they were sitting at the top of the world, away from everything and everyone, being with Dylan made her feel like she was home.

"Does The Starlight feel like home yet?" she said. "You spend so much time here."

"My goal is to make it a home for McKenna. It was always my dream to run a family business, something I could share with my children."

"Always? Is that what you wanted when you were a kid?"

He nodded. "My dad used to tell stories of tagging along with my grandparents when they went to work. They owned a dance studio and used to come to The Starlight before big events to give dance lessons to the patrons. He spoke so longingly of those days, working alongside his parents in one of the most beautiful places he'd ever seen. I would listen and wish for the same experience, being a part of a family business, but my parents didn't teach dance lessons. Far from it and for good reason.

"When The Starlight closed, my grandparents lost most of their business and fell on hard times financially. The experience taught my dad to be pragmatic, practical. He gave up on his dream of owning a family business and instead became a trial lawyer, killing himself every day to make money so he wouldn't fall on hard times the way his parents had. I grew up dreaming some of his same dreams, and then following in his same misguided footsteps. It was only after we had McKenna that I reconsidered all the things I thought I wanted."

"When we were growing up I never would have pegged you as becoming a lawyer," Caroline admitted. "I think running this place suits you much better."

"Really?" He looked so hopeful she guarded her next words until she was sure they rang true.

"Absolutely. You should feel proud of yourself for not just reviving this place, but saving it. You're preserving a piece of Roseley history that no one else valued. But when everyone sees it on Christmas Eve, they'll see it for the treasure you saw first."

"I hope so," he sighed. "I don't have a backup plan."

"When The Starlight is complete and you officially open for business, you'll start getting bookings. I know it."

He grinned. "I love that optimism, Red. Galas, parties, weddings—"

"Ugh," Caroline groaned. "*Weddings*. Have fun with those."

He shoulder-bumped her.

"Okay," he said. "Come clean already. What's the deal with you and weddings? Did you have a quickie marriage and divorce I don't know about?"

"No, nothing like that," she said. "There's no big reason. I just don't like them."

"Why? Most people love weddings."

"I don't. They feel like a big facade. When I watch a couple get married, I think about how the party will end and real life will sock them hard in the jaw. They'll learn too late that getting married was a bad idea all along."

"Do you feel that way about all marriages?" he asked.

Caroline gasped. She'd had a dislike of big weddings for years. But hearing him narrow her dislike from wedding ceremonies to marriage made her uneasy.

"Well, no," she began, "I guess not. I've seen people happily married before, I guess."

"But it's not for you?"

Caroline hated to admit, in the midst of one of the most romantic places she'd ever sat, that her hope for marriage and family was miniscule.

"I've seen the ugly side," she admitted. "I don't see weddings and marriage through rose-colored glasses like some people."

"That implies that you once did. What changed?"

Caroline formed her mouth to respond, though she didn't know how. Had she once believed in the happy ending when it came to love? Why did Dylan's conclusion make her break out in a cold sweat? Why could she not remember when she'd started to change her mind about the possibility of a happily-ever-after?

"Well, what about you?" she said, scrambling for redirection. "Do you believe in taking the plunge again after divorce?"

He hesitated. "Maybe if I find the right person. I have to choose more wisely this time."

Caroline nodded. He had McKenna to think about and picking a new partner was not something he could take lightly. She understood that all too well.

"I wish my mom had had your perspective," she said sadly.

"Didn't she?"

"Nah," Caroline mumbled.

"Don't you like your stepdad?"

Caroline felt the tears forming just at the mention of her mother's remarriage to Darren. "He's fine, I guess."

But he wasn't. At least not in her mind. The truth was, she hadn't been invited to spend much time with Darren and her mom so she couldn't speak for the guy. If anything, it was his existence that bothered her.

Dylan leaned closer. "You guess?"

"He's the reason my parents' marriage broke up so I can't exactly love the guy."

"Yeah," Dylan said. "I remember folks talking about him and your mom."

Caroline nodded. "A lot of people saw them out together before Trig and I knew they were dating. Definitely before my dad knew his marriage was over."

"They had a big wedding," Dylan said softly. "I remember that."

Caroline groaned. "Yeah. Three months after I got the job with Sheila, my mom got engaged and insisted I stand as her maid of honor. I didn't want to do it, but she kept pushing until I agreed. I hated every minute of it.

She didn't have the decency to slip away and get married quietly. Instead, she made a big, obnoxious spectacle of moving on from my dad. Moving on from Trig and…" Caroline covered her mouth, shocked when the tears slid in streaks down her cheeks.

"You?" Dylan said, his voice swelling with empathy. Caroline nodded as she struggled to hold herself together.

Weddings were supposed to symbolize a union between two families, but all her mother's remarriage had symbolized to her was that her family was permanently split. Instead of Darren and her mother welcoming her and Trig into their fold, they'd drifted away to live a life separated from them.

Dylan scooted close and wrapped his arms around her, conveying in the simple gesture that she didn't need to hold it together. He felt so warm and strong she couldn't help but melt into his embrace. His scent enveloped her like a hug, kind and nourishing, just what she wanted.

He held her there, on the catwalk, with the stars keeping watch overhead. After a minute, she felt her composure return.

"You're not supposed to cry in such a beautiful place," she managed, heaving a giant sigh.

"You're not supposed to shoulder a painful

memory like that on your own." His words re-assured and she knew there was nothing to be embarrassed about, nothing to regret.

"I think I know why I don't like big weddings," she said, forcing a tearful laugh. He gave her a squeeze before pulling away to study her. He gently wiped the tears off her cheeks, his hand like velvet against her skin.

"Caroline Waterson," he said in mock authority. "I hereby declare that you never have to plan another big wedding again."

"Promise?" she said, giggling with relief that the tears had stopped.

"Promise. If you ever decide to get married you can just piggyback your marriage vows on a party already in progress."

"Like that gala."

"Exactly. I can't wait to see it, by the way."

"Well, that makes one person." Caroline finished wiping her eyes as Dylan's face contorted in concern.

"What do you mean?"

"My dad doesn't want to come to the gala with me," she said glumly.

"Oh." His shoulders hunched in empathy. "Well, I'll be there for a little while."

"Will you bring your family?" The possibility that she could show off her gala to Delia and Isabel sent a sudden thrill through her. "I would love for them to see it. And McKenna too."

Dylan frowned. "A gala is not the kind of thing McKenna does well with."

"Of course," Caroline said, kicking herself for even asking in the first place. She'd gotten so wrapped up in her own hurt feelings she didn't stop to think of what the gala might feel like to McKenna. "I understand. It would have been nice having all of you there for Christmas Eve, but the music will probably be too loud."

"Right." He scratched at his chin and peered at her, thinking. "Still…"

"Still?" Caroline said, hopeful. If there was a time to not seem too eager, it was now, when she should be supporting Dylan's diligence to protect McKenna. However, she just couldn't help but dream. Celebrating Christmas Eve with her new friends, McKenna included, sounded like a wish come true.

"McKenna *does* have a pair of headphones she wears sometimes," Dylan said, thoughtfully. "She wears them when we go on airplanes."

Caroline brightened, anticipating his next thought.

"I suppose," he continued, carefully, "if she's well rested and having a good day that day, she could come for a little while if she wears them."

"Oh, I would love that! She can see the Christmas trees and decorations and get her picture taken with Santa Claus..." Caroline was already imagining the fun of it all. If her own family wouldn't attend the gala, sharing it with Dylan and his family hardly felt like a consolation prize. It was exactly what she now wanted for Christmas, but only if McKenna would enjoy it too. "Do you really think McKenna would be okay?"

Dylan shrugged. "We can give it a try."

Caroline slung her arms around Dylan's neck, folding him into a giant hug.

"Thank you, Dylan. I know it will be wonderful."

"You're the one who's wonderful, Red," he said with a laugh, squeezing her back. She beamed, holding him there. He and his family were becoming so important to her, so quickly. Though she felt the urge to slam on the brakes for now, she felt content.

As she clung to his neck, letting more time pass as she held him, she slowly became aware of how his body felt with each inhale and exhale. The pace had increased, as hers had too. The fondness of their hug was transforming, and as she adjusted her hold, to get a better look at him, she knew that her fondness had shifted to longing.

He tightened his hold on her. It wasn't to keep her from slipping away, but to show her his intention. He lowered his head, bringing his cheek to hers. His stubble scratched gently against her skin, pricking her senses.

"Don't," he whispered in her ear. "Not yet."

Her skin instantly chilled as the vibration of his words shivered down her neck.

She didn't want to pull away, or let their date come to an end. But as much as she didn't want to fight the urge to kiss him again, to entwine herself more into his life and his family, a part of her, the dominant part that had protected her heart for years, whispered that eventually she would get hurt. As much as she didn't want to believe it, wanted to believe that Dylan had only the best of intentions for her, she wondered just how long it would be until he abandoned her too.

He peppered a kiss to her ear, the gentle puckering sound crystallizing against her skin. It was divine, delicious. All at once her body went hot.

"We should be careful," she said, muttering the words more for herself than for him. She needed to be careful with all that was developing between them. She cared about him and McKenna too much now to slip away without getting hurt. But as he skimmed his warm lips along her cheek, working his way to her parted mouth, she knew he didn't read her meaning.

"I won't let you fall." He smoothed a practiced hand to the small of her back, shifting to wrap her up in his embrace. "I've got you, Caroline."

Did he? If things got difficult, and in her experience, things always got difficult eventually, wouldn't he drop her like everyone else in her life had at one time? She wanted to believe him, even if she wasn't sure either of them should be making any promises.

He cinched her closer as she felt all the oxygen suck from her lungs. All at once her head felt fuzzy, and she couldn't manage a response that made much more sense than, "I've got you too."

She wasn't sure if it was her breath that caught or his, but when his mouth covered hers, she drifted away with his kisses. For as long as he held her, she knew her head would stay suspended in the Milky Way constellations that transformed above them. Try as she might, finding her way to solid ground again seemed nearly impossible.

CAROLINE HELD A small red gift box and followed Dylan into Delia's house. She had prepared a gift for McKenna and though she had intended to send it home with Dylan after meeting him at The Starlight, he had insisted that she follow him home to give it to McKenna herself. She had agreed partly because she had wanted to see McKenna's face when she opened the gift and partly because after her kiss with Dylan, she wasn't quite ready to call it a night yet.

"What on earth are you two doing here?" Delia called as they kicked off their boots and traipsed into the living room. Caroline knew they would be surprising Dylan's family. What she hadn't realized was that the Christmas tree, *her* Christmas tree, would take her by surprise.

Caroline swallowed a lump in her throat as she stopped to admire it. It was stunning. In the house it looked much more impressive than it had at the tree lot. The branches had opened and Dylan's family had decorated every inch with hundreds of lights, sparkly ornaments and silver tinsel. Around the red tree skirt was a little train running with a collection of cartoon safari animals in each car. At the top of the tree was a star that slowly changed its light from blue to purple to pink.

It was all so beautiful, and it wasn't hers. Nothing about Christmas had felt like hers in a very long time. Even though she was now in a position to throw the most spectacular Christmas event of the season, it still didn't feel like hers, especially when her dad had declined to attend.

Now, standing in Dylan's living room, staring up at the tree, a lump began to grow in her throat. What was the point of putting yourself out there and inviting someone to be a part of your life if they didn't want to be there in the first place? Her dad certainly didn't. Trig had moved away and her mom focused all her time on Darren and his children.

"Are you okay?" Dylan said, studying her. Caroline tried to swallow the lump, but it came floating back up like a fishing bobber. She hadn't mentioned anything about her conversation with her dad. Dylan had alluded to some difficulties with Giana when they'd first arrived at The Starlight so she sensed it would be too much to lay her problems on him as well.

Caroline nodded, choosing instead to squat down several feet from McKenna. The little girl was playing with Russian nesting dolls, fitting one doll inside the other.

"I have a little present for you, McKenna," Caroline said, softly. "Would you like me to bring it to you?"

She understood that McKenna needed a light touch when it came to social interaction, so she would give her the control to decide for herself. McKenna studied her nesting dolls as if she hadn't heard Caroline. Finally, after several seconds, she made her way over to examine the box. Caroline sat down on the ground and opened it for her.

"These used to be my ornaments when I was a little girl. They reminded me of you."

McKenna lifted out the first ornament. It was a little mouse holding a giant chocolate chip cookie. She held it up for Delia to see.

"Oh, how darling," Delia said. "It's perfect for our Little Mouse."

Caroline next lifted out a string of five rainbow-sequin butterflies. "McKenna, can you hang this on the tree?"

The rainbow butterflies had been one of her favorite ornaments when she'd been a child. She'd loved to lie under the Christmas tree and watch how they glittered under the lights. But as it had been several years since she had decorated her dad's house for Christmas, she thought it was a shame that they were packed away in the basement gathering dust. If she couldn't enjoy them the way they were meant to be enjoyed, she suspected there was a three-year-old little girl who might.

McKenna's face lit up as she turned the butterflies over in her hands. When she giggled and scrambled to place them on the tree, Caroline's heart leaped with a satisfaction she hadn't felt in a long time. Her suspicions had been right; if anyone would cherish her ornaments the way she had, it was McKenna.

"How did you know?" Dylan said. Caroline peered up at him, as his eyes intensely searched hers.

"Know what?" she said.

"She loves butterflies."

"Really?"

"*Loves* them."

Caroline watched McKenna hang the ornaments on the lowest tree branches, the butterfly string nearly grazing the ground. She'd noticed the butterflies on McKenna's tent but hadn't thought they were more meaningful to her than that. What little girl didn't love rainbow butterflies? She certainly had when she'd been McKenna's age.

McKenna approached Caroline and took her hand. Then she led her to sit next to her Russian nesting dolls. Caroline looked up at Dylan with a wide smile.

"You might want to get comfortable," she said. "I have a feeling we may be here for a while."

Dylan joined them and gave Caroline's hand a gentle squeeze. "I don't mind if you don't."

Caroline accepted a nesting doll from McKenna. She really didn't.

CHAPTER TWENTY

DYLAN THREW AN arm over his eyes as his alarm clock, a silent one that slowly brightened to signal the time, shone in his face. He rolled over and dimmed it before noticing McKenna. She was already awake playing quietly in a dark corner of the room.

"Mornin', Little Mouse," he said, clearing the sleep from his eyes. McKenna fumbled to her feet and raced to jump onto his bed. Since his date with Caroline, he'd been putting in long hours all week, trying to get as many renovations finished before the opening. He worried that his time away at work was taking a toll on McKenna, but with so much to get done, he felt at a loss for what to do about it. He had to satisfy himself that he was doing right by her in the long run. Launching the venue successfully would be his ticket to starting over with a secure job in town, which would provide for his family.

"Daddy," McKenna said. She pulled back his comforter and scooted to snuggle into the crook of his arm. "Do you have to work today?"

He wished he didn't. Being gone for the day was one thing. If they were living in the city, he'd have to work a day job like all working parents. But he'd been working through dinner most nights, sometimes not making it home until after McKenna's bath time. Their little rituals, playing and doing sensory integration activities together, had taken a back seat to the looming Christmas Eve deadline.

"I have to go to work, yes."

"I could come with you," she offered. "I can help."

"You would be a great help to me," he said. "I know you would. But there's a lot of construction at my work. Remember when we were driving and saw that big truck?"

He and McKenna had been stopped at a traffic light when an excavator in a nearby job site had begun digging into the earth. Even in the safety of his pickup truck, the excavator's noises had not been muffled enough for McKenna. She'd been completely terrified.

She nodded, eyes wide as if remembering.

"There aren't any big trucks like that at my work now," he said. "But sometimes things can get loud."

McKenna stuck her thumb in her mouth and

peered up at him. He knew Giana wanted him to break her thumb-sucking habit. As much as he wanted to, he recognized what a comfort it was to her.

"You've been doing such a good job playing your games with Ms. Callie," he continued. "I hope you're proud of yourself."

McKenna nodded. Delia had subbed in for him all week, helping Ms. Callie with the sensory integration, but once the gala was over, he planned to get back on schedule with McKenna. He wondered what on earth he would do without his mom and sister. They were helping him raise his baby girl and he could never take that for granted.

"I've been thinking," he said. "The construction at my work will be done in time for Christmas Eve. Would you like to come see it then?"

"No trucks?" McKenna mumbled, thumb still in mouth.

"No trucks," Dylan said. "There will be music, but you can wear your headphones."

"If there are trucks, I can go home," McKenna said. Dylan squeezed her. He'd been coaching her to ask for what she needed, giving her as much control in a situation as was possible.

"That's right. If it's overwhelming, we can go

home. Grandma and Aunt Izzy will come with us too. And your friend Caroline will be there."

"And Mommy." It wasn't a question but a declaration.

Dylan's heart sank. He had no idea when McKenna would get to see her mother again and it pained him.

"Not this time, but we'll see her another day. Okay?"

McKenna pulled the covers over her head before peeking out at him again.

"You're a big mouse," she said, giggling. Dylan's face broke into a surprised grin as he poked a finger to her side and gave a little tickle.

"A what? Says who?"

"Big Mouse!" McKenna cried, pointing at him and laughing. "Big Mouse! Big Mouse!"

Dylan couldn't help but laugh, not just because of how she joked, but because she shouted so happily. McKenna always did better with sound when she had control of it. He tickled her and played along, happily disappearing into her world before the demands of the day began.

CAROLINE RACED THROUGH Sheila's office, a phone pressed to her ear. With less than a week to the gala, she hadn't had much more than a few minutes to herself in days. It hadn't given her much time to process the sweet moment she'd had with McKenna and Dylan in front of the Christmas tree or the time she'd spent with Dylan under The Starlight sky…

Caroline bit her lip remembering the way Dylan had held her. He had concentrated on her as she talked about her mom.

Caroline collapsed onto Sheila's office chair and gave herself a quick hug just to keep the tingles from overtaking her body. She'd been kissed before, but the emotional connection she had felt with Dylan before their first kiss made her hopeful about what was developing between them.

For the first time in a very long time, she'd felt seen and understood. Trust was building up slowly with Dylan, but she hoped it was progressing as rapidly as her feelings for him were. They had both been so busy since their night under the stars, they'd had to limit their interactions to quick work visits at The Starlight. And, as Caroline heard her phone chime, she smiled at another one of his text messages.

Heading up to the catwalk. Thinking of you. xoxo

Caroline blushed as she read it, wishing she was climbing up there with him right then. As she struggled to think of a response, Sheila barreled into the office.

"Caroline," she burst, clasping her chest. "That applicant you scheduled for a follow-up interview was no good. No good at all."

Caroline jerked back on her chair. Though she had worked for Sheila for a number of years, she was still never prepared for Sheila's drama.

"Sheila," Caroline said, trying to maintain her professionalism, "I told you that after the first interview."

Sheila's face drew back in mock horror. "Then why did you set up a second interview?"

"You asked me to."

Her boss waved off her statement, gliding around the room with a huff.

"Who else do we have?"

Caroline closed out her email inbox and ran a hand through her hair as she thought. Few people had applied for the position and though she had placed several more ads online and on social media, it seemed she was the only person foolish enough to work for her boss.

"There is no one else. I've interviewed everyone who applied, and I've tried head-hunting a few people in town who I thought might be a good fit—"

"Think bigger, broader." Sheila pulled out

her cell phone and began to text. Caroline's phone chimed at such an inopportune time, she thought it was Sheila texting *her*. She glanced at her own cell and found another text from Dylan.

I'm taking McKenna to lunch. Come meet us.

She winced, not sure if she'd have time to even eat, let alone slip away for a proper lunch break. She sadly replied:

Can't. Finding my replacement.

"There's a job fair at the beginning of January," Sheila continued though engrossed in her phone. "You can probably find some great applicants there."

Caroline cringed. If she didn't find a replacement soon, she could see herself starting the new year still under Sheila's thumb. That was something she had promised herself she wouldn't do. Where did it end?

You gave her longer than two weeks, Dylan texted. Quit. Boundaries.

Caroline checked her phone calendar. To be completely prepared for the gala, she couldn't devote one more minute to Sheila's problems.

She'd spent years doing that, and now she was done. She had to move on.

"Sheila," Caroline began. Her boss continued to text furiously on her phone. "Sheila?"

"Hmm?" Sheila managed, still distracted.

"Months ago I told you I was leaving, but you didn't take any action to find and train a replacement. I've done my best to help you. I really have. I've searched for a new person. I haven't slept in weeks—"

"And I appreciate that, Caroline," Sheila said, not looking up from her phone. "I don't know what I would do without you." Caroline sighed and stood. She knew that was all true, but it didn't mean she had to put her own dreams on hold any longer.

She packed her bag and gathered her purse and coat as Sheila powered on.

"Grab lunch and we'll rendezvous in an hour. I need your eyes on some things for the Dingleman wedding—"

"I'm done," Caroline said quietly.

Sheila blinked, finally looking up from her phone. "Pardon?"

"I've been very loyal to you, and I wanted to leave you in a good place, but I'm done now."

"I don't understand. We agreed you wouldn't leave until you found a new person, a new *you*."

"I wish you all the best, Sheila," Caroline

said, offering the most genuine smile she could muster. "I really do."

Then, feeling freer than she had in a long time, she walked out of the office. She felt that her feet barely touched the ground as she glided out into a new era, an era where she ran the show.

DYLAN READJUSTED THE headphones on McKenna's head and relaxed into the restaurant booth. He had learned that the best time to eat at The Nutmeg Cafe was just after two o'clock. The lunch rush was over and the restaurant was usually empty, except for a few stragglers. The grandfather clock and cuckoo clocks had also already sounded the hour. As long as he and McKenna could eat and get out before three o'clock, a meal was usually quiet and enjoyable for the both of them.

Be there in a few.

Dylan read Caroline's text message and placed his cell phone back into his pocket. He picked up a crayon and began to color McKenna's paper menu alongside her.

The café was dripping in all things Christmas and judging by the aromas wafting out from the kitchen, the staff was preparing the roasts and gravies and potpies for dinner.

Dylan took a sip of water and glanced around the restaurant, stopping when he saw the one face he didn't want to spot.

Bianca Behr had just stood up from a far corner booth and had turned just in time to lock eyes with him. He hadn't seen her on his way into the restaurant, much to his regret. He had become accustomed to looking for their car whenever he took McKenna out and had somehow also missed it.

Bianca waved as Tex also stood. It looked like they had been meeting with another couple. Dylan groaned and readjusted in his seat, grateful that McKenna was engrossed in coloring.

"Good to see you again," Bianca said as she approached his table. Dylan drew in a patient breath. His breathing techniques had helped him so much since McKenna had been born. He'd never realized how anxious and upset Giana had made him over the years until he'd found his way to counseling and had learned how to handle himself around her. Counseling was something he had never done—until they'd had McKenna. For him to be the best possible dad to his daughter that he could, he had to get his feelings and struggles in order first.

"Bianca," he said, keeping his face blank with control. "Merry Christmas."

She smoothed her face into a smile and fluttered a wave to McKenna.

"Hello, sweetheart," she said. "I love your headband."

Dylan side-glanced at McKenna's headphones. At first glance, it did look like a headband, a wide one that a child might possibly wear in the winter. It was a thick fabric with a mouse face stitched onto the top of the crown. She was his little mouse, after all.

McKenna lowered her face closer to her coloring page, suddenly shy. She tended to get that way when strangers talked to her in public and though Bianca had spoken to McKenna at The Starlight recently, she was still very much a stranger. Unfortunately, for Dylan, Bianca was not a stranger to him.

Bianca clasped her hands together and waved again. "What a shy little one you are. Hard to believe you're Giana's."

"We'll see you later," Dylan managed. He hoped Bianca would take the hint that he had no desire to speak to her or Tex, who couldn't stop smiling at McKenna.

"Yes, we will," Bianca said. "We heard the news from Caroline. Tex and I are ecstatic."

"What news?" Dylan said, frowning.

"She said McKenna and your family would attend the gala. I knew she'd convince you, come hell or high water. We found a gem in Caroline, didn't we, Tex?"

Dylan leaned back from the table, in shock. He'd been touched by Caroline's appeal for him and his family to attend the gala because he thought they were doing it for her. But if she'd been *tasked* with getting his family there, it cued an uneasiness he usually felt with interacting with Giana.

Tex nodded. "McKenna will make the donation more meaningful. Thank you."

"Donation?" Dylan shook his head, not quite understanding. "What donation?"

Bianca happily explained. "Tex and I are making a personal donation to the children's wing of the hospital. Having McKenna onstage with us when we give it will mean so much." Tex wrapped a supportive arm around Bianca's shoulder as she continued. "I know we've had our differences over the last couple of years," she said. "But I think we're all ready to bury the hatchet, for McKenna's sake. Don't you agree?"

Dylan felt the heat rise in his face. It had

started in his throat at the mention of McKenna being onstage in front of a giant crowd of people and had continued to creep up his neck with each word Bianca spoke. She and Tex were standing tall looking so…so…*not* like two people who had tried to ruin his life a year ago.

Under the table he balled his hands into fists and tried to remember his breathing. He couldn't have an angry outburst because of McKenna, who was still intensely focused on her coloring page. She deserved at least one parent who could hold their emotions in check.

"Let me be clear," Dylan said through gritted teeth. "McKenna is not going onstage with anybody. I would not do anything for either of you considering what you tried to do to me this time last year. Bury the hatchet? Are you kidding me?"

Bianca's eyes widened, her thin peach lips wavering. He couldn't stand to watch another person cry, but as Tex rubbed her back, he didn't know how else to convey that they'd done him wrong and had never acknowledged it.

"We didn't do anything to you," Bianca whispered, cautiously glancing between him and McKenna to keep from alarming her. "Children belong with their mother and you were trying to keep McKenna from seeing hers."

Dylan ran a hand down the length of his face. In a matched whisper, he said, "As I've tried to explain to you several times now, I moved McKenna here because that's what is best for her."

"We'll let you get back to your lunch," Tex said, tipping his head proudly in the air. "Come on, B."

Dylan stared straight ahead as Tex and Bianca quietly buttoned their coats and made for the door. Once they were out of his line of sight, he wondered what promises had been exchanged between them and Caroline.

He was used to Giana manipulating him, doing or saying what she needed to get her way. She'd messed with his head for years before McKenna had come along. Giana hadn't liked parenting or spending time with McKenna or giving two seconds of her time to learning what could be upsetting their child so much. Despite Dylan's pleads for help, for understanding, she hadn't liked how McKenna had thrown her world, her social life, her career into turmoil. All she'd cared about was what needed to happen day to day to keep her own schedule on track.

When he'd suggested he get full custody and

move McKenna to Roseley so they could have family support, Giana hadn't been opposed to the idea. In fact, she'd casually mentioned that it saved her the trouble of interviewing live-in nannies. Dylan had felt grateful to Giana for seeing his reasoning—until her aunt and uncle had intervened. Without knowing McKenna or fully understanding the situation, they'd persuaded Giana to blindside him with a petition for full custody.

Even after he'd called them to explain that McKenna's extra needs could best be helped with him caring for her, they'd pushed Giana to fight, believing that their niece was the better choice. For months he'd been sick with worry, believing Giana would win, and why wouldn't she? On the surface she was a beautiful, intelligent, responsible woman. Leaning on his professional experience, he knew that unless he could prove that Giana was hurtful to Mc-Kenna, the courts wouldn't think twice about siding with her. *She*, as Bianca had pointed out several times, was the mother and the obvious choice.

Dylan was still grappling with his thoughts, with the fact that Caroline had discussed him with the Behrs, when he saw her enter the restaurant.

"Hey, stranger," she said, sliding into the

seat across from him. "I did it. I officially quit my job."

She grabbed his water glass and took a quick sip, smacking her lips with satisfaction. She looked so proud of herself, unaware that his world, his view of her, had been completely thrown off-kilter.

"I was very calm," she continued. "But I told Sheila exactly what I thought. I did my best and invested a lot of extra time but it's time to move on. Boundaries, right?"

Dylan worked his jaw. Boundaries. He'd relaxed one of his most important rules when forming a new relationship. He'd let someone into his and McKenna's life too soon and look where it had gotten him. He hadn't seen it coming with Caroline and looking back he couldn't think of where he'd gone wrong. Sure, she'd been so passionate about starting her own business and landing the contract with the Behrs, but he could have never imagined that she'd prioritize that over McKenna's well-being. Or over his trust in her.

"Boundaries are important," he said, now guarded. What did a future with Caroline mean if he couldn't trust her? Couldn't trust that she wouldn't manipulate him the way Giana had? He'd promised himself he would proceed slowly with any new relationship, not just for his sake, but for McKenna's. Neither of them could stand another broken heart.

Caroline walked two fingers across the table to McKenna and tickled her on the knuckles. McKenna giggled and moved her hand, teasing Caroline to try it again.

Dylan reminded himself that one of the things he'd grown to admire about Caroline was her kind heart. She was generous and self-sacrificing, and in a short time he'd sensed she cared for not just him but McKenna as well.

"Bianca is happy we're attending the gala," he said. Caroline startled and stared at him. He tried to read her expression, wanting to see if she felt any remorse.

"When did you talk to Bianca?"

"Before you arrived."

"That's great," Caroline said, brightly. Her positivity plucked at an irritated nerve he didn't know he had. "I'm glad."

He cleared his throat, leaning forward to discern her meaning.

"Really? How so?"

"Bianca has mentioned to me on more than one occasion how she wants to get to know McKenna. Both she and Tex are hoping for a relationship with her. With you too, I think."

Dylan blinked, trying to understand. "You two talked about us?"

"Just in passing." Caroline lowered her voice, checking to make sure McKenna was distracted coloring. "We prepared a private meeting for the both of you with Santa. He understands how to quietly ho ho ho."

"Why would you do *that*?" Dylan said, instantly regretting his accusatory tone.

Caroline readjusted on her seat, noticeably surprised. "It was my idea," she said. "Bianca said they've never shared a Christmas with McKenna so I thought it might be a nice, low-stakes way for all of you to—"

"Let's get something straight," he snapped. "I don't need a relationship with Giana's extended family. I have my own family."

He immediately regretted the dark tone his voice had taken when Caroline shifted her eyes to McKenna. She was staring up at him, fully aware that her dad was upset about something. Just remembering how hard he'd had to fight to preserve the kind of life for McKenna she deserved brought up all the old emotions like a wildfire raging out of control.

"Of course," Caroline said. "Your family is such a good support to her. To you."

"Right. So what do I need Bianca 'know-it-all' Behr for?"

Her brow had furrowed so deeply he knew she was trying to ascertain what was going on.

"I don't get that impression from her." He'd never shown her his anger before, not the kind that surfaced whenever he thought of what the Behrs and Giana had tried to pull. As much as he tried to push it back down again, the turmoil turning his gut over and over again reminded him that it was always lurking in his swampy feelings, just waiting to jump out like a crocodile and attack.

"I agreed to bring McKenna to the gala because I thought *you* wanted us there, not the Behrs."

Caroline's eyes widened in horror. "I *do* want you there. I told Bianca to invite you herself. I didn't run interference for her, Dylan. I promise."

He searched her eyes trying to decide if she was being honest. He had a hard time imagining she would pull such a sneaky stunt and he wanted so much to believe her.

"Fine," he said flatly, suddenly exhausted. "I believe you."

She leaned forward, unconvinced. "But do you? Do you really?"

He checked his feelings. He wasn't quite sure. All he was sure of was that he'd lowered a boundary at a time when he should have stayed diligent.

McKenna tugged at his arm. "Daddy," she said, eyes pleading. "Can you talk to me now?"

Dylan wrapped his arm around his daughter, frustrated that their lunch had been hijacked with old frustrations and buried wounds.

"Of course, Little Mouse. Our food will be here any minute."

Dylan rubbed McKenna's back. She was still young and didn't know all the background context to what he said, but he knew she picked up on subtle shifts in his demeanor.

Caroline had too. After a few moments, she quietly gathered her coat and purse.

"I'll let you two enjoy your lunch together," she said, slipping out of the booth. He had expected her to work harder to convince him of her innocence or even guilt him into believing her. Giana had played many different cards over the years, always finding the one thing to say that would make him reconsider and doubt that he'd been wronged by her at all.

Caroline, however, did nothing. She waved to McKenna and hurried out of the restaurant. He hated her leaving with the disharmony between them, but reestablishing boundaries to better guard his heart moving forward sometimes stung.

CHAPTER TWENTY-ONE

IN THE DAYS leading up to the gala, Caroline's head swirled with all the decisions she had to make. After she'd hurried out of her lunch with Dylan and McKenna, she'd had to meet him at The Starlight to admire the new Marley floor that had been installed and realized very quickly that he had no desire to talk.

Caroline had decided to table any conversation between them since there was so much to do. Laying the floor had been the last renovation in the hall, which meant Caroline was now free to begin directing the hospital crew to move in all the tables and decorations. It was a quick three-day sprint, a thrill that was only dampened by Dylan's cold shoulder.

Among the dozen Christmas trees that needed arranging, miles of garland that needed to be strung or fireplace mantels that needed decorating, Caroline collapsed into bed every night feeling like she'd spent the day running a marathon. She figured this was best since it left her little time to think about Dylan and the emotional divide that widened by the day.

A day before the gala, Caroline let herself into her dad's house and glanced around. She had plenty to do without adding her dad's mantel decorating to her list. But after another afternoon painfully passing by Dylan a dozen times without really talking to him, she had needed to escape to something, anything, cheery.

"Dad?" she called. "Where are you?"

"I'm in here," he said. She had intended to only stop by for a minute. Her dad had texted to tell her that the lights strung through the garland had burnt out. As she shopped for a replacement, she tried to keep from ruminating over the fact that her dad knew how to correctly use a cell phone. He could call or text when he needed something, yet he appeared to lack the ability to respond to *her* calls and texts. He was constantly on the move, and she worried about him. Couldn't he pick up the phone more often to catch up, let her know how he was doing?

Caroline made her way to the living room to find Gus in his recliner, reading a book about muscle cars of the 1950s.

"Planning your next purchase?" she said, removing the box of lights from the shopping bag. She opened it and began unwinding the lights as Gus held up the book.

"I wouldn't get much use out of one," he said. "No place to store all my fishing gear."

"True," Caroline said with a smile. She began stringing up the first collection of lights, working as quickly as she could, when Gus stopped her.

"Wait a minute. What's that on the box?" he said, making his way over to examine it. "Are those *white* lights?"

"Yeah," she said. "They're LED so they should last."

"We need the multicolored ones, sweetie," he said. "You remember, don't you?"

Caroline held the white lights in her hands and stared back at him. It was two days before Christmas. The stores were sold out of most decorations, which was why she had special-ordered everything for the gala weeks ago.

"They didn't have multicolored ones, Dad. Just white, purple or red."

"What about The Hardware Store? Don't they carry lights?"

"I don't know," Caroline said, hesitant about what to do next. Her father had never before cared about what kind of Christmas lights were hanging up in the house. He had made it clear that he didn't want a Christmas tree, even one picked out and hauled to his house by her. But now he wanted the mantel decorated, specifically with multicolored lights? "Does it matter that much to you?"

"Well," Gus said, grinning earnestly, "do you think Trig will like 'em?"

"Trig?"

"He's coming to see me in a couple days, ain't he?"

Caroline clenched her jaw before quickly gathering the lights up into a tangled clump. She knew there was no way she'd be able to get them back into the box without painstakingly coiling them and there was no way she had the time to do that.

"That's what I hear," she muttered. If plans for Christmas changed, she figured she'd be the last one to know. Her father never felt the need to keep her in the loop.

She shoved the clump of lights back into the grocery bag as Gus fumbled into his pocket.

"Let me give you some money for those," he said. "Maybe you can use them for your… your… What's that thing called again?"

Caroline turned, raising a brow. "My Christmas gala?"

"Yeah. That's the one," Gus said. He held out a wad of cash, smiling. "My contribution to the cause."

"The cause?" Caroline stared at the cash like it was a wad of snotty tissues. She refused to accept it, to pretend like he was doing something helpful or kind or meaningful for her, because he wasn't.

"It's some sort of fundraiser, ain't it?" he said. "It's the least I can do."

Caroline worked her jaw, wondering if her father really believed that she would appreciate him donating a string of white lights to the biggest event of her life.

"You've certainly got that right," she said, her voice breaking. "It is the least you could do. What I don't understand is why."

"Honey?" Gus said, noticeably confused.

"This Christmas gala—" Caroline heaved a large breath "—has been a dream of mine for years, and I'm going to have to attend it all alone because I don't have any family willing to celebrate with me."

Gus took a half a step back, the one-two punch of her statement landing square on his nose.

"I'm glad you care so much for Trig," she continued, braving her hurt as her eyes moistened with tears. "But I don't understand why you always call and text him when *I'm* the one who worries the most about you. I don't understand why you always invite him to go do stuff when I'm the one who's always trying to spend time with you. And when I invite you to the biggest night of my life, because I want you to see something I've created, you refuse to go."

She pressed her fingers to her temples as all of her frustration finally made its way to her lips.

"So no, Dad," she continued, "I don't want money for these dumb lights. I want a relationship with you that's balanced, give *and* take. I want a family for Christmas."

There was plenty more she wanted to say and explain, like all the hurt she'd been repressing for such a long time. But as she'd already begun to shake, she knew she had to leave before the emotional current coiling inside her broke free.

She placed the bag of lights on his recliner and made her way out of his house silently. As she returned to her car and pulled out onto the road, she wanted to tell someone what she'd just said, just done. She wanted someone to reassure her that she had been brave to speak the truth to her dad. Her words had flowed when she had least expected them to, but at least they had helped her acknowledge that her hurt was real.

The one person she most wanted to talk to was Dylan. He seemed to understand so much of what she felt with her dad, and he always left her the space, the silence between words, to find her voice.

But after their conversation at The Nutmeg Cafe, he had gone to great lengths to work alongside her without really having to talk to her. By his behavior she could only assume he and his family wouldn't be attending the gala either.

What she wanted for Christmas more than anything was to celebrate her gala with family and close friends who had been supporting her like family. Instead, she had to prepare herself for the dark, cruel reality that the only people who would see her gala for Christmas were Tex and Bianca—and they were paying her.

She steered the car toward home, prepared to hole herself away for the evening as she worked out the last-minute gala details. But as she approached the entrance to her apartment development, she knew that squirreling herself away all night to work wouldn't mend the ache in her heart. She knew she had to talk to Dylan and try to set things right.

Caroline swung her car around and drove toward Dylan's house. Even if he wanted to pull away from her like everyone else in her family had, she had to give their friendship one more try.

DYLAN STOOD ON the sidewalk in front of The Starlight with McKenna sitting on his shoulders.

The front marquee had finally arrived that afternoon and not a moment too soon. Bobby and the crew had just finished installing it over the main entrance. He'd told them not to turn it on until he'd picked up his family and returned for the big reveal.

Though McKenna was still a little girl, still too young to understand the symbolism of the marquee, he wanted her with him. He could only hope that when she was older she'd remember the night her father had turned the lights of The Starlight back on and brought the shining star of Roseley back to its full glory. Perhaps someday she'd smile nostalgically when remembering the marquee in the same way he still did when recalling his dad's Starlight stories.

"Are you ready?" Bobby called over the radio. Dylan squeezed McKenna's hand as Delia clapped with anticipation. It was dark and still on the street, except for the four of them. By the partial moonlight, they could see their breaths in the frigid air.

He was happy to have his mother and sister with him, sharing in a moment that would signify that The Starlight was finally ready for opening. He'd daydreamed about buying the old dance hall ever since he'd seen the gleam in his dad's eye when he remembered it. His dad had driven him by the abandoned building countless times, shaking his head every time he saw how such a glorious place could quickly fall to ruin. Secretly, Dylan had always dreamed that *he* could renovate a place so magical it could touch the heart of a man as rigid and hard to please as his dad.

As Dylan stared up at the dark marquee and counted how many years it had been since he'd first wished to buy the dance hall, he tried to keep his excitement at the forefront of his mind. Seeing a dream fulfilled after so many years was enough to make your heart explode with joy, but as he shivered on the street, bouncing McKenna on his shoulders, he couldn't ignore that a part of his heart was secretly sinking. With all the work he had done over the last several weeks with Caroline, it didn't seem right to turn on the marquee without her there.

Caroline had been a good friend, but he'd moved too quickly to turn that friendship into something more. He figured that the ache he felt was no more than just his consequences for having put his heart on the line in the first place. He had taken a risk he shouldn't have.

With time, he hoped, to reconstruct his boundaries. He would move on. He'd be happy—one day.

"Are we ready, ladies?" Dylan asked. Delia and Isabel each gave a thumbs-up. He craned his neck to look up at McKenna. "Little Mouse? Are you ready to see Daddy's lights?"

McKenna squealed wildly, most likely unsure of what exactly was about to happen.

"Is it a go?"

"Go!" she cried.

Dylan brought his walkie-talkie to his mouth and radioed.

"McKenna says it's a go, Bobby!"

Dylan stared up at the dark marquee. The anticipation in his stomach flurried like butterflies as he waited for the voltage to go hot. The seconds ticked by one after another. Just as he held the walkie-talkie to his mouth, ready to radio Bobby again to see if something had gone wrong, the marquee illuminated.

It was brilliant. The giant, golden bulbs outlined the words he'd been seeing in his dreams for so long.

THE STARLIGHT

The neon blaze knocked him back a few steps as Delia and Isabel did a soft cheer and hugged each other. He wanted to scream and holler at how glorious it looked but instead, for

McKenna's sake, he did a little jig right there in the middle of the empty street with McKenna giggling on his shoulders.

"Isn't it beautiful, baby?" he cried. "I made this for us."

"Daddy, it's so bright."

"It is bright," he said, wiping a tear from his eye. "People will see it from the far end of the street. Tomorrow night the searchlights are going to signal that The Starlight is back and better than ever. This place is going to give us the life we want."

It would. He was sure of it. The dance hall would become the crowning jewel of Roseley once again and it would be his. His and McKenna's. It would be their Starlight.

Delia hurried over to hug Dylan.

"I'm so proud of you," she said. "Are you happy?"

He nodded, wanting to be as happy as he thought he could be at this moment. He knew he should be thrilled. And he was for the most part.

But another part of him felt like the moment was lacking. It was missing a very important, meaningful link. He knew Caroline had only been in his and McKenna's life for a short while, but not having her with them now, when the moment on Egleston Drive felt bigger than any of them, made him wonder if the regret he was feeling was for making a terrible mistake.

CAROLINE STEPPED OFF the front stoop of Delia's house just as Dylan's truck pulled up next to her car. She offered a polite wave as Dylan and his family piled out of the truck.

"Caroline!" McKenna called, waving frantically as Dylan lifted her out of her car seat. Out of sheer instinct, Caroline squatted down to greet her. Once out of the car, McKenna scampered up the walk. When she reached Caroline, she stopped, hesitating. After lingering on the sidewalk, she gave Caroline a big grin.

"We saw Daddy's lights," she said.

"Did you?" Caroline said, realizing the evening had been a big one for both of them.

"Caroline," Delia said as she and Isabel approached. "Are you staying for dinner? You're always welcome."

Caroline searched Dylan's face as he lingered on the front walk. By the seriousness she saw on it, she very much doubted that.

"I don't think so," Caroline said. "But thank you."

"Come help me set the table, McKenna," Isabel said, offering her hand. "It's good to see you, Caroline."

Delia and Isabel took McKenna into the house as Caroline faced Dylan. She was used to being the one who put herself out there for the sake of the relationship. She was the one who texted and called her dad even when he didn't respond. She was the one who had stood in her mom's wedding even though her new marriage had broken up her family. She was even the one who had stayed at a lifeless job for years because she didn't want to put her boss in a tough spot.

But as she studied Dylan and still found him distant, she didn't know if she had it in her power to put herself out on the line one more time. She'd changed for the better since meeting him, and maybe all that change was to prepare her for a life she didn't know she needed. She still wasn't sure what that life was, but if she was going to be worthy of it, she needed to be worthy of every moment leading up to it too.

"How have you been?" he asked, shoving his hands into the front pockets of his coat. He had his hat tugged down over his ears and his coat zipped to his throat. Bundled up for winter, his stature unwelcoming, the cold had seemed to harden the lines of his face and the warmth that had once existed between them.

Still, she thought, as she searched for some

glimmer of hope in his eyes, she knew the Dylan she had been getting to know over the last few weeks. He was still there, just avoiding her now. He'd once accepted her heart for what it was and he'd handled it so gently. Something might have changed between them, but could they return to what they'd once had?

"Tired," she said. "I've been working so hard I didn't do any Christmas shopping."

He offered a polite grin. "When you're a parent you can't afford to forget that."

"True." She managed a smile of her own. "What did McKenna ask for this year?"

He seemed to bristle at the question before responding. "She wants to see her mom."

"Oh," Caroline said. "Of course. That's not so easy for Santa to deliver, I imagine."

"No." Dylan looked past her to the front window and gave a little shiver. "Did you need something?" he said.

He hadn't invited her in and that subtlety was not wasted on her.

But as she shivered on the front walk, gathering up her courage, she wanted to tell him she needed him. If he would attend the gala and spend Christmas Eve with her, she wouldn't ask Santa for another thing. If the distance between them could just disappear, that would be the Christmas miracle she'd dream about.

But saying all that was too much for one night. Especially when she was still reeling from the aftermath of talking to her dad.

"I told my dad how I felt," she said. "I thought you might…" She wondered if he would feel happy to hear her news. On the drive over it made sense that he would, but now, with growing awkwardness, she worried her instincts had been very wrong.

"That's good," he said. "He deserved to know."

"Yeah," she said. "I think he did."

"I was thinking about you earlier," he began, studying the ground before continuing. "We hung the marquee tonight. You'll be able to see it tomorrow."

She now found herself staring at the ground too. He'd been so excited to finally see The Starlight in bright lights that she'd found herself looking forward to it too. He apparently hadn't wanted her there to experience the first lighting. It stung.

"That's wonderful," she said, shifting her weight as she fumbled for something more. Even though she could feel him pulling away from her and had been feeling it for days, she wanted him to know that she still cared. "I'm proud of you."

He perked. "Yeah?"

"After all you've worked for? It's fantastic. You must feel so proud of yourself."

His face softened and for a moment she forgot that he'd been distant. She spotted the same familiar Dylan who could connect with her so easily. "Thanks," he said. "I appreciate that."

She wavered on her feet, wanting to be bold. "I didn't want you to come to the gala because of Bianca," she said. "I wanted you and McKenna to come for me. I care so much about both of you and having you there for my big night, our big night, is something I want. Me."

He lowered his eyes again. "I know. I believe you."

Did he? He seemed genuine, but he was still pulling away. She'd spent years reinforcing the wall around her heart, so she felt confident he couldn't break it if they ended things now. But as he refused to look her in the eye, she realized he was certainly capable of bruising it.

"As long as you know," she said, nibbling the inside of her cheek. "I gotta get to…"

She trailed off, unable to come up with an excuse quickly enough. When Dylan pulled his hands out of his pockets, she thought maybe she wouldn't have to. She thought he might be preparing to hug her, to invite her inside, to pull her into the family that she'd been growing to love over the last few weeks. Instead, he crossed his arms over his chest.

"I'll only be by for a little while tomorrow night," he said. "Just to make sure you and the gala are all set."

Caroline's spine stiffened. He was protective of McKenna so it made sense that he was falling back on his original decision to not bring her to the gala. But the realization that he wouldn't attend for very long made her loneliness swell. "You won't want to stay?"

He shrugged. "My part will be done."

A well of disappointment began to fill in her chest. He wasn't just saying that his part with the gala would be done. He was saying that they were done.

"Just say it," she said. Her voice went gravelly, making her wonder just how deep the well went.

His eyes narrowed. "Say what?"

"Where to begin?" she said, sucking a breath before rattling off every excuse she could think of. "You have to focus on McKenna right now. You can't devote time to pursuing a close friendship with me. Family and The Starlight are all you can handle. The timing is bad. The time we spent together was a big mistake." She leaned closer, a wry smile on her face. "Am I getting warm?"

He settled back on his feet. "Caroline, you and I moved too quickly and yes, the timing for me is…"

"I wondered once."

"Wondered what?"

She squeezed her eyes shut. "What it would feel like to be pushed to the other side of your…" She popped her eyes open, letting her resentment settle in them. *"Boundaries."*

"I care about you, Caroline, and I appreciate your friendship." He ran a hand over his face. "I've always appreciated it, even since we were kids and—"

"Ha," she spat, tipping her chin in the air. If he didn't like where the things between them had been heading, that was fine. She didn't need any more reminders of how love could go wrong. She could chalk up the last few weeks to a good learning experience. It hurt, but their sweet moments would serve as a cautionary tale the next time she considered getting close to someone.

What she didn't appreciate was the idea that he was going to rewrite history to protect her feelings. She didn't need that kind of protection. She wouldn't tolerate it.

"You were friends with Trig, Dylan," she said, raising her voice louder than either of them was prepared for. "Not me. I was just the dumb… What did you call me once? Side-kick?"

That's what she had felt like in too many people's lives for way too long. She was tired of being second string in her family's life, in her job, and she sure wasn't going to try to convince Dylan that she was worth more than that to him now.

His sullen expression did little to slow her momentum.

"That's the pattern of my life, I guess. I'm the sidekick who gives and gives and…" She laughed hard, though it was out of sheer desperation to keep herself under control. "You were the first person who valued me and made me realize I'm no one's sidekick." She straightened her shoulders. "I deserve more from you."

"Caroline, don't leave like this. I'm trying to explain that I value your friendship but I—"

"No," she snapped, unwilling to listen to one more person tell her how great she was while choosing to not be there for her when she needed it. "I have a Christmas gala to throw. If I see you, I see you."

What did it matter now if he even showed up to the gala? Her Christmas wish had been foolhardy from the beginning. Christmas Eve at the gala would be just another day, just like Christmas and just like Thanksgiving.

She hurried to her car and climbed in. She couldn't stand to look back and check to see if he was watching her leave. Because if he wasn't, all was lost for their friendship, and she couldn't handle that kind of blow right before Christmas.

CHAPTER TWENTY-TWO

On Christmas Eve, Dylan had arrived home from The Starlight hoping for some time with McKenna before returning for the grand opening. The day had been harried at best.

For most of the morning, he and Caroline had been like ships passing in the night, politely managing to avoid each other. But as the momentum of the day began to build and the hours quickly dwindled until guests would arrive, they'd had no choice but to talk.

Caroline had been kind, a true class act, whenever she had had to address him. On the surface, she seemed optimistic and excited about the gala.

"The Hometown Jamboree just arrived to set up. Is the band stage clear?" she asked as Dylan directed his crew to lower the height of the center chandelier.

"Last I checked they were just sweeping up the pine needles from all the trees," he said. "Should be all set."

"Great." Caroline consulted the earpiece on

her headset, listening to someone before talking into the microphone. She'd been electronically tethered to Bianca, the caterer, and the head of the decorating crew all day. After answering a quick question, she turned to him and smiled brightly. "We might actually pull this thing off."

He tried to project the same optimism, but inside, his gut was coiling. Not sharing the day with Caroline, really sharing it the way he had imagined they would, made him feel like his world was falling apart.

Instead of dwelling on that, however, he hollered to his electrician to tighten the stage spotlight.

After standing in the driveway last night, trying to explain his reconstructed boundaries, he realized that he'd made a mess of it with her. He could tell by the look on Caroline's face the night before that he'd hurt her deeply.

In the daylight he watched her float around the dance hall, delegating tasks to her hired crew and ordering people around, and he saw that she had grown into a strong, self-assured woman since they had been children. She'd certainly taken him by surprise when he'd met her again at Tyler and Olivia's wedding, and since then, she'd grown so important in his life, he had been starting to forget what life had been like without her.

"Caroline," he'd said, waiting for her to focus on him. Though her eyes were wide in surprise, they seemed hollow. By the way her eyes darted to other things happening around them, he could tell he needed to do something better than just apologize. If he was going to clean up the mess he'd made of things, he couldn't just tell her how much he cared. He had to show her.

Caroline pressed fingertips to her ear as if concentrating to hear. After a moment, she held up her hand apologetically and hustled for the loading dock. "They're delivering the place settings, Dylan. I have to go!"

He had watched her run off and knew it wasn't the moment for him to try to reconcile. It was her moment. Her day to shine.

When he'd finally returned home, he had expected to find his family settling in for the evening, perhaps doing things to prepare for Santa's arrival that night. Delia usually liked to bake cookies, a tradition she'd started when Dylan had been a small child and had informed her that Santa Claus preferred freshly baked peanut butter blossom cookies with his milk. It had not been a coincidence that he and

Santa liked the same cookies, but Delia had not seemed to notice.

He strode through the back door, ready to steal a few cookies before dinner, when he found his mother and sister twirling in their finest dresses. When they spotted him, they giggled and his mother gave him a little curtsy.

"How do I look?" Delia asked. Dylan couldn't wipe the surprise off his face as his sister coached him to respond.

"When a woman asks you that, Dylan, you always say *beautiful*."

Dylan gathered his composure again and let out a whistle. "You do, Mom," he finally said. "You do look beautiful…" Delia fluffed her hair as he continued. "But what are you two *doing*?"

Delia huffed a laugh. "What does it look like? We were invited to the biggest event of the year, which just happens to be held at my son's Starlight dance hall, and we're going."

"That's right," Isabel said, taking Delia's hand and doing a spin of her own. "Christmas Eve on the town!"

"You can't go to a gala," he said. "I have to go, and I need you to watch McKenna." He glanced around, realizing his daughter wasn't there. After checking her tent, he turned to them. "Where is she?"

Delia and Isabel exchanged a smirk and motioned toward the staircase. He paused and heard a little voice call from the top of the landing.

"Daddy," McKenna anxiously whispered. "Come see me."

Dylan looked from his mother to his sister before making his way to the bottom step. He looked up to find his baby girl standing at the top, giggling. She was dressed in a red-and-black velvet Christmas dress. Her hair was pinned up in the front, baby curls spiraling around her shoulders. She pointed a foot, modeling her black patent leather dress shoes.

"Do I look pretty?" she asked eagerly. Dylan sighed, wistfully. She was growing up so fast, too fast. One day he'd blink, and she'd be standing at the top of the stairs ready to go to prom or leave for college or get married. He wished time would slow down—just a little.

"You look beautiful," he said, offering his hand. As she descended the stairs, still too young to alternate steps like an adult, she grinned. She navigated her way down to him and held out her arms for him to pick her up. He did and carried her to his mother and sister. They had obviously been making plans in his absence, but he still had his reservations about taking McKenna to a place like the Christmas gala.

Even if she wore her headphones, he worried the sounds and commotion would be too much for her. As she kissed him sweetly on the cheek, he knew she didn't have an understanding of where they were going or what she would do there. Otherwise, she would be frightened to go.

"You all look beautiful, and you certainly deserve a night out," he said. "But I don't know how we're going to…"

Delia clasped her hands together like a prayer and explained. "Sensory integration means navigating new situations and noises with patience and intention," she said. "We do a great job of that at home, but we must navigate new situations out in the world too." She winked at McKenna. "We will all help McKenna tonight and if things become too overwhelming…"

McKenna took Dylan's chin in her hand. "We can leave, Daddy," she said.

"And you'll wear your headphones?" Dylan asked. He didn't want to limit her or impose his own fear, but she was still very much a little girl who needed protection.

"She'll wear them," Isabel said. "We'll help her."

Dylan hemmed and hawed on his feet, still

uncertain. He supposed they could at least try to attend the gala. It was true that they could leave at any time.

"Can we just try it?" Isabel said. "For Christmas Eve?"

"I want to see Santa," McKenna said. "And Caroline."

He hummed a sigh. "Caroline will certainly be happy to see all of you," he admitted. He just didn't think she'd be thrilled to see him.

"Is she attending with anyone?" Delia asked. Dylan shook his head sadly. As far as he knew, she wasn't. It was a shame. A woman like Caroline deserved the world, and at the least, a date for the biggest night of her life.

FAITH ZIPPED CAROLINE into a long plum-colored, chiffon gown that she'd borrowed from her sister-in-law, Samantha.

"It's a good thing you and Sam are the same size," Faith said, helping her step into strappy heels. "And that you look amazing in purple."

"It's the red hair," Caroline said, turning toward the mirror. She'd had such a small window of time to get dressed, she couldn't believe Faith had styled her curly mane to look so beautiful, so quickly.

"Faith, it's hard to believe you spend most of the day repairing motorcycles." She turned from one side to the other. "If you ever want to change careers—"

"No, thanks," Faith said, slipping a golden comb accent into Caroline's styled hair. "I happen to like grease under my fingernails."

"Well," Caroline said, smoothing her hands down her hips. "I clean up pretty good."

"More than good, cousin. You're gorgeous." Faith turned Caroline to face her. "Are you sure you don't want me to come with you? I can be dressed in ten minutes, and I'll even hang up my motorcycle boots for the night. I make one hot date."

"I'm fine," Caroline said, forcing a smile. "It's better that I can give my full attention to the gala. You'd just get bored wandering around without me."

She had gotten used to living life mostly on her own. Why would the biggest night of her life be any different?

She slipped into the bathroom for finishing touches as the buzzer to her apartment sounded.

"Would you get that?" Caroline called. "Someone has the wrong apartment number again."

The buzzer had been sounding off and on since she'd returned home. One of her neighbors was having a Christmas party and guests kept buzzing her apartment in error.

"No problem!" Faith called, hurrying to the door.

After a minute, Caroline emerged from the bathroom, slipping on gold rhinestone earrings.

"Do you think this jewelry is too fancy?" she called. When Samantha had sent the dress and shoes, she'd also sent the most obnoxious costume jewelry Caroline had ever seen. Samantha's bold, bright wardrobe fit with her big personality, but on Caroline, she felt like the jewelry was wearing her.

As she admired how much her ears and neckline now sparkled, she reminded herself of the note Samantha had sent along with the jewelry: *If you can't go all out for a Christmas Eve gala, when can you? You are born to shine!*

Caroline had just grabbed her handbag and was making her way to the front door when she realized Faith was not alone. She was speaking to someone with a deep voice and by the few words Caroline could make out, Faith was reassuring someone that he was right to visit. As she got closer, she saw a man standing in a dark suit. Her breath caught.

"What are you doing here?" she gasped. "It's getting late."

He turned around to face her, nervously fiddling with the lapel of his jacket as his eyes hesitantly searched hers.

"Hi, honey," he said. "Oh my, don't you look beautiful."

It was her father.

He was dressed in an old suit that he probably hadn't worn in a decade. His sparse hair had been slicked back and in his hand he held a little clear box.

"Dad?" she said, coming forward. "I don't understand."

But she did. All at once she understood the lengths he'd gone to—pressing the suit, getting a haircut, buying a—

He opened the box and pulled out a hand corsage. Caroline bit the inside of her cheek as she realized it was for her. She had only ever seen one in pictures.

"I was hoping you didn't have a date yet," he said. "I know I should have called and properly asked you to the gala a long time ago, but I thought maybe…" He rasped a hand over his smoothly shaved chin. "You could still do me the honor?"

Caroline swallowed hard, feeling her tears

welling. "I just did my makeup," she said. "Don't make me cry, okay?"

"Oh, no, honey," he said, fumbling for his handkerchief. "We don't want any of that. Not on your big night."

As Caroline dotted her eyes, Gus slipped the corsage onto her wrist. It had a white rose and an accent of red Christmas holly berries. She chuckled to herself, unable to imagine him at a floral shop, let alone picking out a wrist corsage.

Gus frowned as he considered the corsage against her dress.

"I didn't know what color your dress was," he said. "With it being Christmas, I took a gamble and told the gal at the floral shop that it would probably be red."

"It matches perfectly." She held it up to her nose. She'd always loved the scent of fresh roses. "I love it."

Gus beamed as Faith helped Caroline slip into her coat. Then he offered her the crook of his arm.

"Your Christmas gala awaits, honey," he said. "I can't wait to see it."

Caroline took his arm and squeezed it tightly. She could hardly wait either.

CHAPTER TWENTY-THREE

DYLAN STOOD JUST inside the entrance of The Starlight as guests began to arrive. He recognized a few faces he had known while growing up, but most people, all dressed to the nines, were new to him. Whether familiar or not, what they all had in common was how delighted they looked when they stepped into the lobby of The Starlight.

Everything from the fresh paint to the recently laid carpeting still had that new smell, despite the cinnamon-scented pinecones and fresh pine scents wafting from the Christmas trees, wreaths and garland. Gold and silver tinsel clung to every branch. Strung lights from the ceiling highlighted every step. And just as they had discussed, classic Christmas songs played on an antique record player that Betty Jenkins had loaned them for the night.

Since arriving, Dylan hadn't yet seen Caroline. His eyes darted every time he thought he saw a glimpse of red hair.

McKenna, who was wearing her mouse headphones, tugged on the sleeve of his jacket.

"Daddy?" she said. "Are we going to stay out here the whole time?"

Dylan peered toward the lobby doors that led to the dance hall. The music and chattering of people was muffled for McKenna but he knew it would get louder once they entered the dance hall and made their way closer to the stage.

Delia and Isabel had already gone inside. He had wanted them to take a look around on their own. The evening would require all of them taking turns with McKenna, never leaving her to feel like she was being ignored or overlooked.

He took her hand. "It'll get a little louder in there so give my hand a squeeze if you want to leave."

She nodded and let him lead her through the antique brass doors. He'd saved and refinished the doors, as they were one of the things that helped give The Starlight its character. They stood as gatekeepers into the hall, but also into another era.

Inside, guests mingled under the constellation lights twinkling in the ceiling. The stage lights transitioned from red to purple to blue as The Hometown Jamboree played its first set.

Christmas trees were strung in various-colored lights and adorned with gold and red and silver ornaments. And stationed by the fireplace at the far side of the hall was a very jolly-looking Santa Claus.

"How come there are no other kids to see Santa?" McKenna asked.

Even though McKenna was right and there were no other children at the gala, Santa was still a very busy man. The patrons seemed to love the scene Caroline had designed for Santa, complete with stacks of wrapped presents and a side table of every assortment of Christmas cookie, all ripe for the taking.

"You're the only child invited because this is your Starlight," Dylan said with a grin. "Would you like to see Santa?" Despite all the bright sights, McKenna had been laser focused on him as soon as they entered the hall.

She shook her head, making Dylan nod with understanding. Sometimes it was best for McKenna to process things on her own for a little while. No kid would accept a spoonful of ice cream if you forced it into their mouth.

Instead of cutting a line to Santa, Dylan let McKenna lead him as they meandered around the back of the hall, slowly winding their way closer to the stage. Round tables with eight place settings each had been placed around the perimeter of the dance floor. Guests were already dancing, talking and tipping back the specialty drink of the evening, a nonalcoholic Christmas punch.

As Dylan surveyed the room, McKenna tugged on his hand and pointed to Caroline and Gus.

"Daddy, there's Caroline." She waved excitedly. "Caroline!"

Caroline jerked at the sound of her name. When she spotted them, her face broke into a wide smile and for a moment, all he could see was her. She took her dad's arm and hurried to greet McKenna.

As she sashayed across the dance floor, the chiffon fabric skimming her hips and floating around her heels, she was a vision. If he could watch her cross a room like that for the rest of his life, he would consider himself a lucky man. Unfortunately, she wasn't crossing to see him.

Once Caroline reached them, she squatted down to get eye level with McKenna. By her positioning, Dylan could tell that Caroline had not expected to get a hug. He appreciated how Caroline showed interest in McKenna without overstepping.

Boundaries.

Dylan kicked himself for adhering so

strongly to his own. He'd done exactly what she had accused him of. He'd gotten scared and had pushed her away without giving her, or them, a real chance.

What was worse was that he had believed her. Getting to know her over the last several weeks meant getting to know her heart. She was not the sort of person who would have gotten into the Behrs' good graces at the expense of McKenna's well-being. But his fear had never been about not believing Caroline. It had been about him protecting his vulnerable heart. He couldn't afford to get himself, or McKenna, hurt again.

McKenna, however, did not seem to understand that things had changed. After wavering on her feet for a moment, she crept closer and leaned into Caroline, letting her friend hug her. She stayed there, melting into Caroline's arms for so long, Caroline glanced up at Dylan. Her relaxed face conveyed she was touched at receiving such affection.

Dylan felt his own face soften at the sight of them. He had never thought that he could fall in love with someone just by watching how they treated his child. But when his daughter finally released Caroline and let her stand, he looked into her gleaming blue eyes and wondered if that was what had just happened.

The moment, however, had not seemed to have the same ethereal effect on Caroline as it had had on him.

"We did it," she sang, motioning to the hall. "Somehow we pulled it off."

"We make a good team," he said. He wanted to say that he meant it. He wanted to say he'd made a terrible mistake and had just gotten scared, but he didn't. He couldn't.

Instead, he greeted Gus.

"Good to see you, Gus," he said, shaking his hand. Gus patted Dylan on the shoulder.

"I have some fond memories of this place, Dylan. You did well, son."

"Thank you, sir. Your daughter and I both did. People will be talking about this event for a long time."

Caroline bit her lip, but he knew how proud she was of her gala. At least, he thought that she ought to be. Before he could continue, Tex and Bianca hurried over to greet McKenna.

"McKenna, sweetheart, we're so glad you're here!" Bianca said. She bent down to touch McKenna's hand. For as light a touch as Caroline had had, Bianca's energy was startling. "Did you see Santa yet?"

McKenna slipped behind Dylan's leg to hide.

"She doesn't like when people come up

too close to her," Dylan explained. "And she doesn't like all the noise."

Bianca laughed. "It's a gala. I'm afraid we can't do anything about that."

"What's that on her head?" Tex said as Delia and Isabel joined them. "Does she always wear that headband?"

Dylan didn't want McKenna to become a spectacle, a focal point he'd have to answer questions about. But with several people now standing around and making her the center of attention, he was afraid she was.

"It's to soften the noise," Caroline explained. "Isn't that a good idea?"

Tex frowned. "It's just music."

"Not to her," Caroline continued. "It can be overwhelming."

"Nah," Tex said. "Giana has reason to believe that coddling just makes it worse. She wants to break her of it just like you would thumb-sucking."

Dylan crossed his arms over his chest, widening his gait to better shield McKenna.

"As a matter of fact, Tex—" he began but Bianca had already moved in front of him.

"Delia," she said. "I'm so happy you could make it. You can hear about our special surprise for McKenna."

Dylan frowned, now remembering some

nonsense about pulling McKenna up onstage for a financial donation. He reached for McKenna's hand and found it already waiting.

"McKenna will *not* be going onstage," he said as Caroline held up her hand.

"It's okay," she said. "I already told them that."

"That's right," Bianca said. "McKenna does not have to do anything she does not want to do. However, our surprise is something she will be very happy to hear."

Bianca glanced excitedly from Dylan to McKenna. He could see that she was bursting to tell them all something important, but because he had no idea what it was, it made his stomach flip-flop with queasiness.

"Tell them already," Tex said, chuckling. "You've been talking about nothing else for two days."

Dylan tried not to squeeze McKenna's hand nervously as he braced for impact. Bianca addressed McKenna directly. "McKenna, sweet darling, your mommy is coming to the gala tonight!"

Dylan felt a nerve in his jaw tighten as he stared at Bianca's proud expression. Once again, she and Tex had no understanding of their situation, yet they were inserting their judgment and their influence into his and McKenna's life.

McKenna released Dylan's hand as she began looking around the room. He could tell she didn't understand that Giana was not at the gala just yet.

McKenna grabbed Isabel's hand and began to tug her toward the lobby. He knew she was searching for Giana and the most comfortable place to begin her search was in the foyer.

"We'll be right back," Isabel said with a laugh, hurrying to keep up with McKenna.

"Look at how excited she is," Bianca said, squeezing Tex's arm. "I knew she'd love it."

"Giana had better show," Dylan said tensely. Every ounce of him was straining to keep his composure. "If you just promised her she'd see her mother for Christmas and Giana doesn't walk through those doors—"

"Why, of course she'll show," Bianca said, raising her brow. "Why would you say such a thing? Her flight was at three o'clock. She'll be here shortly."

"Giana hasn't been interested in being a mother for the last three years," Dylan replied. "If she walks in tonight, it will be a Christmas miracle."

Tex wrapped an arm around Bianca's shoulders. The two stood before him as a united front. "Giana talks of nothing but McKenna," he insisted. "She cries and cries to us all the time about how much she misses her."

Dylan certainly hoped she did, but not because he wanted to bring Giana any pain. He wished Giana really did care strongly for their daughter.

As he couldn't muster a response that didn't make him sound like he was raining on their Christmas parade, he excused himself and went to find something to drink at the bar. Once he'd grabbed a glass of Christmas punch, he felt someone scoot up beside him.

"Do you think Giana really won't show?" Caroline asked. Her eyes were etched in worry, the same kind he also couldn't shake.

"If past behavior is the best predictor of future behavior—" he threw back a gulp of punch "—she never got on the plane."

Caroline took his hand in her own. The softness of her touch cooled something angry and bubbling inside him. Just the way she conveyed her concern made him hope that things with Giana could be managed to protect McKenna. He also hoped things between him and Caroline could be resolved.

"What can I do?" she asked.

He flickered a glum smile. Unfortunately, there was nothing she could do. She had a gala to run and he had a little girl to comfort when her mother didn't arrive as promised.

"The Behrs just make plans without asking," he grumbled. "They don't have the faintest idea what's best for McKenna."

"Have you ever tried telling them that?"

"Yes, but they're not my family. I shouldn't have to keep trying."

"No," Caroline said slowly. "But they are McKenna's family. They're also living in Roseley and from what I've seen and heard, they desperately want to be a part of her life. Take it from me, Dylan. A family can get small pretty quickly. You might want to talk to them again so they can learn how to support both of you. I'd bet anything they really want to."

"What about you?" Dylan said, turning her hand over in his. "Do you still want to be in our lives too?"

Caroline withdrew her hand. "I will always be your friend," she said. "And McKenna's friend..."

"Caroline, I drew my boundary lines to protect McKenna. But I made a mistake and I know now that I want something more than friendship with you."

She touched her cheeks and he could tell she was trying to stay composed. When he leaned closer, wanting to show her that he wanted her, she held up a hand to keep him at bay.

"I have to check on dinner," she said. "We'll be serving soon."

Before he could stop her, she slipped away from the bar and disappeared through the crowd.

CHAPTER TWENTY-FOUR

CAROLINE COULDN'T ENJOY her food as her stomach had been in a vise all throughout dinner. By the time dessert had arrived and the hospital board had started a slideshow presentation of what the new children's wing of the hospital would look like, she felt certain that a little fresh air would set her to rights.

Slipping out the back doors into the hall, she roamed the long hallway to a back lounge. Tucked in a quiet corner of the building, it had originally been something of a cigar lounge back in the day. Dylan, however, was still in the process of renovating it to be a private place for escape. He'd explained weeks earlier that having McKenna in his life had taught him that every hall needed a place for people to escape to, to unwind and recalibrate their feelings when the excitement of the crowd became too much.

Caroline had loved listening to him talk about his plan. He'd shown a real understanding of not just his daughter, but the struggles some people had when being in a crowd.

The lounge was dark, still off-limits to guests, since its renovations weren't finished. Power cords and equipment were still strewn in the corners. The workers had made it a temporary break room and had even brought in a couch, which was now stationed in front of a large, newly installed picture window.

Caroline beelined through it to the back exit door and pushed it open. The cold air whipped against her exposed skin. It reminded her of the first time she'd seen Dylan since he'd returned to Roseley. The thrill he'd given her just with his smile had sent tingles down her spine.

While his smile could still make her skin prick with goose bumps, his thoughtfulness and care could also make her swoon. She'd grown to care about him more than she'd cared about anyone. Realizing that he could shrug her off so quickly, so easily, now terrified her. Nothing about love felt safe. Not when it could be withdrawn so easily and with such little provocation.

"Honey?"

Caroline turned and pulled the exit door shut as Gus made his way across the room.

"Be careful," she said, pointing to the ground.

In the dark it was difficult to see the obstacles. "I don't want you to get hurt."

"That's what I was just thinking about you." When he reached her, he offered her his handkerchief again.

"I'm not crying," she said. "I just needed a minute to clear my head."

"What's the matter? Is your gala not going well?"

Caroline realized that her gala was perfect. Everything she had dreamed of and everything she had planned was working. As long as they reached the Behrs' fundraising goal, and she had every reason to believe they would, she could consider her first event a success.

It made her wonder, then, how she could leave her own party. If succeeding as an event planner was supposed to make her feel ecstatic, why was she wishing for something more?

"When you were a little girl," Gus said, dipping his hands casually into his trouser pockets, "you used to make extensive lists for Santa Claus. They were epic, usually three times longer than Trig's. He wanted simple things like a new fishing pole or a video game. But you…" Gus tipped his head back as if fondly remembering. "My Caroline wanted the world. But, your mother and I, and Santa, of course, couldn't deliver all that. After a while I think we stopped trying to come close at all."

"I didn't want the world," Caroline said. "I wanted your attention."

"I thought I gave it to you."

She smiled sadly. "You mostly gave it to Trig."

Gus clicked his tongue, considering. "I loved you, honey. I still do. You got my attention now. I promise."

Caroline nodded as he patted her cheek and continued.

"I might be getting kind of old to notice these types of things," he said, dipping his head closer. "But was there someone else in there whose attention you wanted most?"

Caroline wrapped her arms around herself and plastered on the most innocent-looking face.

Gus quietly hooted with laughter. "Just so you know, you've got his attention. Any fool, even an old one like me, can see that. Don't go throwing out your Christmas list just yet."

Caroline rolled her eyes, ready to explain that she was content just the way things were in her life. Just because she wanted something more with Dylan didn't mean she could trust it.

But before she could open her mouth, she spotted Dylan standing in the doorway. The backlight of the hall was pooling in behind him, casting him in shadows, but from his frame and stance, she knew it was him.

Gus moseyed across the room and patted Dylan on the shoulder.

"I have to get back to my dessert," he said. "I haven't had pecan pie in ages."

Once they were alone, Caroline made her way to Dylan.

"I was looking for you," he said, studying her.

"Why?"

"At dinner you didn't look okay."

She wanted to explain that nothing about the evening, the biggest night of her life, felt okay when things between them weren't right. As much as she wanted to pull him into her arms and pretend that she wasn't scared of getting hurt, of getting rejected, she knew holding him too quickly would be a lie. She was still scared of giving herself fully over to love when she couldn't guarantee, without a doubt, that it would be returned—forever. She'd made a choice to live a life she loved, building a career she loved. If she thought she could be happy with just that, then wasn't that safer than risking her heart?

"I should check on things," she continued.

"They'll be wrapping up the slideshow soon and collecting donations."

"I'll join you." They fell into step, walking back to the hall.

"How's McKenna doing?" As she and Gus had been seated at another table, she hadn't had a clear view of McKenna or Dylan all through dinner.

"All she'll talk about is Giana."

"The Behrs were trying to deliver her Christmas wish," Caroline said. "You can't fault them for trying."

Dylan nodded. "That's the sentiment I landed on too."

When they reached the dance hall, the band was playing again. Guests were digging for their checkbooks and making donations through their phones.

"Fingers crossed," Bianca said once she hurried up to them. "I have a feeling we're going to hit our goal tonight, Caroline."

"Bianca," Dylan said. Pulling his shoulders back. "I've been thinking about what you did for McKenna. I know you had the best intentions in mind when you invited Giana—"

"Of course we did," Bianca said, grabbing his arm. "Tex and I always do."

Dylan shook his head, starting again. "What I mean is, McKenna is a very special little girl.

If you're going to be a part of her life, you have to understand that…"

"What?" Bianca's face contorted in confusion. Caroline watched Dylan again try to put words to all he wanted to explain. In the hubbub of the gala, how could he make Bianca understand that McKenna needed support that most people weren't familiar with?

Caroline stared at Dylan, struggling so hard to bridge the divide between him and Giana's family. He didn't have to do it, and from what he'd mentioned in the past, she knew he didn't want to do it. But for the sake of his daughter, he was willing to try. If he was willing to take a risk with people he didn't even like, people who had hurt him in the past, what would he be willing to risk for her?

Hanging on his every word, listening as he again tried to explain McKenna's condition, Caroline felt a growing sense of hope. In Dylan's words she saw that love was about doing the hard things, the messy things. In his face she saw the man she'd been starting to trust. She'd enjoyed all the time they'd spent together since he'd returned to Roseley, but as she watched him ask for the Behrs' support and understanding, she realized that it wasn't until just then that she had fallen completely in love with him.

"Giana never explained things that way," Bianca said quietly once Dylan had finished. "She led us to believe that you were blowing things out of proportion just to get custody of McKenna."

Dylan lowered his eyes sadly to convey he wasn't just as McKenna ran up with Isabel and Delia.

"We spied on Santa for a little while," Isabel explained. "But we're still not ready to talk to him."

"That's okay," Bianca said, winking at McKenna. "Santa always knows what we want for Christmas, even if we don't tell him."

Tex strode up and grabbed Bianca's elbow. His face was twisted with disgust as he passed her his cell phone and whispered into her ear.

Caroline touched Dylan's arm and leaned close to whisper. "I know that wasn't easy," she said. "But doing that shows that you're a great dad."

He smiled.

"Giana, dear," Bianca cried into the cell phone. "I don't understand. If you didn't make the flight, why didn't you call earlier? McKenna has been watching for you."

Caroline touched Dylan's shoulder to convey her condolences as he squatted down. He had to explain to McKenna that her mom wasn't going to make it in time for Christmas after all.

He'd no sooner taken the little girl's hands when the band finished playing and a member of the hospital board took the microphone to remind everyone to log their donations. Suddenly, as he adjusted the microphone, a high-pitched sound from feedback squealed, echoing across the entire hall. Many people covered an ear and squinted an eye, waiting for the noise to pass. All of the guests conveyed they disliked the sharp sound but could tolerate it. All of the guests except McKenna.

Instantly, as if in the throes of torture, she covered her ears and began to scream. It was a wail so loud and guttural, her face instantly went red.

Caroline had never seen anyone look so inflicted with pain so quickly. Flooded with adrenaline to help make the sharp noise stop, Caroline raced for the stage to help adjust the volume setting. Once she fixed it, silencing the electronic squeal, everyone in the hall turned to stare at McKenna.

Caroline knew that the intensity of the moment was the exact thing Dylan had wanted to avoid. He tried to comfort McKenna but she flailed violently against him, howling as if the electronic squeal had not yet stopped. Tex and

Bianca stared on in horror. By the shock on Delia's and Isabel's face, Caroline could only suspect they had never seen an outburst so extreme before. Delia squatted to try to soothe McKenna as Isabel hovered behind her, both women desperate to help.

Caroline had never seen anything like it. She had thought she'd understood what Dylan had been talking about whenever he spoke of McKenna's aversion to loud sounds. But seeing the little girl so upset, and Dylan looking powerless to comfort her, shook her to the core.

Finally, as the seconds ticked by and McKenna's cries reached a fever pitch, Dylan scooped her up into his arms and bolted for the back of the hall. Once they'd pushed out into the hallway and the doors closed and latched behind them, the guests began to talk again. The band began to play light instrumental music. Everyone quickly returned to what they had been doing—chatting, drinking and digging into their deep pockets for donations.

"I had no idea," Bianca whispered, as she and Tex met Caroline onstage. "Giana didn't tell us any of *that*."

Caroline nodded. "He's doing his best, you know."

"Well, of course he is," Tex boomed. "By the way he protects that little girl, anyone can see he's a wonderful father. Giana, on the other hand, has always been a...*goofball*."

"*Tex,*" Bianca said, horrified.

"Well, she has been, hasn't she? She's from your side of the family so it's hard for you to see it clearly." He turned to Caroline, a knowing look on his face. "But I see it plain as day."

Bianca slapped him playfully on the arm and covered the microphone as she laughed. "Yes, you're a regular private I, dear."

One of the members of the hospital board reached up to the stage and handed Bianca a note. When she read it, she grabbed Caroline's arm.

"We had a very good night, Caroline. They tallied the online donations." She held open the note to show Caroline that the money raised so far online had already exceeded their goal. "You had a big hand in that. You're going places, dear."

Caroline beamed as Bianca tapped the microphone and got the crowd's attention. She knew there would be an announcement about how much they had raised. The Behrs would proudly announce their own donation, pushing them far above their goal. The Behrs would announce that they had enough to break ground on the new children's wing expansion. It was her chance to take a victory lap, but she couldn't.

As Bianca asked guests to take their seats, Caroline quietly slipped offstage. She had thought her success with the gala would make her happy, but after further review, she knew her biggest wish for Christmas had not yet come true.

DYLAN SANK FARTHER back onto the couch and propped his feet up on the windowsill. He mused at how twelve hours earlier his crew had finished installing the beautiful picture window and had laughed that with the lounge closed, no one at the gala would even get to enjoy it.

He supposed he and McKenna would be the only ones to appreciate it that night.

The room was dark. The scene outside in the snow was still. As the window faced the back lot, not a person or car passed by it. With weeks of snow accumulation, everything outside looked like a winter wonderland.

Snow fell in clumps. Against the moonlight and streetlamp on the far corner, it cast shadows on him and McKenna like they were suspended in a snow globe.

McKenna lay on his chest, soggy thumb hanging from her mouth. Her body was still shuddering, the uncontrolled jerks of a child who had cried hard and wouldn't be able to stop for a while. He rubbed her back softly and hummed quietly, letting his deep voice vibrate and lull her to sleep.

From the corner of his eye, he could see someone approaching. The door quietly opened, and a person slipped inside. He could tell just by the way she latched the door it was Caroline.

She tiptoed across the room and stopped at the edge of the couch, gazing down lovingly at them. She didn't speak or ask if they were okay as anyone could see the worst of it was over. She didn't break the trance he had managed to cast over his daughter.

Instead, she slowly eased onto the couch next to him. She brushed a curly tendril out of McKenna's face as her rounded eyes found his. As he watched her, he felt all that he wanted to say growing in his heart.

"You're missing your gala," he said, his words barely audible. He was good at speaking low enough to not wake his daughter.

I don't care, she mouthed.

Caroline was apparently good at keeping it down, too. She was good at a lot of things, most of all, caring deeply for other people, including him and McKenna. He knew what it felt like to have family who loved and supported him, and he thought that his little family and his work at The Starlight would be enough to make him happy.

But as he stared into Caroline's eyes and saw such tenderness, he knew that his future happiness was contingent on making Caroline a part of his family.

"You worked so hard," he whispered. As much as he wanted her to stay with him, he didn't want her to miss the biggest night of her life, unless…she wanted the same thing he did.

Her face melted in a wistful smile. "Dylan," she whispered, her voice breaking. She brushed fingertips across his temple, affectionately stroking hair back off his face. "Staying here with you and McKenna is all I…oh, Dylan…I…"

He could feel his heart swelling, the longing to hold her again and pull her into his and McKenna's world seizing him. In the words she couldn't say, he found a kindred connection. In her expression, he saw a reflection of his own—a sentiment that he was more afraid of losing her than of getting hurt again.

"Ah, Red," he said as his eyes began to mist. "I already know. And we love you too."

McKenna whimpered, rousing for a moment before settling back to sleep. Caroline kissed her fingertips and grazed them to McKenna's temple. When she nestled into Dylan's side and rested her head on his shoulder, he returned to humming.

They stared out the window together, watching the snowflakes waltz across the heavens, a prelude to the Christmas that was still to come. It would be one he and McKenna would share with Caroline, hopefully the first of many. He breathed a sigh of pure contentment. Everything he wanted for Christmas was right here in this room.

EPILOGUE

A YEAR LATER, Caroline clasped Dylan's hands and peered up into his eyes. She could hardly believe it had been just one week since she'd not only thrown a second beautiful gala for the Behrs but had also opened a Christmas gift from McKenna that would change her life forever—an engagement ring from Dylan. In lieu of saying yes, she had said she didn't want to start another year without him and McKenna as her family—officially.

After a year of their businesses booming, it hadn't taken long to realize that merging their enterprises was the best way to grow them and make time for family. They had gotten a lot of requests to book The Starlight for New Year's Eve, but as Caroline stood in the middle of the dance hall with Dylan, surrounded by a small handful of family and friends, she knew that Dylan's refusal to rent it out had been the best choice.

Dylan had promised her that she would never have to plan another wedding, so he had taken care of all the arrangements, which mostly consisted of ordering their late-night wedding cake and champagne toast.

The officiant checked his watch, keeping track of the time, but Caroline hardly noticed. All she could see was Dylan.

In a black tuxedo, he looked like he'd stepped off the pages of a bridal magazine. But it was the charming upturn at the corner of his mouth as he let his eyes fall over her that really made the nerves skitter across her skin.

"You look beautiful," he whispered, bringing her hand to his lips. He brushed a kiss to her knuckles. The warmth of his breath tickled.

While she had never wanted to plan another wedding, she had known what kind of wedding gown she wanted. She had enjoyed picking out the perfect one, with McKenna's help, of course. And as luck would have it, they had found a miniature coordinating flower girl dress.

"It's almost time, sis," Trig said, grinning with equal parts pride and mischievousness as he elbowed Dylan. "Unless you want to change your mind about marrying this joker."

Caroline gazed at her family and friends as they stood around her and Dylan in a tight circle. The constellations glittering in the ceiling above them were their only light.

After Caroline and Dylan exchanged vows, the small group began to whisper in unison.

"Ten…nine…eight…"

Dylan squeezed Caroline's hands, tears forming in his eyes.

"I love you, Red," he whispered. She loved him too, and McKenna, of course. But how could they start the marriage off on the right foot if she let him get away with calling her Red?

"That's still not going to work," she said with a smile.

"Seven…six…five…" the group continued. Dylan flashed a smile as he thought.

"How about if I call you my bride, then?"

"I now pronounce you husband and wife," the officiant said.

"Four…three…two…"

"One," McKenna said with a giggle as she shook her little bouquet of mistletoe up at them. "Kiss now."

Dylan pulled Caroline into their first kiss as a married couple. She closed her eyes, savoring the promise it represented. She was beginning the new year with a husband and a daughter. If he wanted to call her his bride, she supposed that would do.

* * * * *

Get 4 FREE REWARDS!

We'll send you 2 FREE Books plus 2 FREE Mystery Gifts.

FREE Value Over **$20**

Both the **Love Inspired**® and **Love Inspired**® **Suspense** series feature compelling novels filled with inspirational romance, faith, forgiveness, and hope.

Get 4 FREE REWARDS!

We'll send you 2 FREE Books plus 2 FREE Mystery Gifts.

Both the **Harlequin® Special Edition** and **Harlequin® Heartwarming™** series feature compelling novels filled with stories of love and strength where the bonds of friendship, family and community unite.

YES! Please send me 2 FREE novels from the Harlequin Special Edition or Harlequin Heartwarming series and my 2 FREE gifts (gifts are worth about $10 retail). After receiving them, if I don't wish to receive any more books, I can return the shipping statement marked "cancel." If I don't cancel, I will receive 6 brand-new Harlequin Special Edition books every month and be billed just $5.24 each in the U.S. or $5.99 each in Canada, a savings of at least 13% off the cover price or 4 brand-new Harlequin Heartwarming Larger-Print books every month and be billed just $5.99 each in the U.S. or $6.49 each in Canada, a savings of at least 20% off the cover price. It's quite a bargain! Shipping and handling is just 50¢ per book in the U.S. and $1.25 per book in Canada.* I understand that accepting the 2 free books and gifts places me under no obligation to buy anything. I can always return a shipment and cancel at any time by calling the number below. The free books and gifts are mine to keep no matter what I decide.

Choose one: ☐ **Harlequin Special Edition**   ☐ **Harlequin Heartwarming**
(235/335 HDN GRCQ)   **Larger-Print**
                            (161/361 HDN GRC3)

Name (please print)

Address   Apt. #

City   State/Province   Zip/Postal Code

Email: Please check this box ☐ if you would like to receive newsletters and promotional emails from Harlequin Enterprises ULC and its affiliates. You can unsubscribe anytime.

Mail to the **Harlequin Reader Service:**
IN U.S.A.: P.O. Box 1341, Buffalo, NY 14240-8531
IN CANADA: P.O. Box 603, Fort Erie, Ontario L2A 5X3

Want to try 2 free books from another series! Call 1-800-873-8635 or visit www.ReaderService.com.

*Terms and prices subject to change without notice. Prices do not include sales taxes, which will be charged (if applicable) based on your state or country of residence. Canadian residents will be charged applicable taxes. Offer not valid in Quebec. This offer is limited to one order per household. Books received may not be as shown. Not valid for current subscribers to the Harlequin Special Edition or Harlequin Heartwarming series. All orders subject to approval. Credit or debit balances in a customer's account(s) may be offset by any other outstanding balance owed by or to the customer. Please allow 4 to 6 weeks for delivery. Offer available while quantities last.

Your Privacy—Your information is being collected by Harlequin Enterprises ULC, operating as Harlequin Reader Service. For a complete summary of the information we collect, how we use this information and to whom it is disclosed, please visit our privacy notice located at corporate.harlequin.com/privacy-notice. From time to time we may also exchange your personal information with reputable third parties. If you wish to opt out of this sharing of your personal information, please visit readerservice.com/consumerschoice or call 1-800-873-8635. **Notice to California Residents**—Under California law, you have specific rights to control and access your data. For more information on these rights and how to exercise them, visit corporate.harlequin.com/california-privacy.

HSEHW22R2

COUNTRY LEGACY COLLECTION

19 FREE BOOKS IN ALL!

EMMETT
Diana Palmer

COURTED BY THE COWBOY
Sasha Summers

THE RANCHER AND THE BABY
Marie Ferrarella

Cowboys, adventure and romance await you in this
new collection! Enjoy superb reading all year long
with books by bestselling authors like
Diana Palmer, Sasha Summers and Marie Ferrarella!

YES! Please send me the **Country Legacy Collection!** This collection begins with
3 FREE books and 2 FREE gifts in the first shipment. Along with my 3 free books,
I'll also get 3 more books from the **Country Legacy Collection**, which I may either
return and owe nothing or keep for the low price of $24.60 U.S./$28.12 CDN each
plus $2.99 U.S./$7.49 CDN for shipping and handling per shipment*. If I decide to
continue, about once a month for 8 months, I will get 6 or 7 more books but will only
pay for 4. That means 2 or 3 books in every shipment will be FREE! If I decide to
keep the entire collection, I'll have paid for only 32 books because 19 are FREE!
I understand that accepting the 3 free books and gifts places me under no obligation
to buy anything. I can always return a shipment and cancel at any time. My free
books and gifts are mine to keep no matter what I decide.

☐ 275 HCK 1939   ☐ 475 HCK 1939

Name (please print)

Address   Apt. #

City   State/Province   Zip/Postal Code

Mail to the **Harlequin Reader Service:**
IN U.S.A.: P.O. Box 1341, Buffalo, NY 14240-8571
IN CANADA: P.O. Box 603, Fort Erie, Ontario L2A 5X3

*Terms and prices subject to change without notice. Prices do not include sales taxes, which will be charged (if applicable) based
on your state or country of residence. Canadian residents will be charged applicable taxes. Offer not valid in Quebec. All orders
subject to approval. Credit or debit balances in a customer's account(s) may be offset by any other outstanding balance owed by
or to the customer. Please allow 3 to 4 weeks for delivery. Offer available while quantities last. © 2021 Harlequin Enterprises ULC.
® and ™ are trademarks owned by Harlequin Enterprises ULC.

Your Privacy—Your information is being collected by Harlequin Enterprises ULC, operating as Harlequin Reader Service. To see
how we collect and use this information visit https://corporate.harlequin.com/privacy-notice. From time to time we may also exchange
your personal information with reputable third parties. If you wish to opt out of this sharing of your personal information, please
visit www.readerservice.com/consumerschoice or call 1-800-873-8635. Notice to California Residents—Under California law, you
have specific rights to control and access your data. For more information visit https://corporate.harlequin.com/california-privacy.

50BOOKCL22

Get 4 FREE REWARDS!

We'll send you 2 FREE Books plus 2 FREE Mystery Gifts.

FREE Value Over **$20**

Both the **Romance** and **Suspense** collections feature compelling novels written by many of today's bestselling authors.

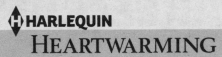
#443 HER FAVORITE WYOMING SHERIFF

The Blackwells of Eagle Springs

by Cari Lynn Webb

Widower and single mom Adele Blackwell Kane must reopen the once-renowned Blackwell Auction Barn—if she can get Sheriff Grady McMillan to stop arresting her on town ordinances long enough to save her ranch. Can love prevail in county jail?

#444 THE SERGEANT'S CHRISTMAS GIFT

by Shelley Shepard Gray

While manning the NORAD Santa hotline, Sergeant Graham Hopkins gets a call from a boy who steals his heart. When he meets the boy's mother, Vivian Parnell, will he make room in his heart for both of them?

#445 THE SEAL'S CHRISTMAS DILEMMA

Big Sky Navy Heroes • by Julianna Morris

Navy SEAL Dakota Maxwell is skipping Christmas—and not just because his career-ending injuries have left him bitter. But Dr. Noelle Bannerman lives to heal. And she'll do that with physical therapy...and a dose of holiday magic.

#446 AN ALASKAN FAMILY THANKSGIVING

A Northern Lights Novel • by Beth Carpenter

Single mom Sunny Galloway loves her job as activities director of a seniors' home—then Adam Lloyd shows up, tasked with resolving financial woes. They have until Thanksgiving to save the home. Can working together mean saving each other, too?

HWCNM0922

HARLEQUIN
PLUS

Announcing a **BRAND-NEW**
multimedia subscription service
for romance fans like you!

Read, Watch and Play.

Experience the easiest way to get
the romance content you crave.

Start your **FREE 7 DAY TRIAL** at
<u>www.harlequinplus.com/freetrial</u>.